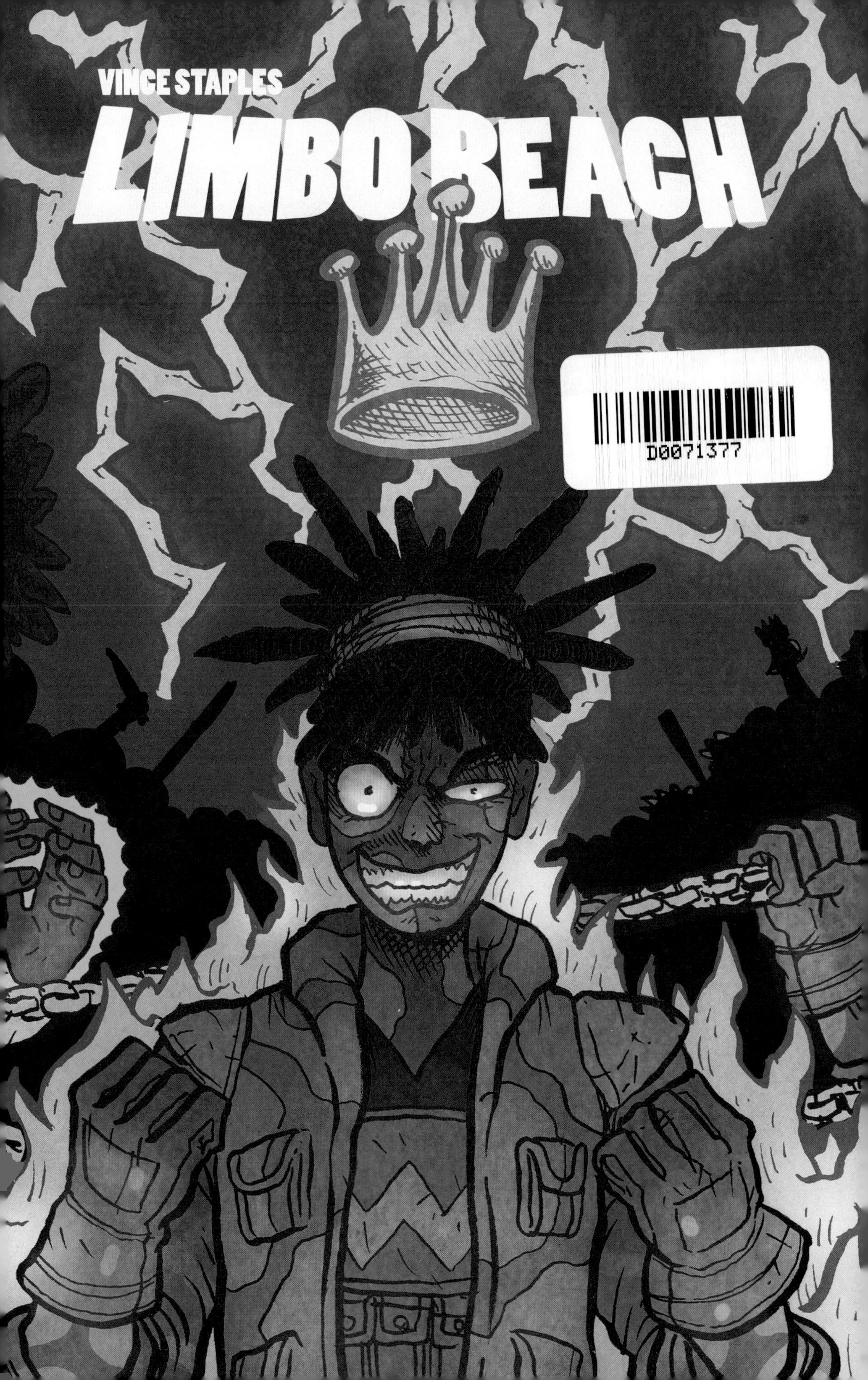
VINCE STAPLES
LIMBO BEACH

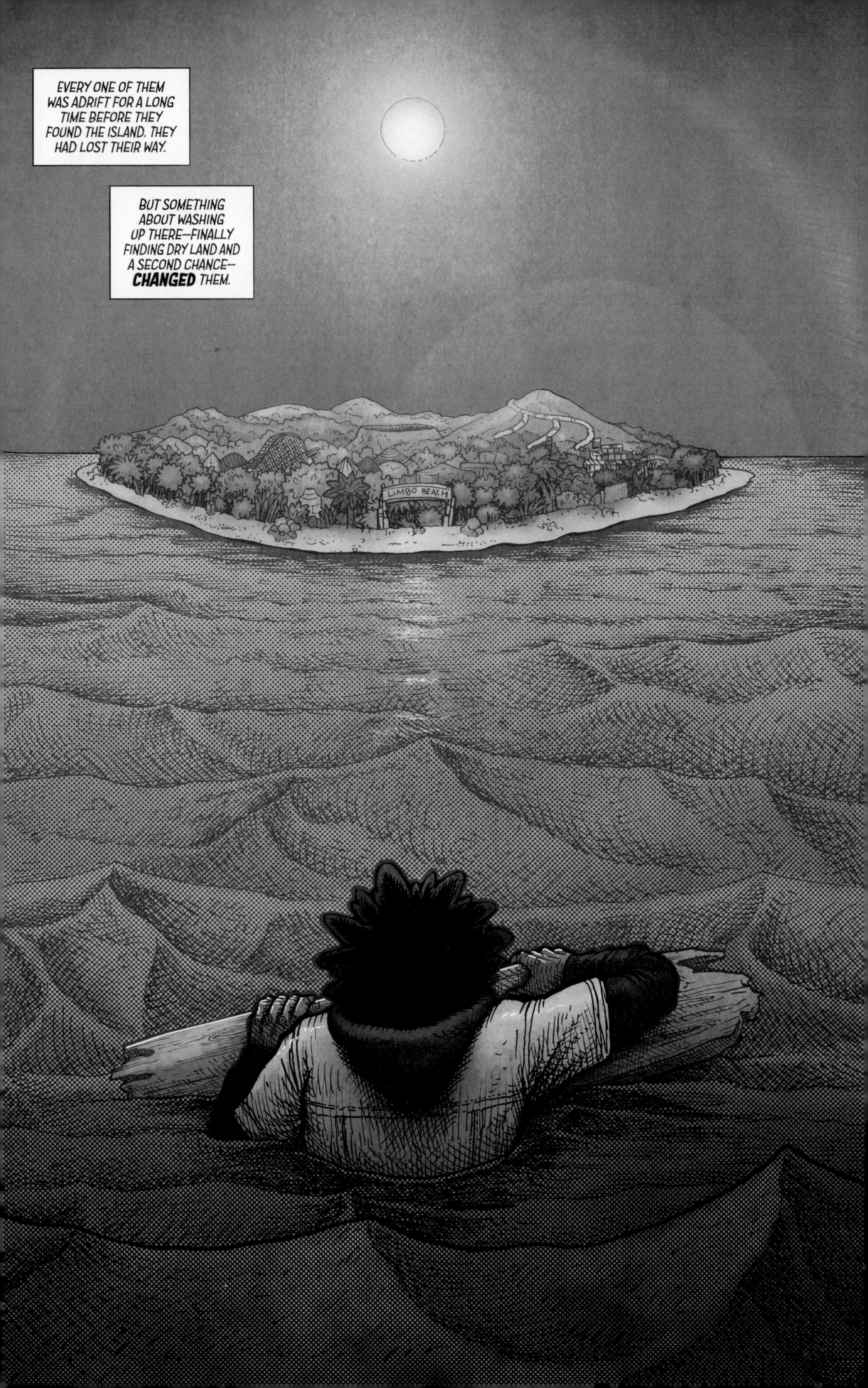
EVERY ONE OF THEM WAS ADRIFT FOR A LONG TIME BEFORE THEY FOUND THE ISLAND. THEY HAD LOST THEIR WAY.
BUT SOMETHING ABOUT WASHING UP THERE--FINALLY FINDING DRY LAND AND A SECOND CHANCE-- **CHANGED** THEM.
LIMBO BEACH

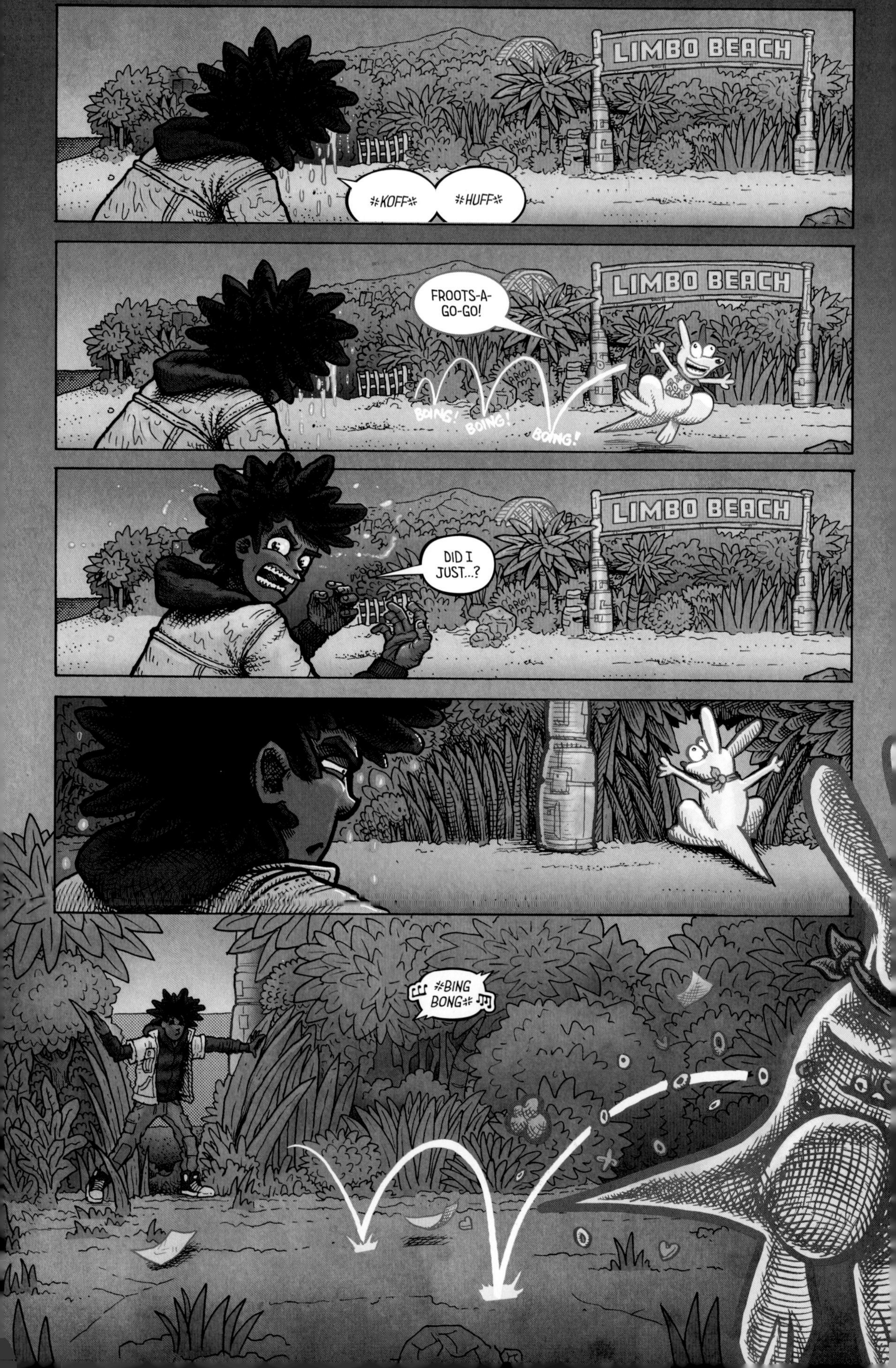
LIMBO BEACH
#KOFF#
#HUFF#
LIMBO BEACH
FROOTS-A-GO-GO!
BOING!
BOING!
BOING!
LIMBO BEACH
DID I JUST...?
#BING BONG#

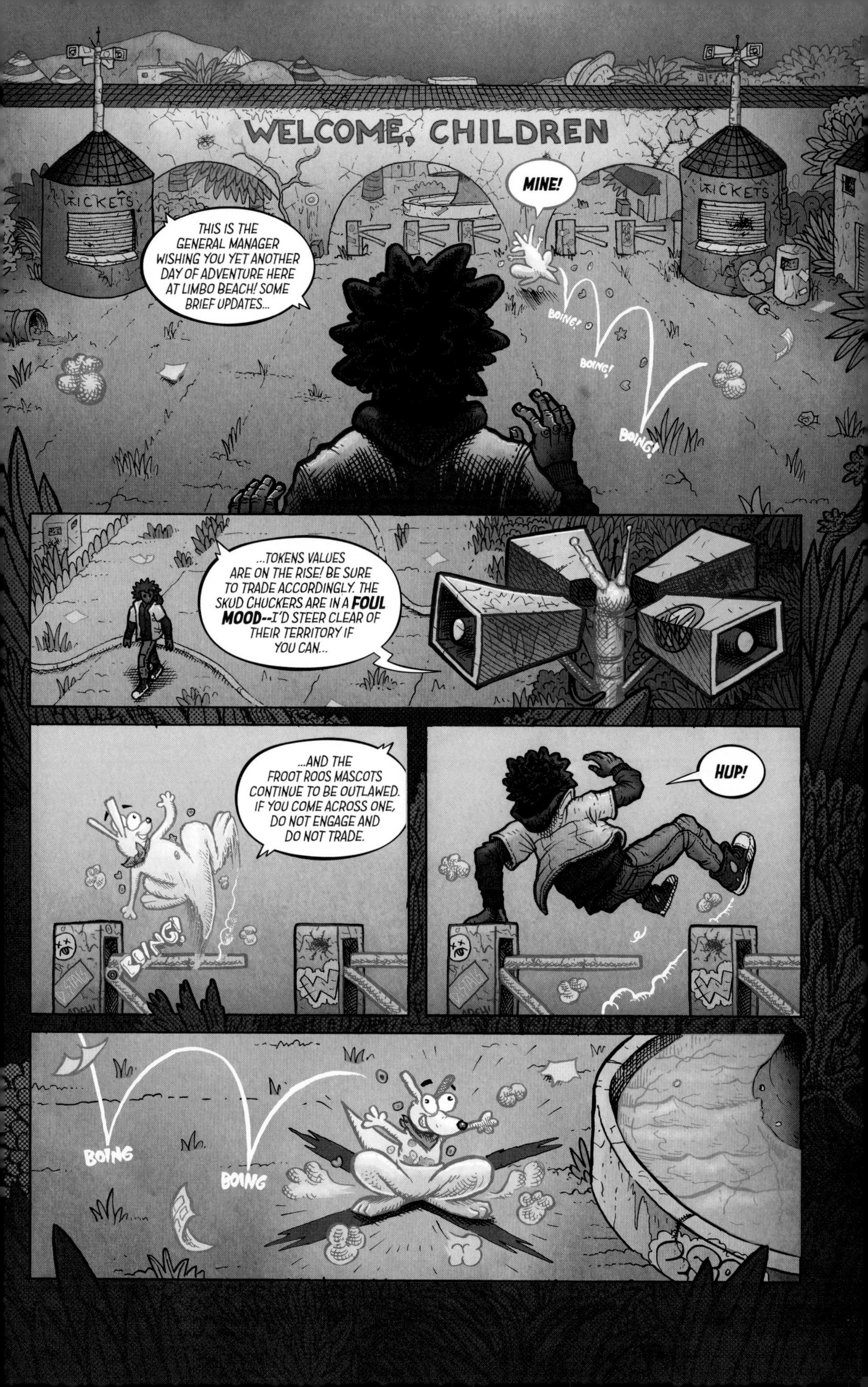
WELCOME, CHILDREN
TICKETS
TICKETS
THIS IS THE GENERAL MANAGER WISHING YOU YET ANOTHER DAY OF ADVENTURE HERE AT LIMBO BEACH! SOME BRIEF UPDATES...
MINE!
BOING!
BOING!
BOING!
...TOKENS VALUES ARE ON THE RISE! BE SURE TO TRADE ACCORDINGLY. THE SKUD CHUCKERS ARE IN A **FOUL MOOD--**I'D STEER CLEAR OF THEIR TERRITORY IF YOU CAN...
...AND THE FROOT ROOS MASCOTS CONTINUE TO BE OUTLAWED. IF YOU COME ACROSS ONE, DO NOT ENGAGE AND DO NOT TRADE.
BOING!
HUP!
BOING
BOING

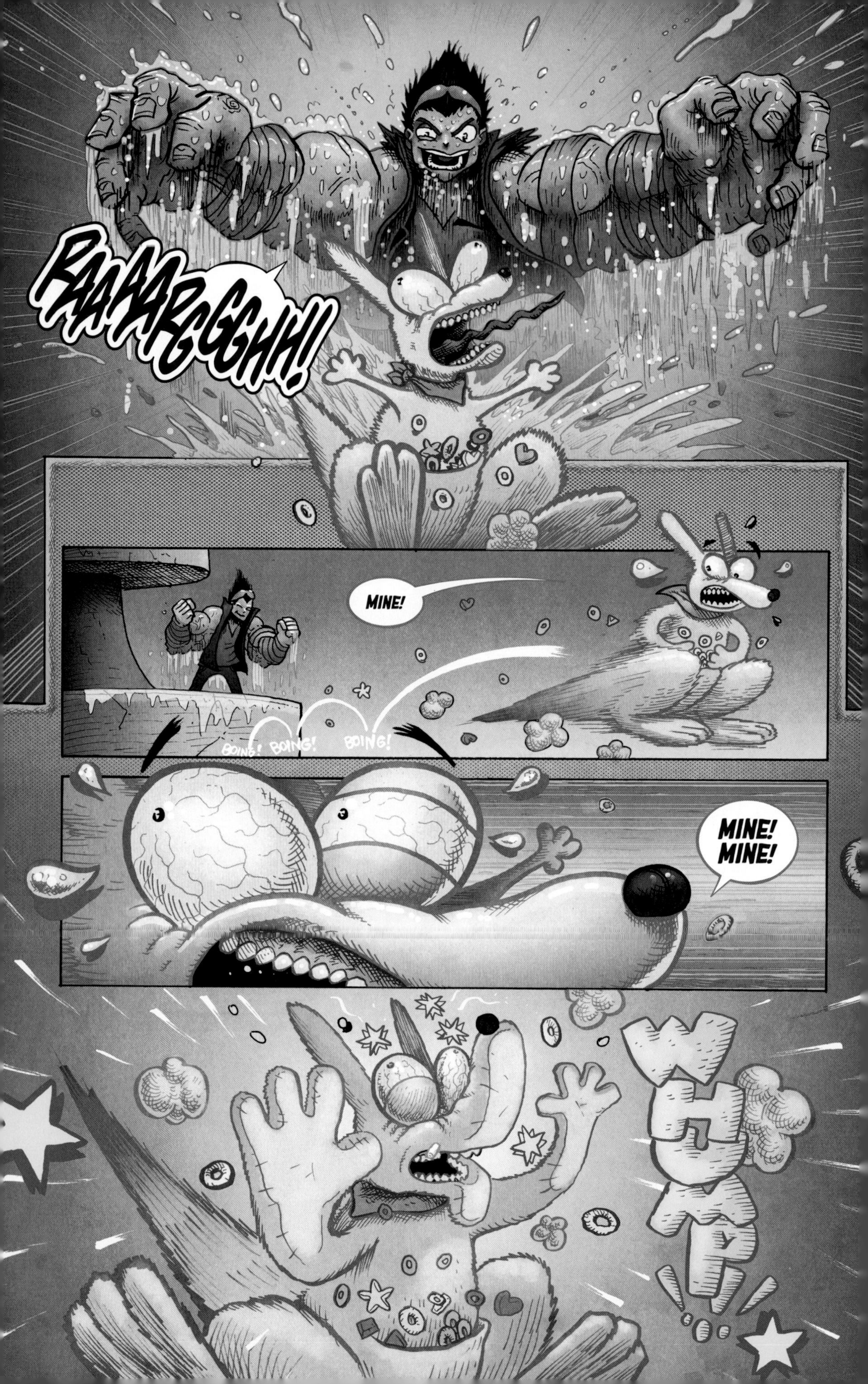
RAAAARGGGHH!!
MINE!
BOING! BOING! BOING!
MINE! MINE!
WHY!!

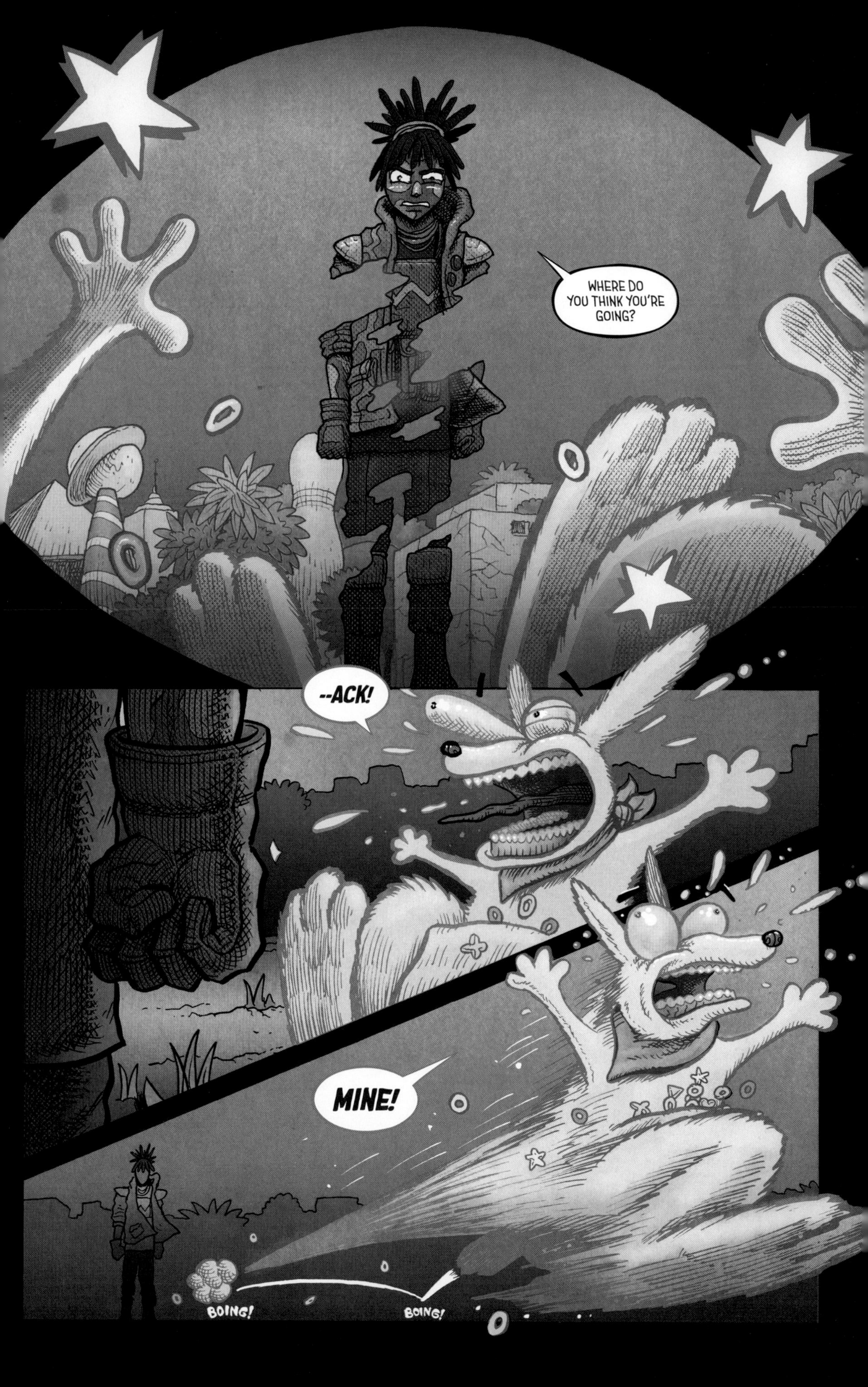
WHERE DO YOU THINK YOU'RE GOING?
--ACK!
MINE!
BOING!
BOING!

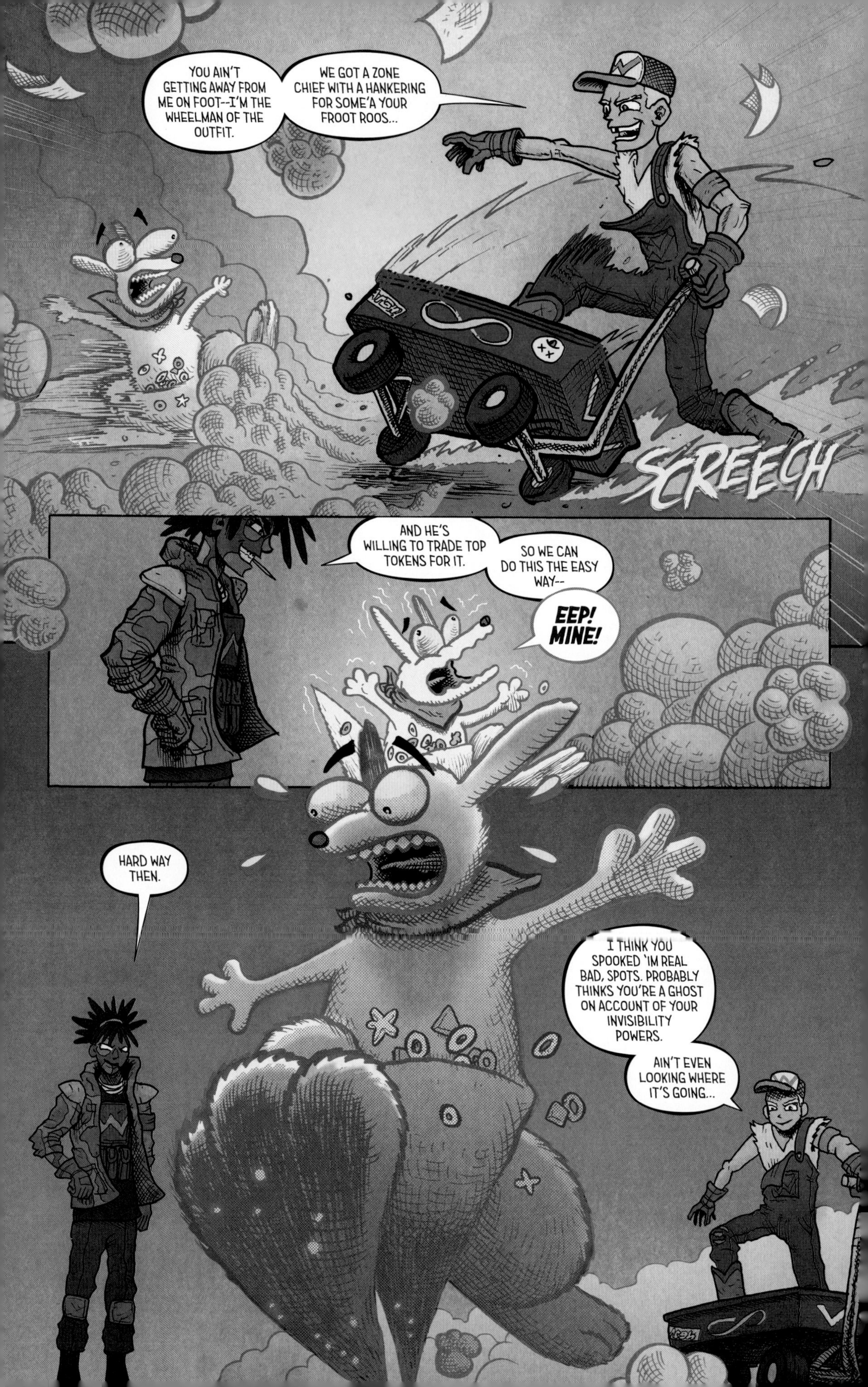

YOU AIN'T GETTING AWAY FROM ME ON FOOT--I'M THE WHEELMAN OF THE OUTFIT.
WE GOT A ZONE CHIEF WITH A HANKERING FOR SOME'A YOUR FROOT ROOS...
SCREECH
AND HE'S WILLING TO TRADE TOP TOKENS FOR IT.
SO WE CAN DO THIS THE EASY WAY--
EEP! MINE!
HARD WAY THEN.
I THINK YOU SPOOKED 'IM REAL BAD, SPOTS. PROBABLY THINKS YOU'RE A GHOST ON ACCOUNT OF YOUR INVISIBILITY POWERS.
AIN'T EVEN LOOKING WHERE IT'S GOING...

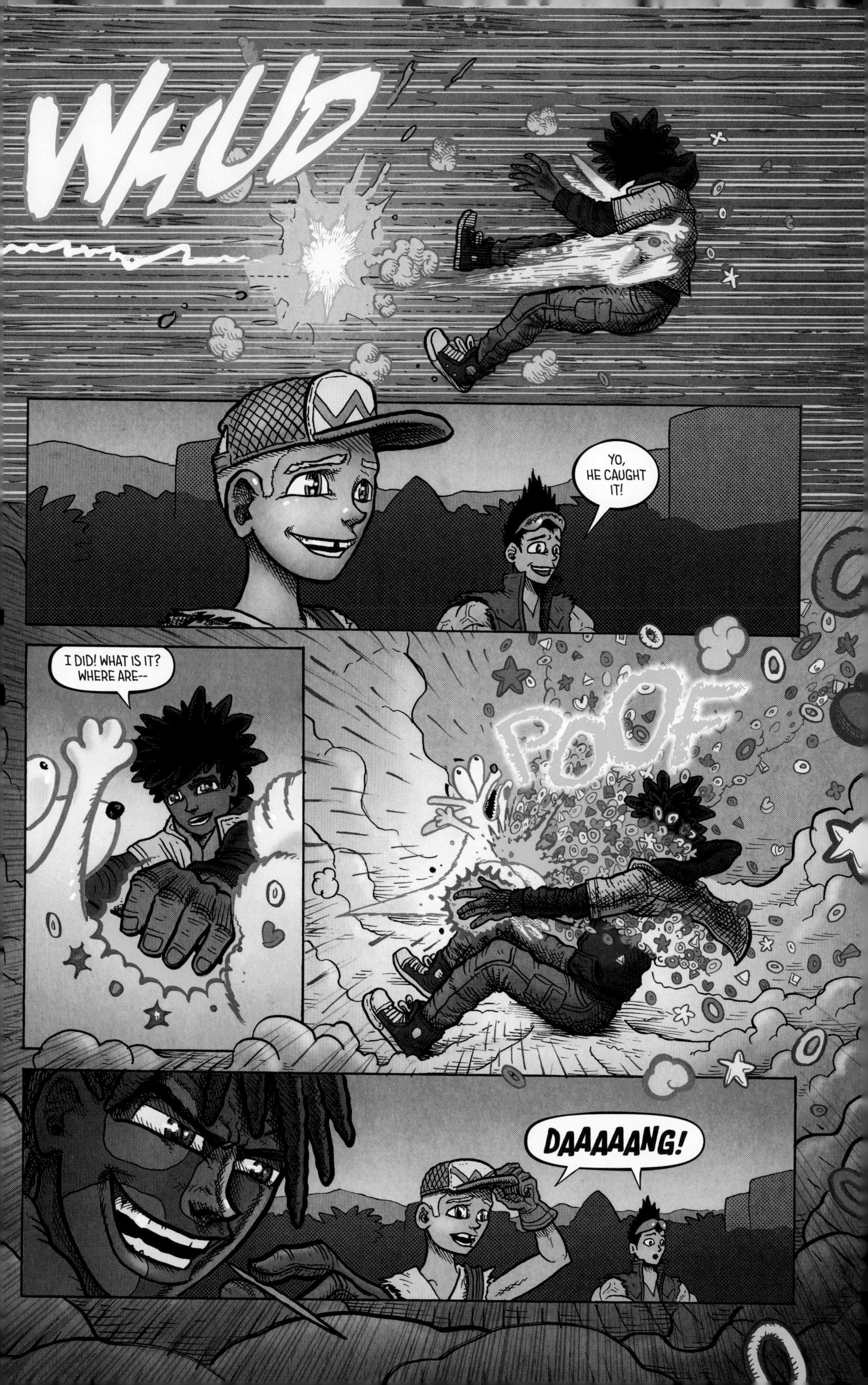
WHUD
YO, HE CAUGHT IT!
I DID! WHAT IS IT? WHERE ARE--
POOF
DAAAAANG!

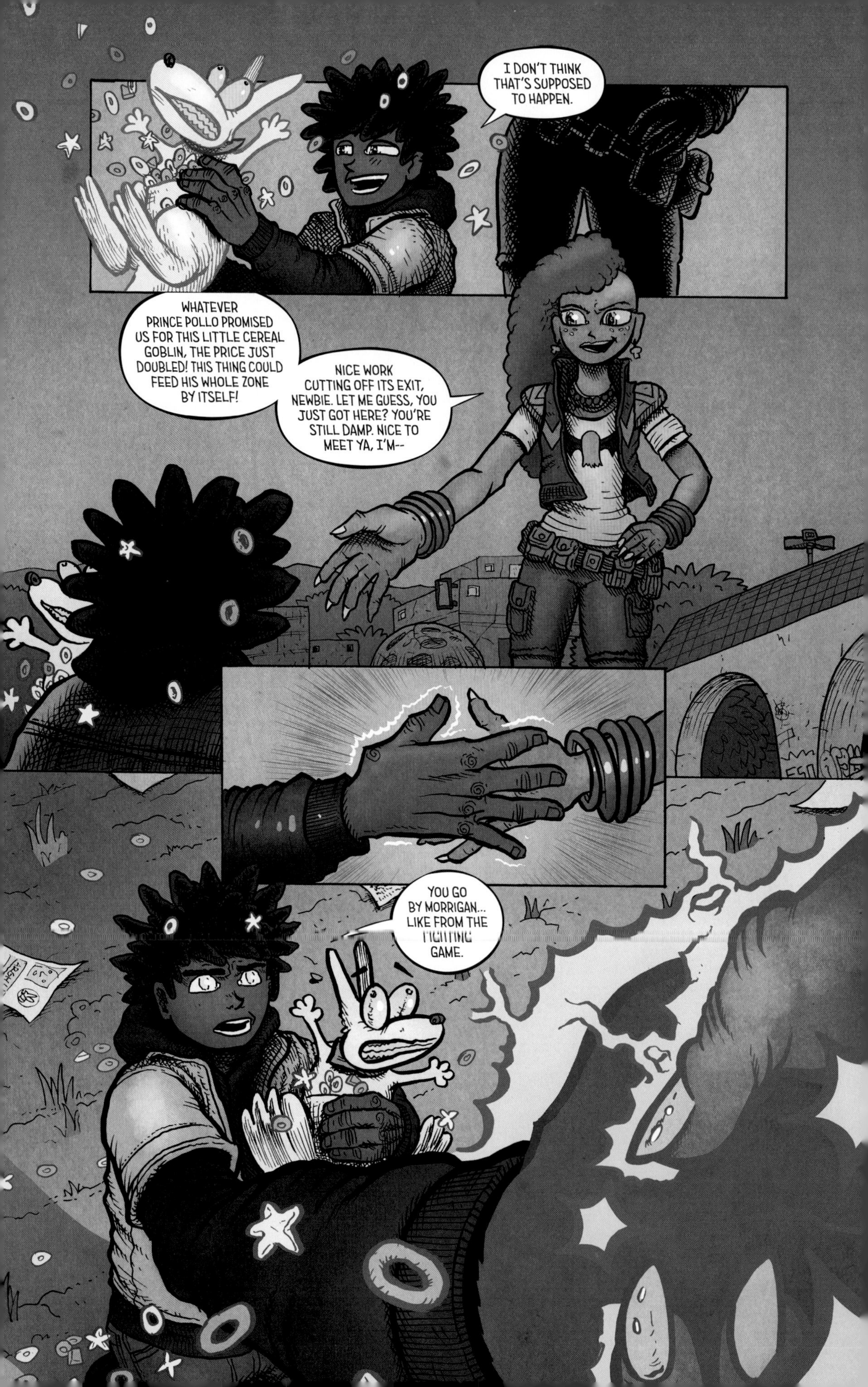
I DON'T THINK THAT'S SUPPOSED TO HAPPEN.
WHATEVER PRINCE POLLO PROMISED US FOR THIS LITTLE CEREAL GOBLIN, THE PRICE JUST DOUBLED! THIS THING COULD FEED HIS WHOLE ZONE BY ITSELF!
NICE WORK CUTTING OFF ITS EXIT, NEWBIE. LET ME GUESS, YOU JUST GOT HERE? YOU'RE STILL DAMP. NICE TO MEET YA, I'M--
YOU GO BY MORRIGAN... LIKE FROM THE FIGHTING GAME.

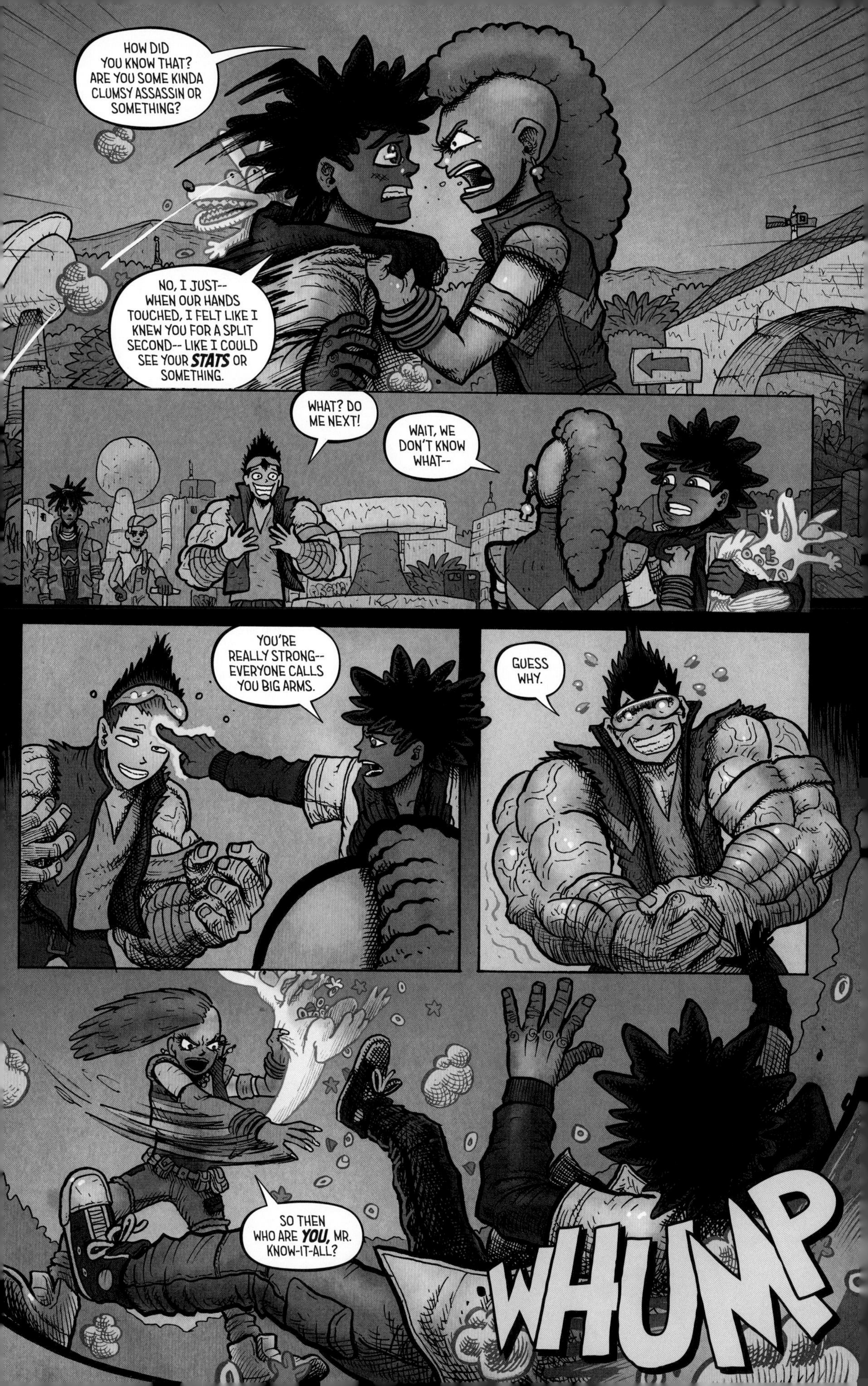
HOW DID YOU KNOW THAT? ARE YOU SOME KINDA CLUMSY ASSASSIN OR SOMETHING?
NO, I JUST-- WHEN OUR HANDS TOUCHED, I FELT LIKE I KNEW YOU FOR A SPLIT SECOND-- LIKE I COULD SEE YOUR STATS OR SOMETHING.
WHAT? DO ME NEXT!
WAIT, WE DON'T KNOW WHAT--
YOU'RE REALLY STRONG-- EVERYONE CALLS YOU BIG ARMS.
GUESS WHY.
SO THEN WHO ARE YOU, MR. KNOW-IT-ALL?
WHUMP

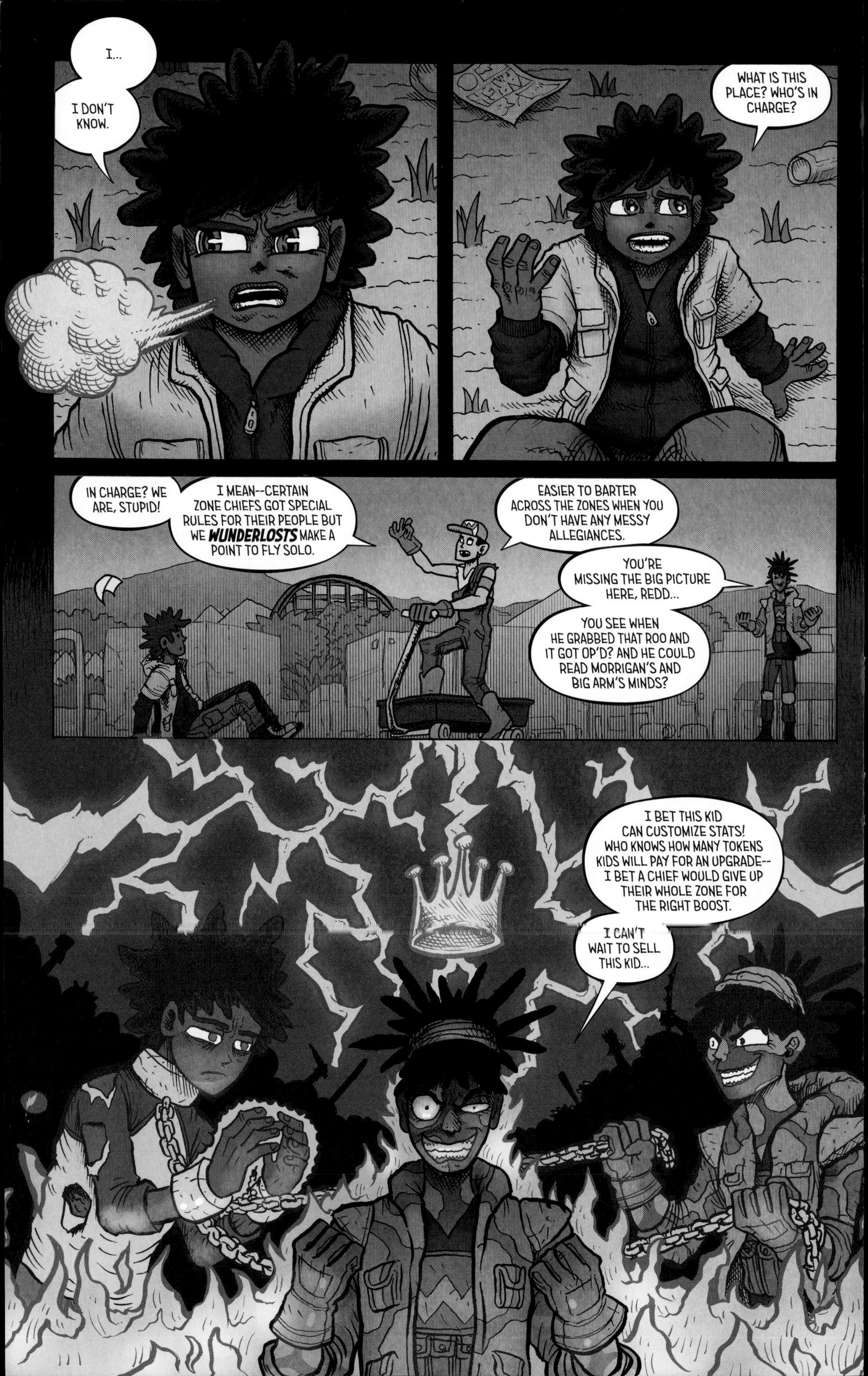
I...
I DON'T KNOW.
WHAT IS THIS PLACE? WHO'S IN CHARGE?
IN CHARGE? WE ARE, STUPID!
I MEAN--CERTAIN ZONE CHIEFS GOT SPECIAL RULES FOR THEIR PEOPLE BUT WE WUNDERLOSTS MAKE A POINT TO FLY SOLO.
EASIER TO BARTER ACROSS THE ZONES WHEN YOU DON'T HAVE ANY MESSY ALLEGIANCES.
YOU'RE MISSING THE BIG PICTURE HERE, REDD...
YOU SEE WHEN HE GRABBED THAT ROO AND IT GOT OP'D? AND HE COULD READ MORRIGAN'S AND BIG ARM'S MINDS?
I BET THIS KID CAN CUSTOMIZE STATS! WHO KNOWS HOW MANY TOKENS KIDS WILL PAY FOR AN UPGRADE-- I BET A CHIEF WOULD GIVE UP THEIR WHOLE ZONE FOR THE RIGHT BOOST.
I CAN'T WAIT TO SELL THIS KID...

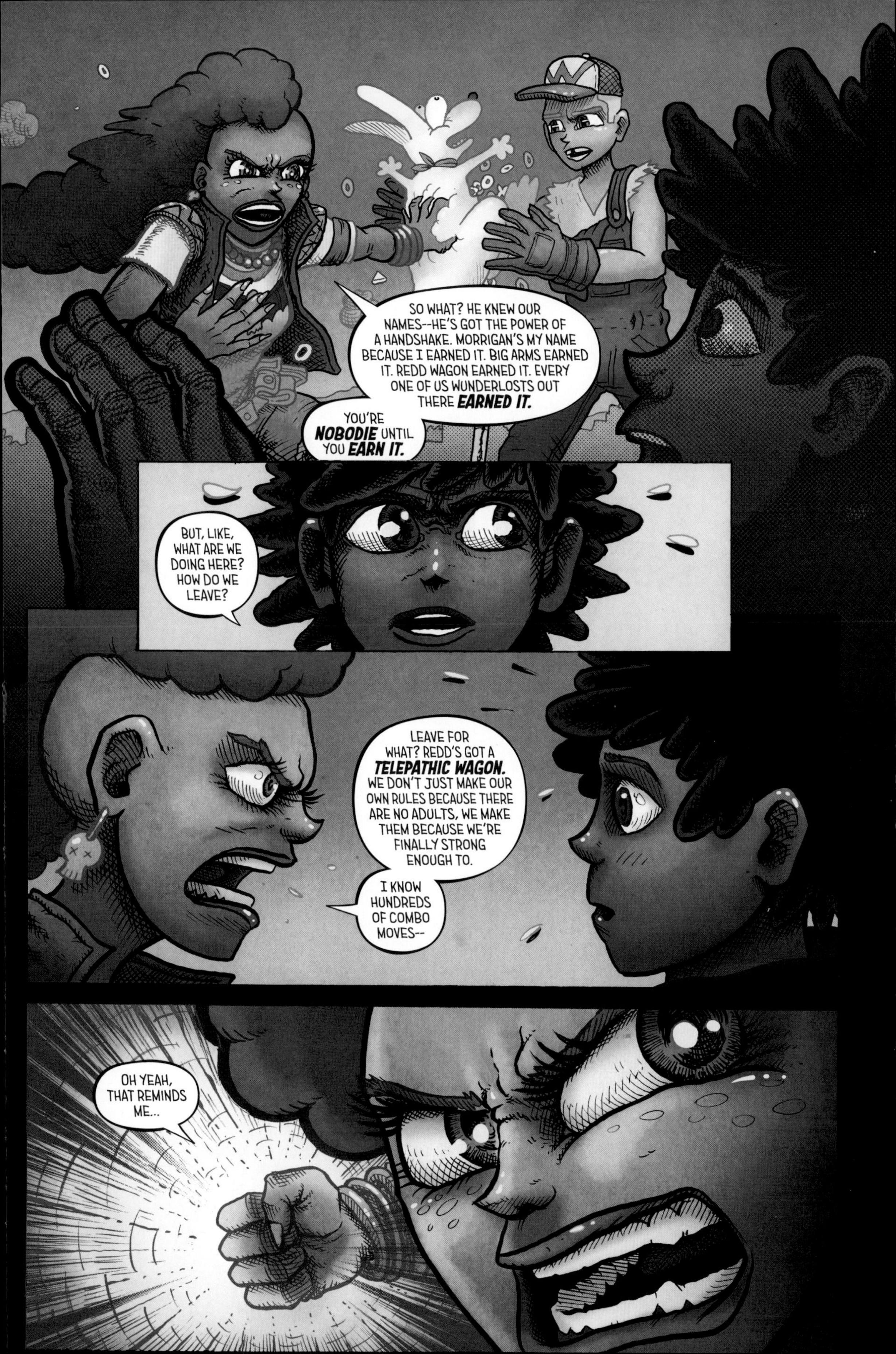

SO WHAT? HE KNEW OUR NAMES--HE'S GOT THE POWER OF A HANDSHAKE. MORRIGAN'S MY NAME BECAUSE I EARNED IT. BIG ARMS EARNED IT. REDD WAGON EARNED IT. EVERY ONE OF US WUNDERLOSTS OUT THERE ***EARNED IT.***
YOU'RE ***NOBODIE*** UNTIL YOU ***EARN IT.***
BUT, LIKE, WHAT ARE WE DOING HERE? HOW DO WE LEAVE?
LEAVE FOR WHAT? REDD'S GOT A ***TELEPATHIC WAGON.*** WE DON'T JUST MAKE OUR OWN RULES BECAUSE THERE ARE NO ADULTS, WE MAKE THEM BECAUSE WE'RE FINALLY STRONG ENOUGH TO.
I KNOW HUNDREDS OF COMBO MOVES--
OH YEAH, THAT REMINDS ME...

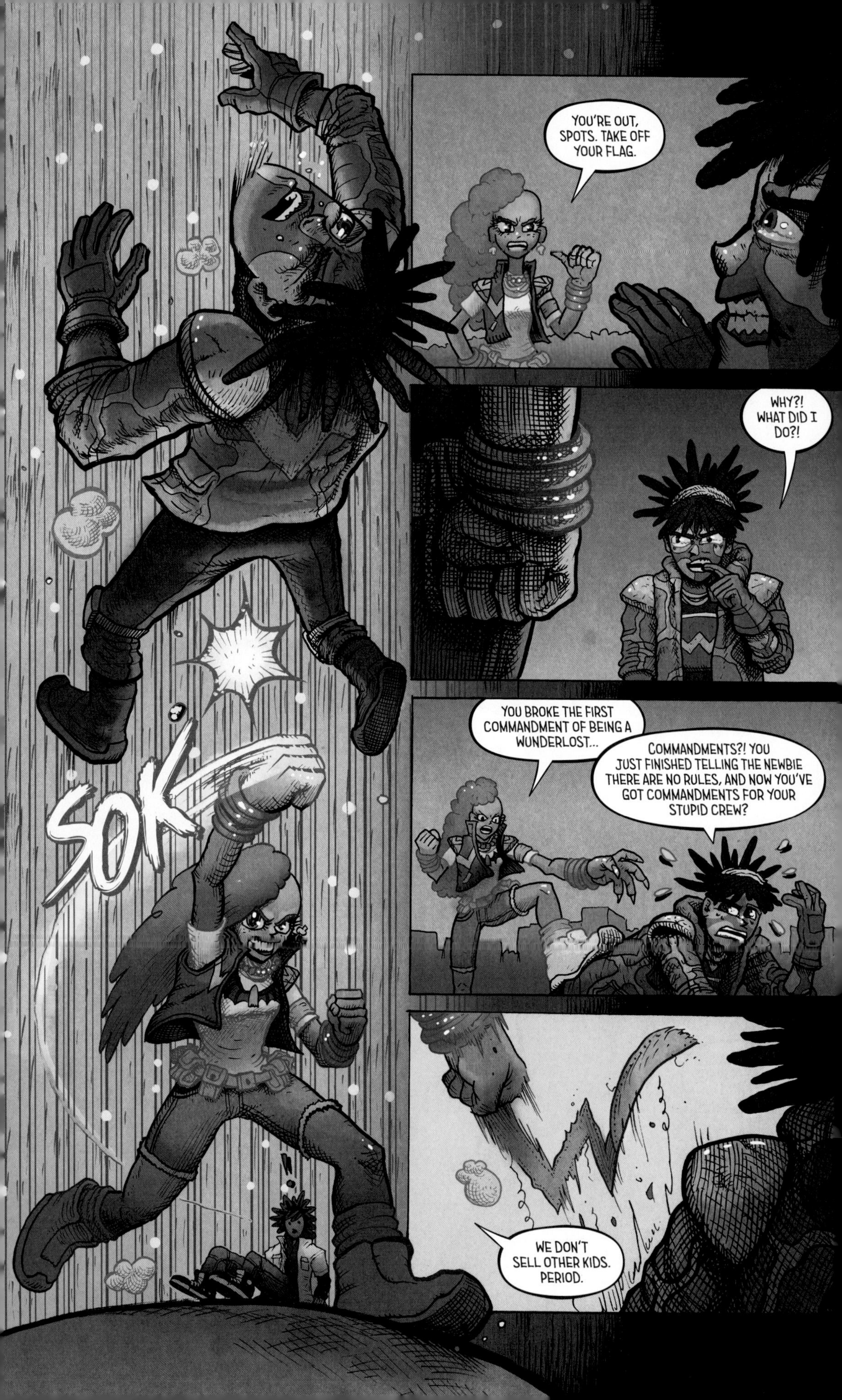
YOU'RE OUT, SPOTS. TAKE OFF YOUR FLAG.
WHY?! WHAT DID I DO?!
SOK
YOU BROKE THE FIRST COMMANDMENT OF BEING A WUNDERLOST...
COMMANDMENTS?! YOU JUST FINISHED TELLING THE NEWBIE THERE ARE NO RULES, AND NOW YOU'VE GOT COMMANDMENTS FOR YOUR STUPID CREW?
WE DON'T SELL OTHER KIDS. PERIOD.

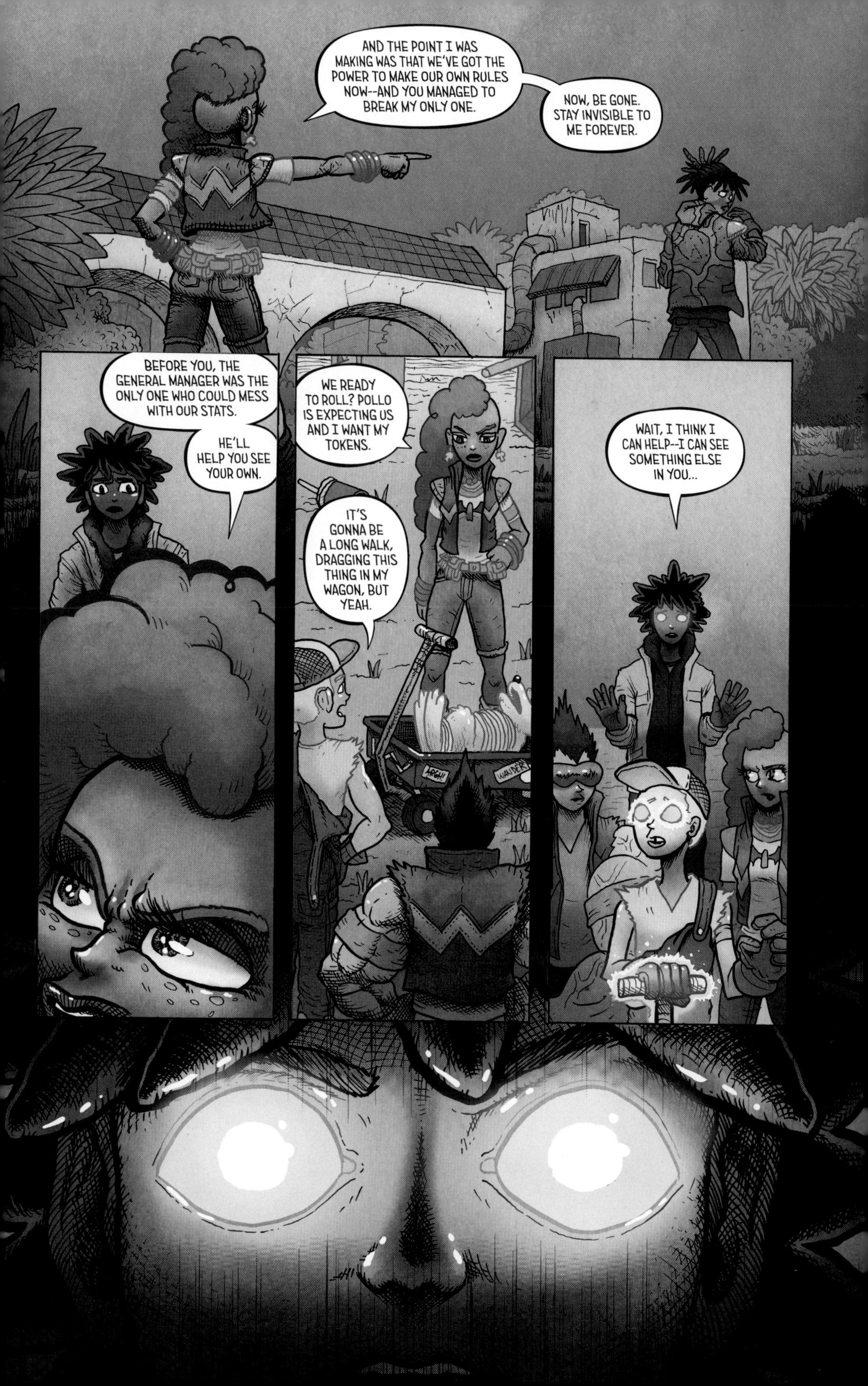
AND THE POINT I WAS MAKING WAS THAT WE'VE GOT THE POWER TO MAKE OUR OWN RULES NOW--AND YOU MANAGED TO BREAK MY ONLY ONE.
NOW, BE GONE. STAY INVISIBLE TO ME FOREVER.
BEFORE YOU, THE GENERAL MANAGER WAS THE ONLY ONE WHO COULD MESS WITH OUR STATS.
HE'LL HELP YOU SEE YOUR OWN.
WE READY TO ROLL? POLLO IS EXPECTING US AND I WANT MY TOKENS.
IT'S GONNA BE A LONG WALK, DRAGGING THIS THING IN MY WAGON, BUT YEAH.
ARGH!
WANDER
WAIT, I THINK I CAN HELP--I CAN SEE SOMETHING ELSE IN YOU...

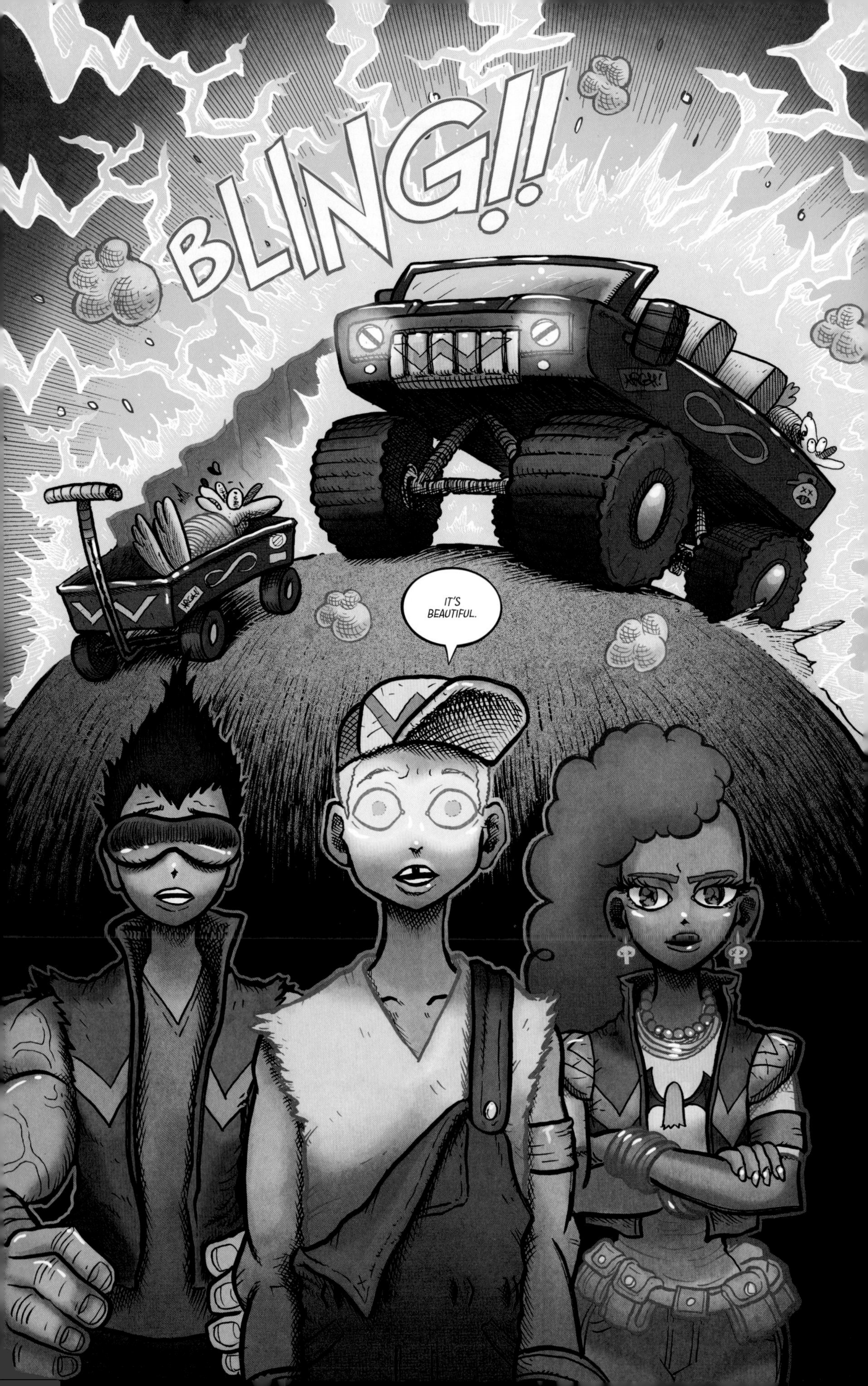

BLING!!
IT'S BEAUTIFUL.

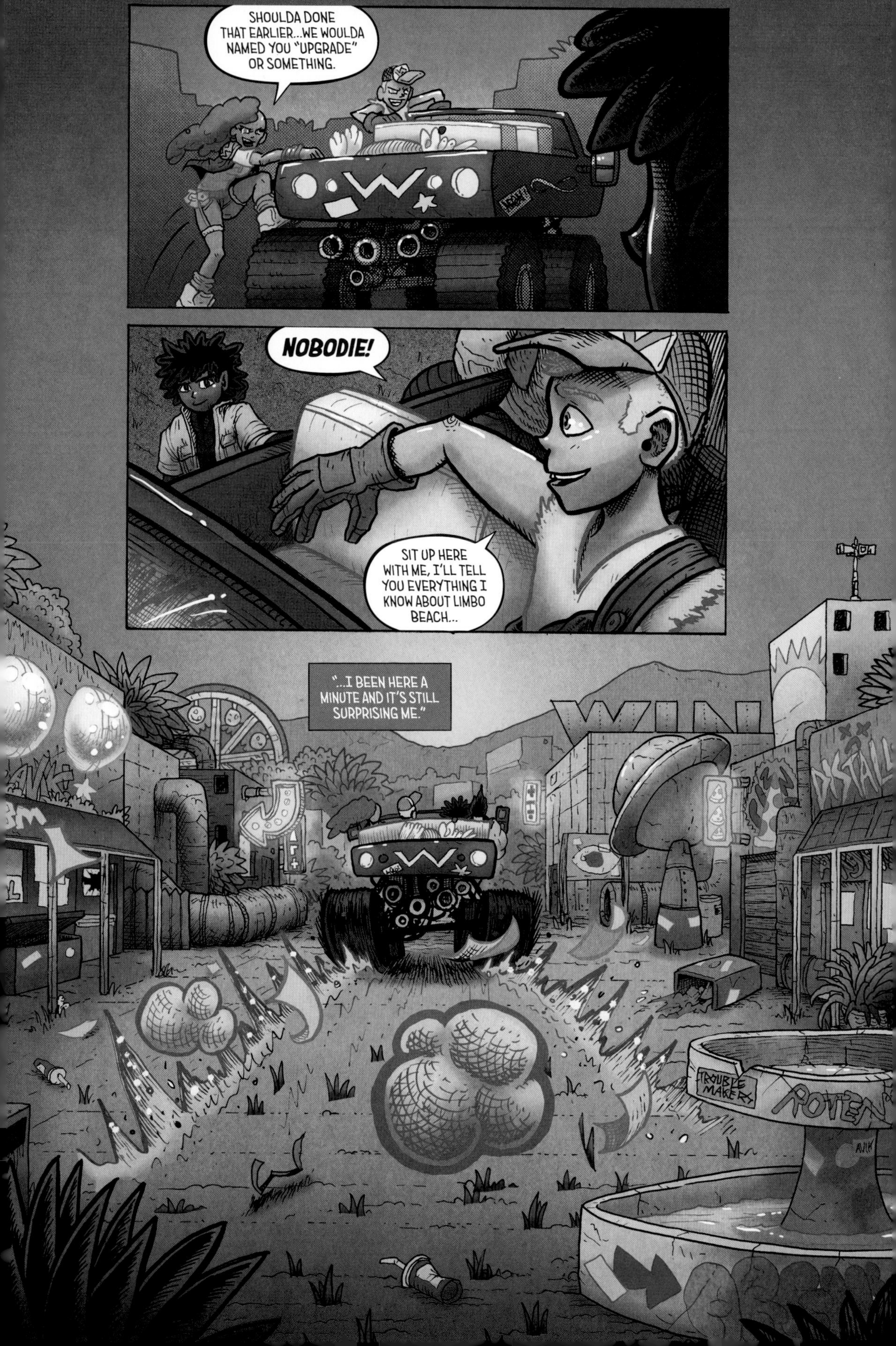
SHOULDA DONE THAT EARLIER...WE WOULDA NAMED YOU "UPGRADE" OR SOMETHING.
NOBODIE!
SIT UP HERE WITH ME, I'LL TELL YOU EVERYTHING I KNOW ABOUT LIMBO BEACH...
"...I BEEN HERE A MINUTE AND IT'S STILL SURPRISING ME."
TROUBLE MAKERS
ROTTEN

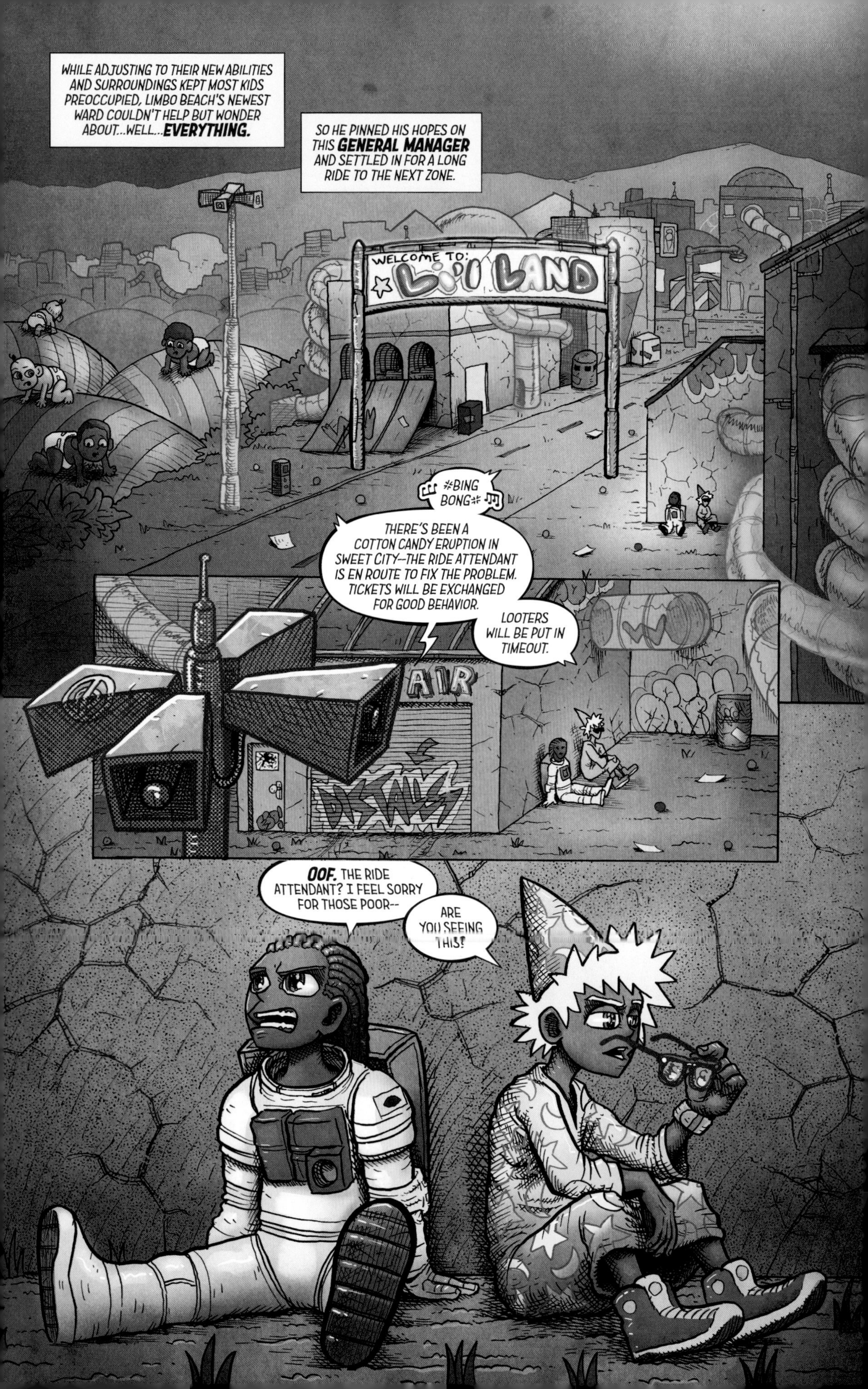
WHILE ADJUSTING TO THEIR NEW ABILITIES AND SURROUNDINGS KEPT MOST KIDS PREOCCUPIED, LIMBO BEACH'S NEWEST WARD COULDN'T HELP BUT WONDER ABOUT...WELL...**EVERYTHING.**
SO HE PINNED HIS HOPES ON THIS **GENERAL MANAGER** AND SETTLED IN FOR A LONG RIDE TO THE NEXT ZONE.
WELCOME TO: LI'L LAND
#BING BONG#
THERE'S BEEN A COTTON CANDY ERUPTION IN SWEET CITY--THE RIDE ATTENDANT IS EN ROUTE TO FIX THE PROBLEM. TICKETS WILL BE EXCHANGED FOR GOOD BEHAVIOR.
LOOTERS WILL BE PUT IN TIMEOUT.
AIR
OOF. THE RIDE ATTENDANT? I FEEL SORRY FOR THOSE POOR--
ARE YOU SEEING THIS?

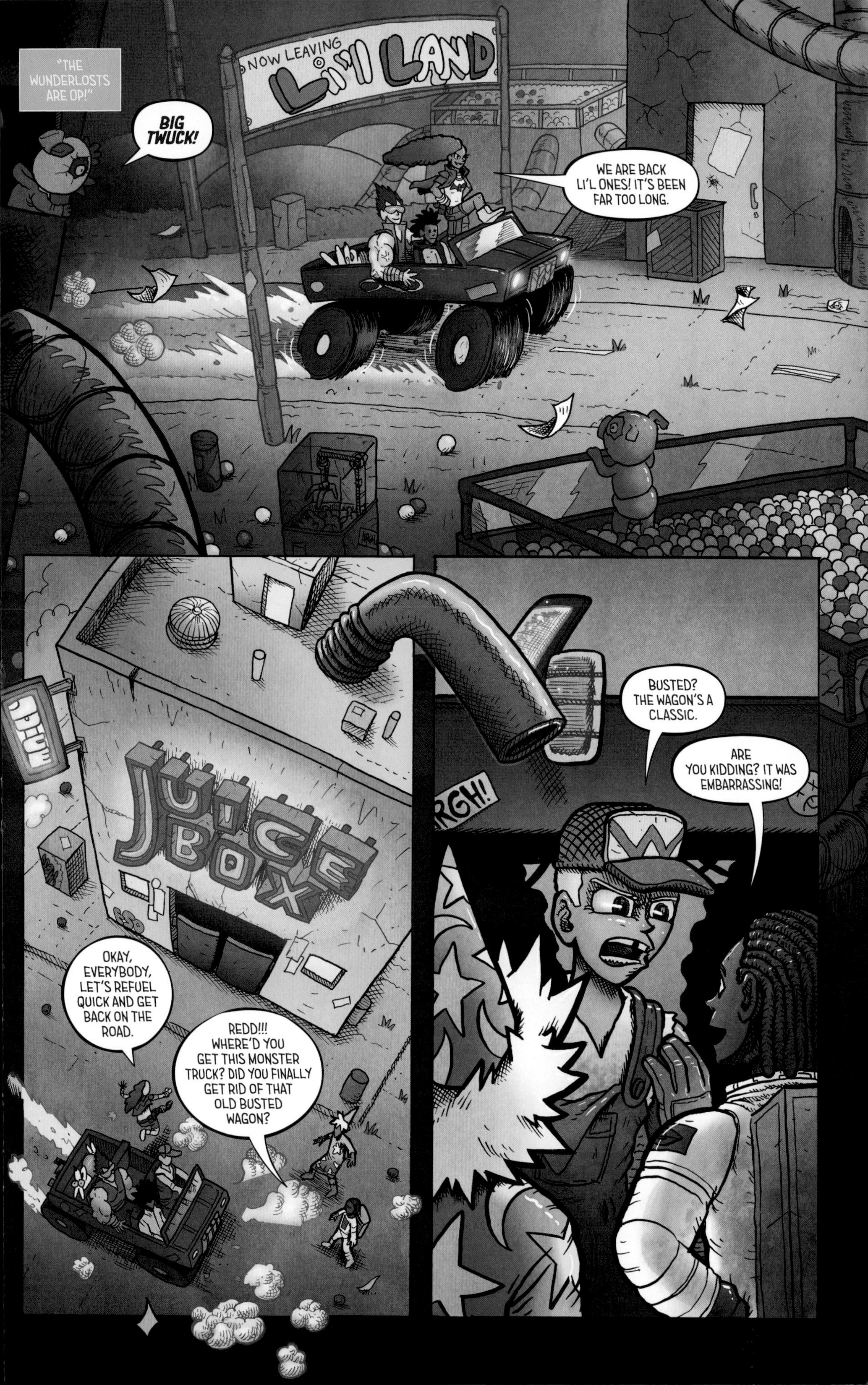
"THE WUNDERLOSTS ARE OP!"
BIG TWUCK!
NOW LEAVING LI'L LAND
WE ARE BACK LI'L ONES! IT'S BEEN FAR TOO LONG.
JUICE BOX
OKAY, EVERYBODY, LET'S REFUEL QUICK AND GET BACK ON THE ROAD.
REDD!!! WHERE'D YOU GET THIS MONSTER TRUCK? DID YOU FINALLY GET RID OF THAT OLD BUSTED WAGON?
BUSTED? THE WAGON'S A CLASSIC.
ARE YOU KIDDING? IT WAS EMBARRASSING!

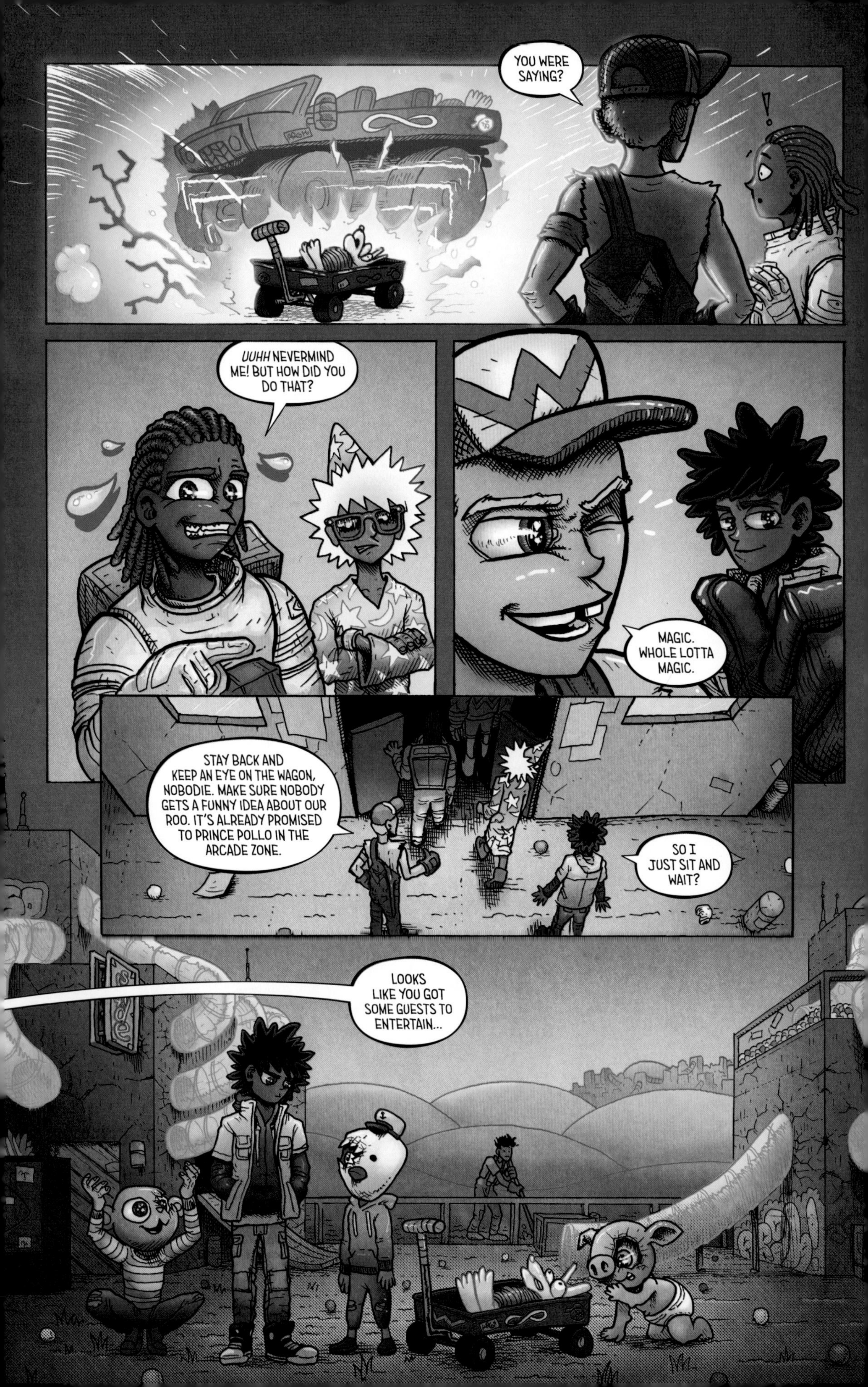
YOU WERE SAYING?
!
UUHH NEVERMIND ME! BUT HOW DID YOU DO THAT?
MAGIC. WHOLE LOTTA MAGIC.
STAY BACK AND KEEP AN EYE ON THE WAGON, NOBODIE. MAKE SURE NOBODY GETS A FUNNY IDEA ABOUT OUR ROO. IT'S ALREADY PROMISED TO PRINCE POLLO IN THE ARCADE ZONE.
SO I JUST SIT AND WAIT?
LOOKS LIKE YOU GOT SOME GUESTS TO ENTERTAIN...

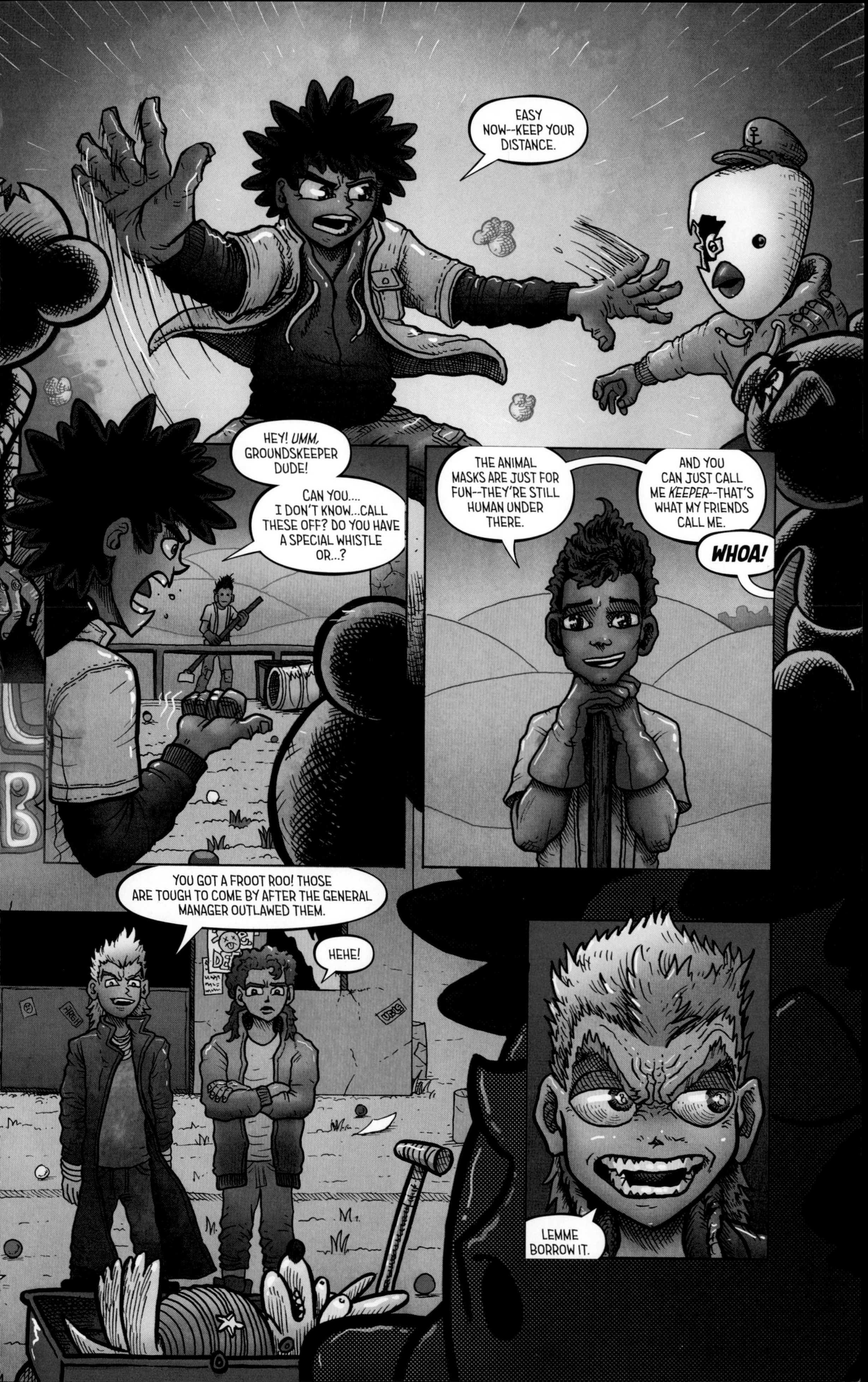
EASY NOW--KEEP YOUR DISTANCE.
HEY! UMM, GROUNDSKEEPER DUDE!
CAN YOU.... I DON'T KNOW...CALL THESE OFF? DO YOU HAVE A SPECIAL WHISTLE OR...?
THE ANIMAL MASKS ARE JUST FOR FUN--THEY'RE STILL HUMAN UNDER THERE.
AND YOU CAN JUST CALL ME KEEPER--THAT'S WHAT MY FRIENDS CALL ME.
WHOA!
YOU GOT A FROOT ROO! THOSE ARE TOUGH TO COME BY AFTER THE GENERAL MANAGER OUTLAWED THEM.
HEHE!
LEMME BORROW IT.

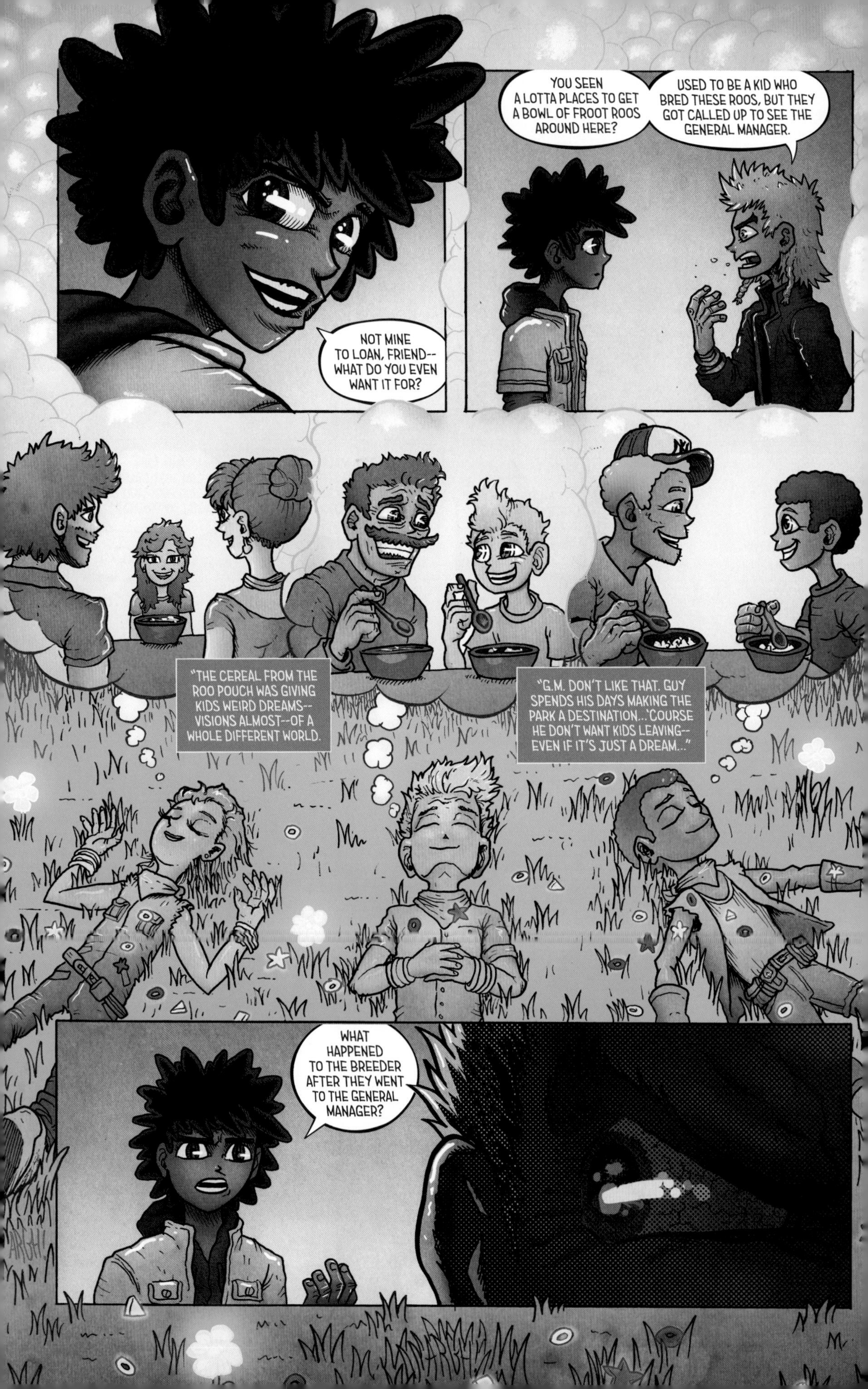

NOT MINE TO LOAN, FRIEND-- WHAT DO YOU EVEN WANT IT FOR?
YOU SEEN A LOTTA PLACES TO GET A BOWL OF FROOT ROOS AROUND HERE?
USED TO BE A KID WHO BRED THESE ROOS, BUT THEY GOT CALLED UP TO SEE THE GENERAL MANAGER.
"THE CEREAL FROM THE ROO POUCH WAS GIVING KIDS WEIRD DREAMS-- VISIONS ALMOST--OF A WHOLE DIFFERENT WORLD.
"G.M. DON'T LIKE THAT. GUY SPENDS HIS DAYS MAKING THE PARK A DESTINATION...'COURSE HE DON'T WANT KIDS LEAVING-- EVEN IF IT'S JUST A DREAM..."
WHAT HAPPENED TO THE BREEDER AFTER THEY WENT TO THE GENERAL MANAGER?
ARGH!

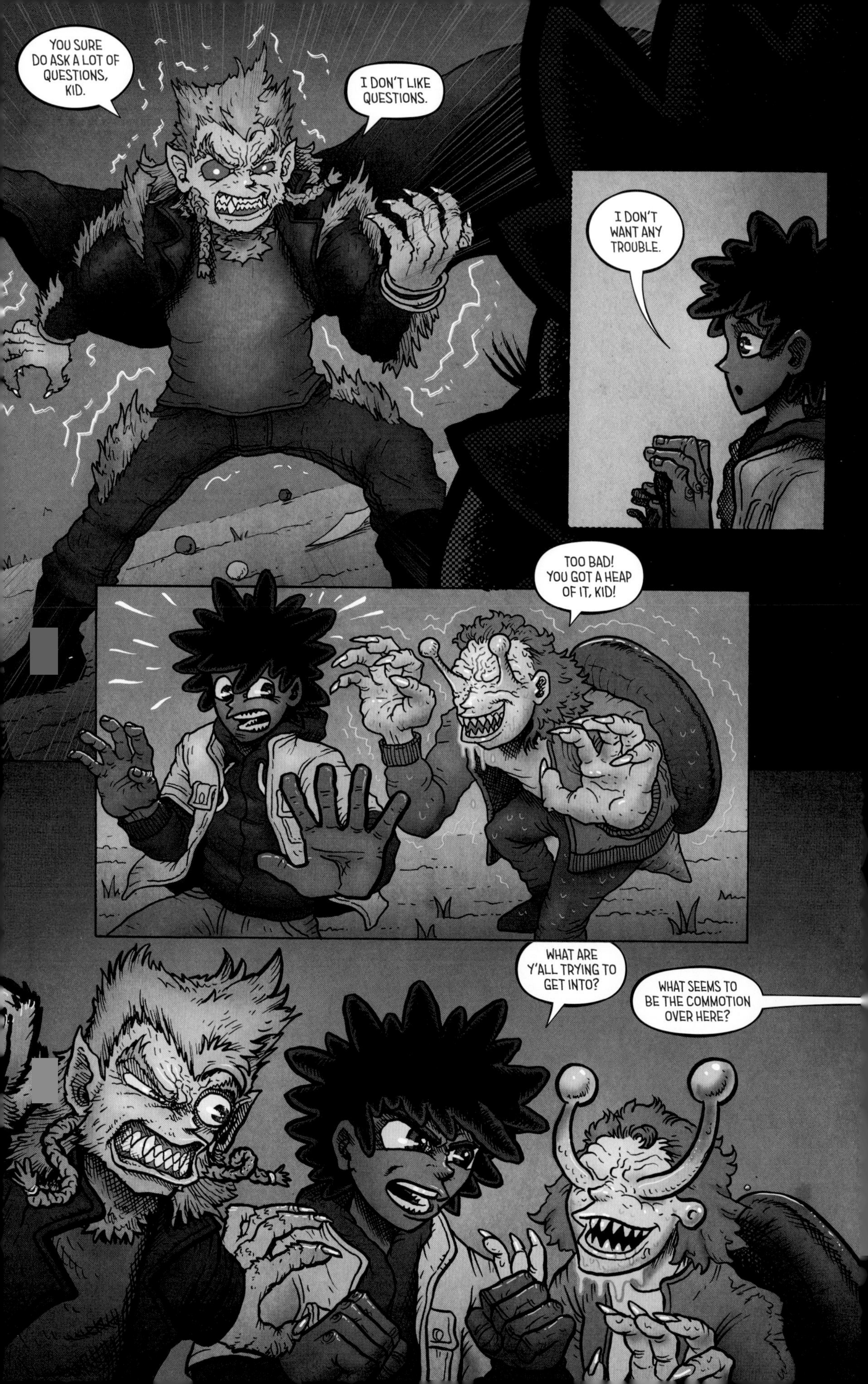
YOU SURE DO ASK A LOT OF QUESTIONS, KID.
I DON'T LIKE QUESTIONS.
I DON'T WANT ANY TROUBLE.
TOO BAD! YOU GOT A HEAP OF IT, KID!
WHAT ARE Y'ALL TRYING TO GET INTO?
WHAT SEEMS TO BE THE COMMOTION OVER HERE?

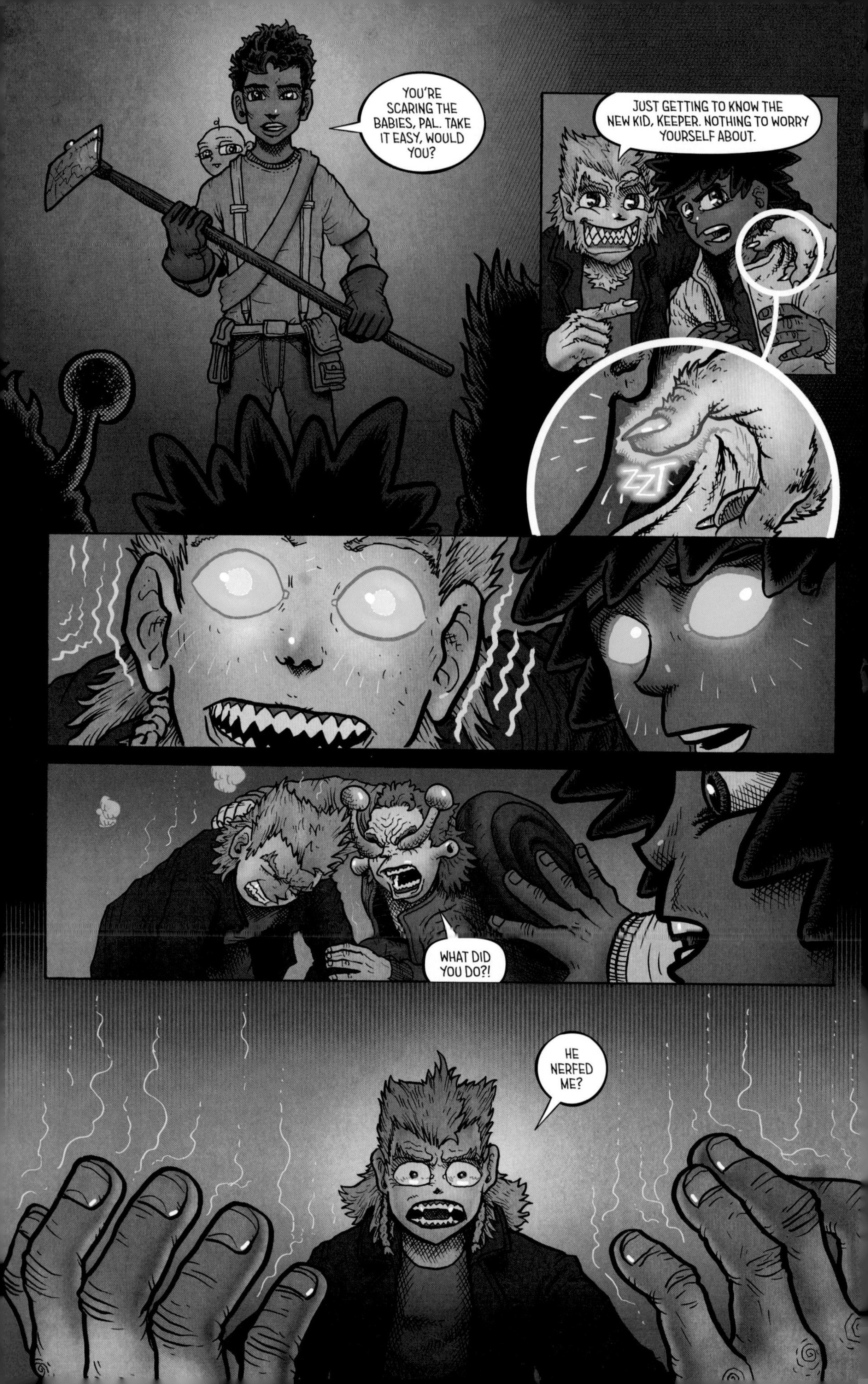
YOU'RE SCARING THE BABIES, PAL. TAKE IT EASY, WOULD YOU?
JUST GETTING TO KNOW THE NEW KID, KEEPER. NOTHING TO WORRY YOURSELF ABOUT.
ZZT
WHAT DID YOU DO?!
HE NERFED ME?

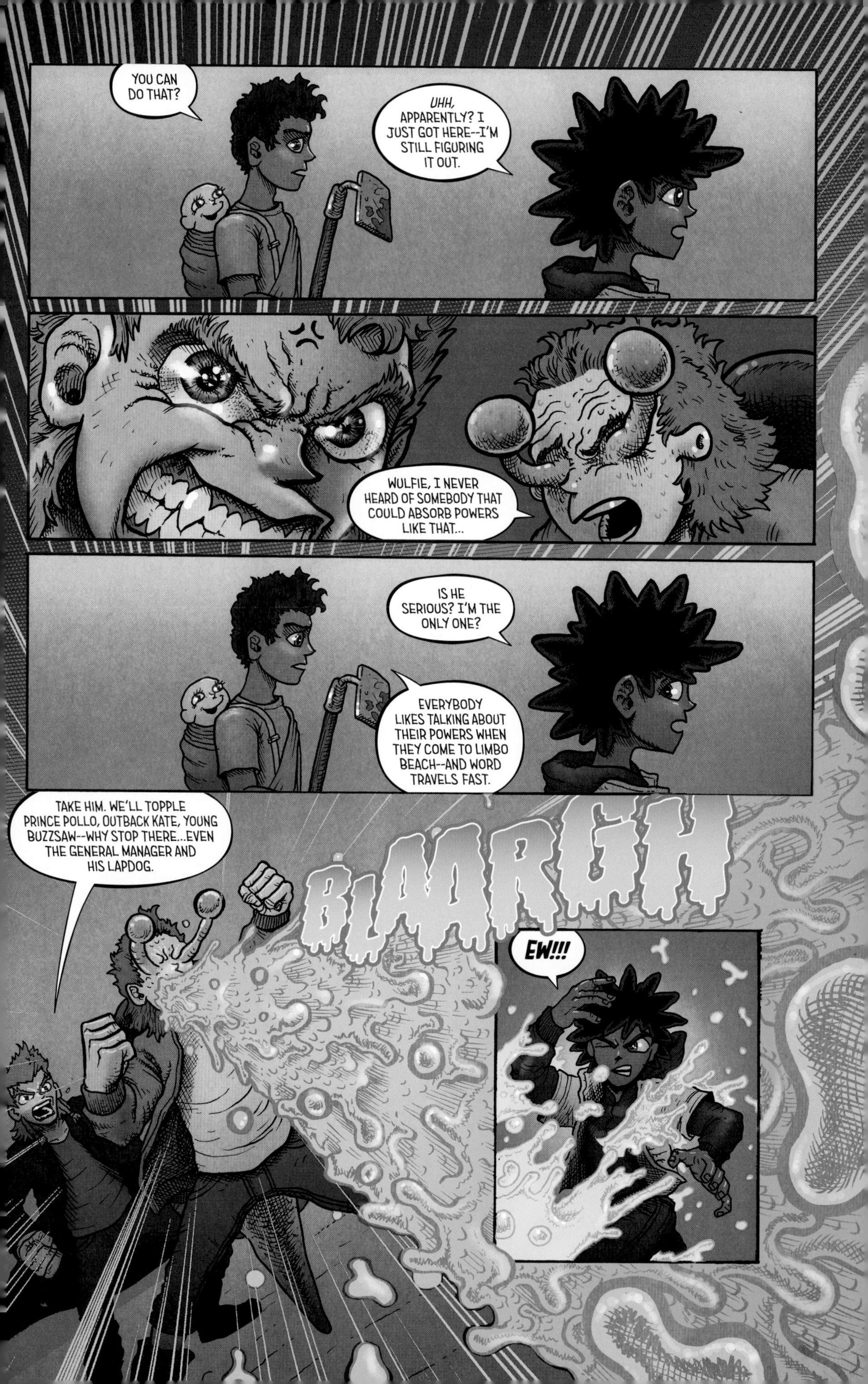
YOU CAN DO THAT?
UHH, APPARENTLY? I JUST GOT HERE--I'M STILL FIGURING IT OUT.
WULFIE, I NEVER HEARD OF SOMEBODY THAT COULD ABSORB POWERS LIKE THAT...
IS HE SERIOUS? I'M THE ONLY ONE?
EVERYBODY LIKES TALKING ABOUT THEIR POWERS WHEN THEY COME TO LIMBO BEACH--AND WORD TRAVELS FAST.
TAKE HIM. WE'LL TOPPLE PRINCE POLLO, OUTBACK KATE, YOUNG BUZZSAW--WHY STOP THERE...EVEN THE GENERAL MANAGER AND HIS LAPDOG.
BLAARGH
EW!!!

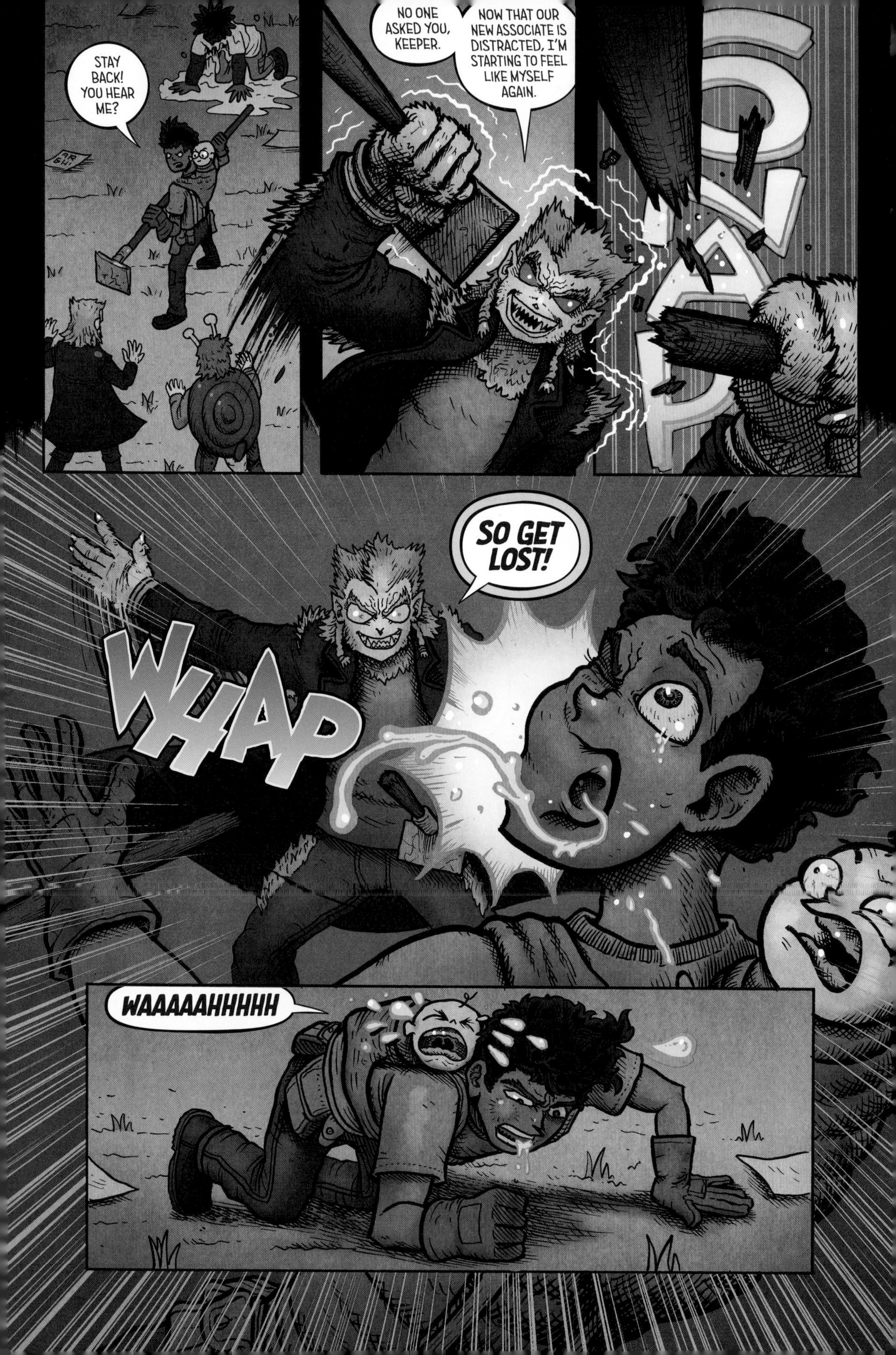
STAY BACK! YOU HEAR ME?
NO ONE ASKED YOU, KEEPER.
NOW THAT OUR NEW ASSOCIATE IS DISTRACTED, I'M STARTING TO FEEL LIKE MYSELF AGAIN.
SNAP
SO GET LOST!
WHAP
WAAAAAHHHHH

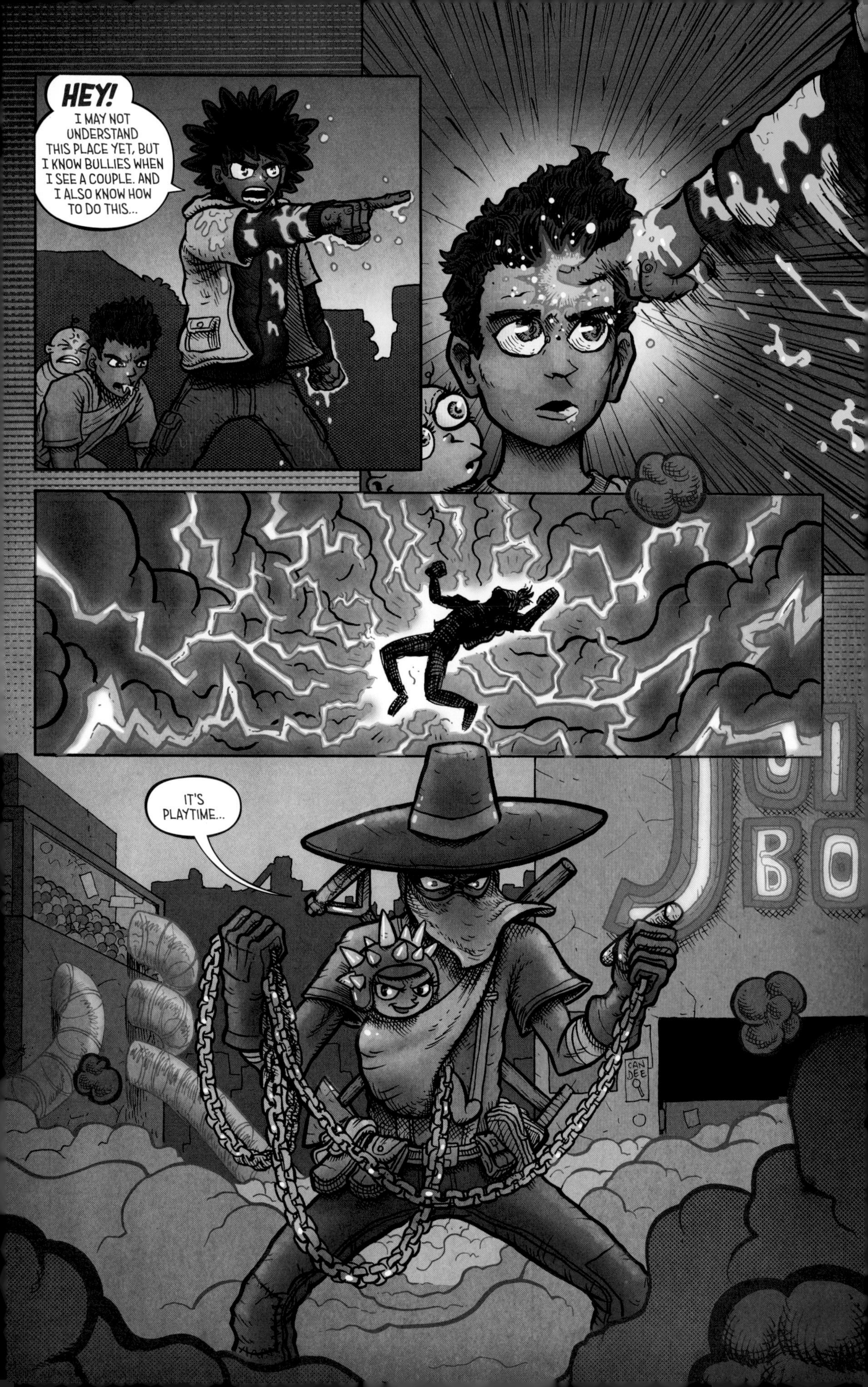
HEY! I MAY NOT UNDERSTAND THIS PLACE YET, BUT I KNOW BULLIES WHEN I SEE A COUPLE. AND I ALSO KNOW HOW TO DO THIS...
IT'S PLAYTIME...

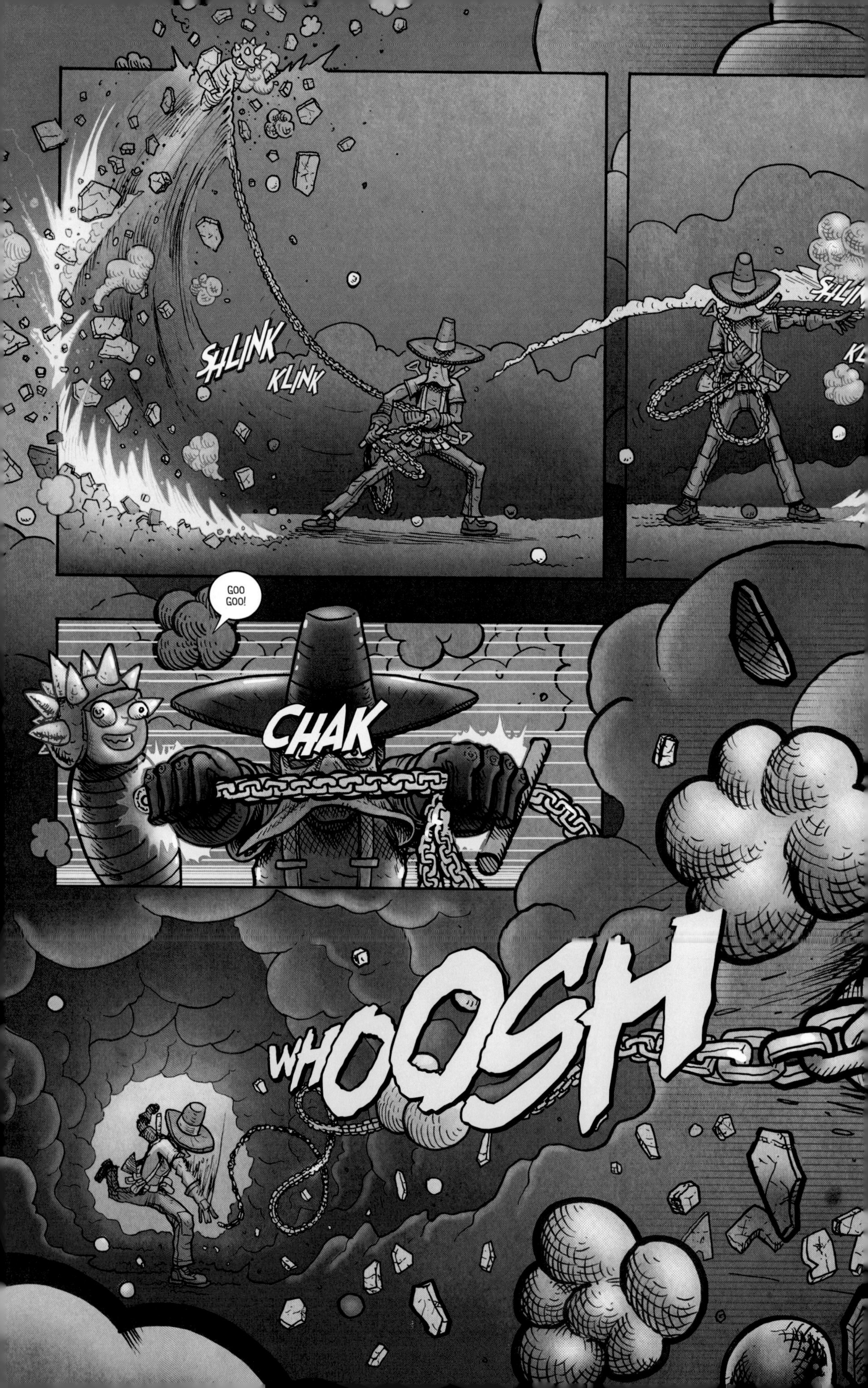
SHLINK
KLINK
SHLINK
GOO GOO!
CHAK
WHOOSH

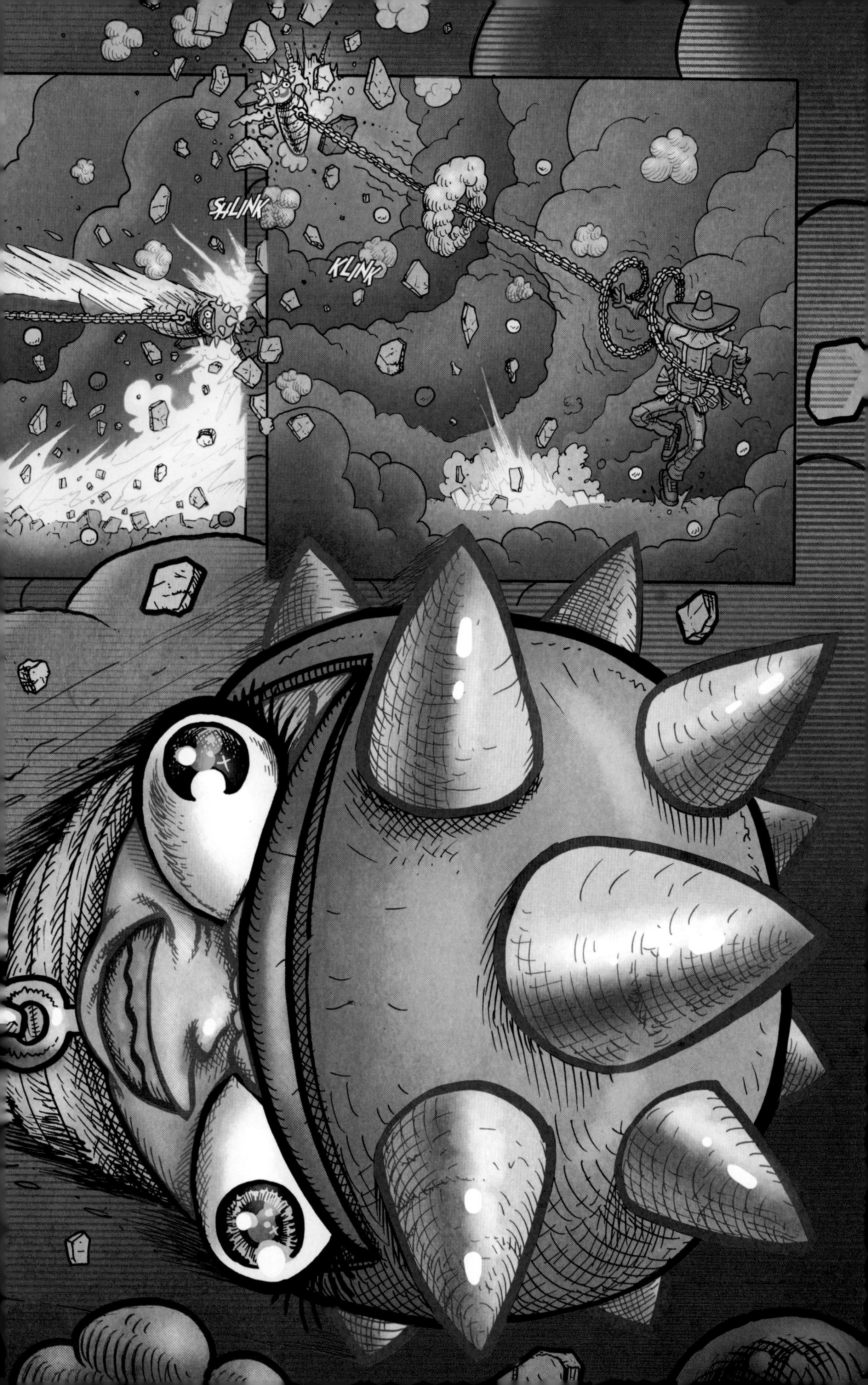
SHLINK
KLINK

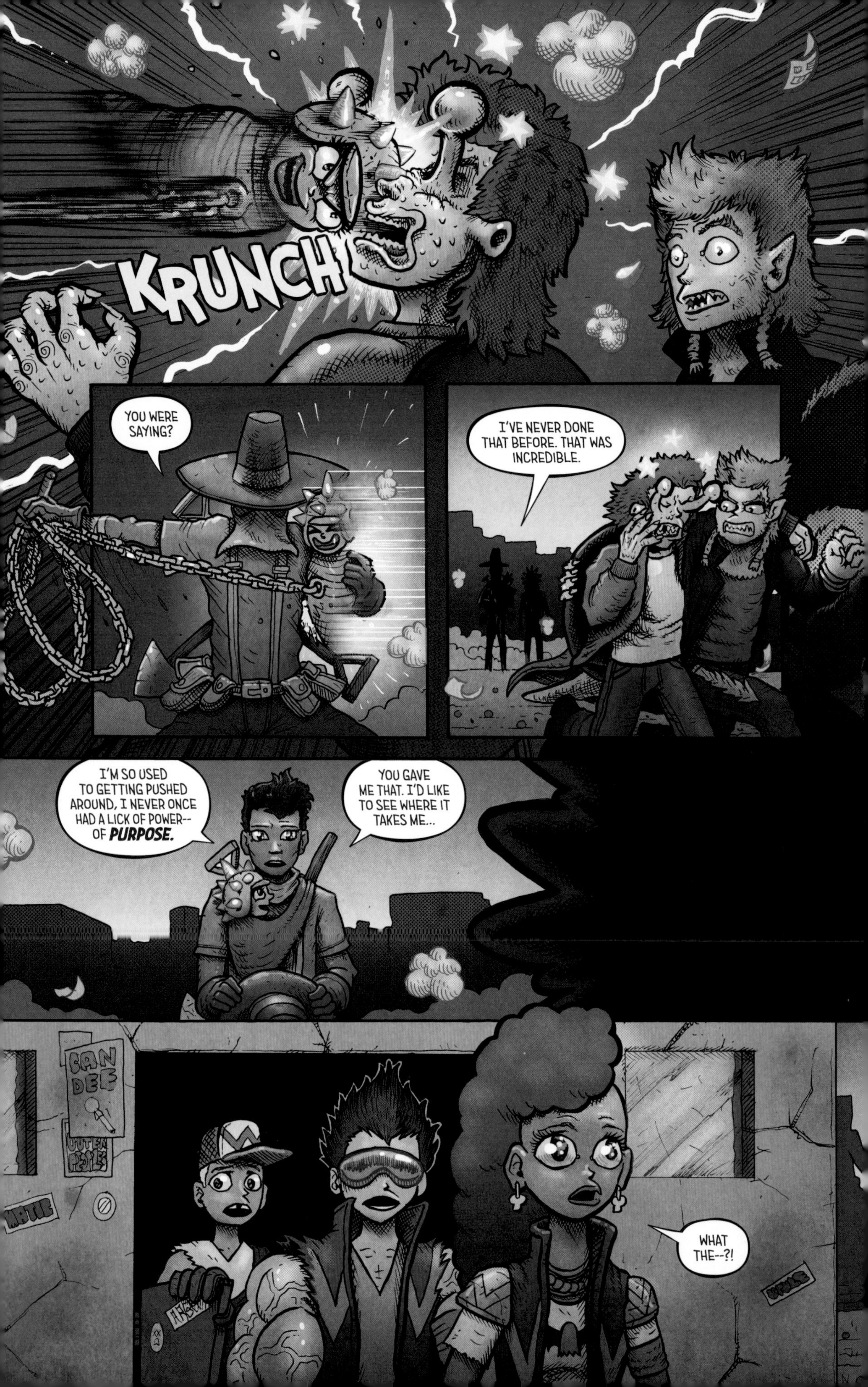
KRUNCH
YOU WERE SAYING?
I'VE NEVER DONE THAT BEFORE. THAT WAS INCREDIBLE.
I'M SO USED TO GETTING PUSHED AROUND, I NEVER ONCE HAD A LICK OF POWER-- OF **PURPOSE.**
YOU GAVE ME THAT. I'D LIKE TO SEE WHERE IT TAKES ME...
WHAT THE--?!

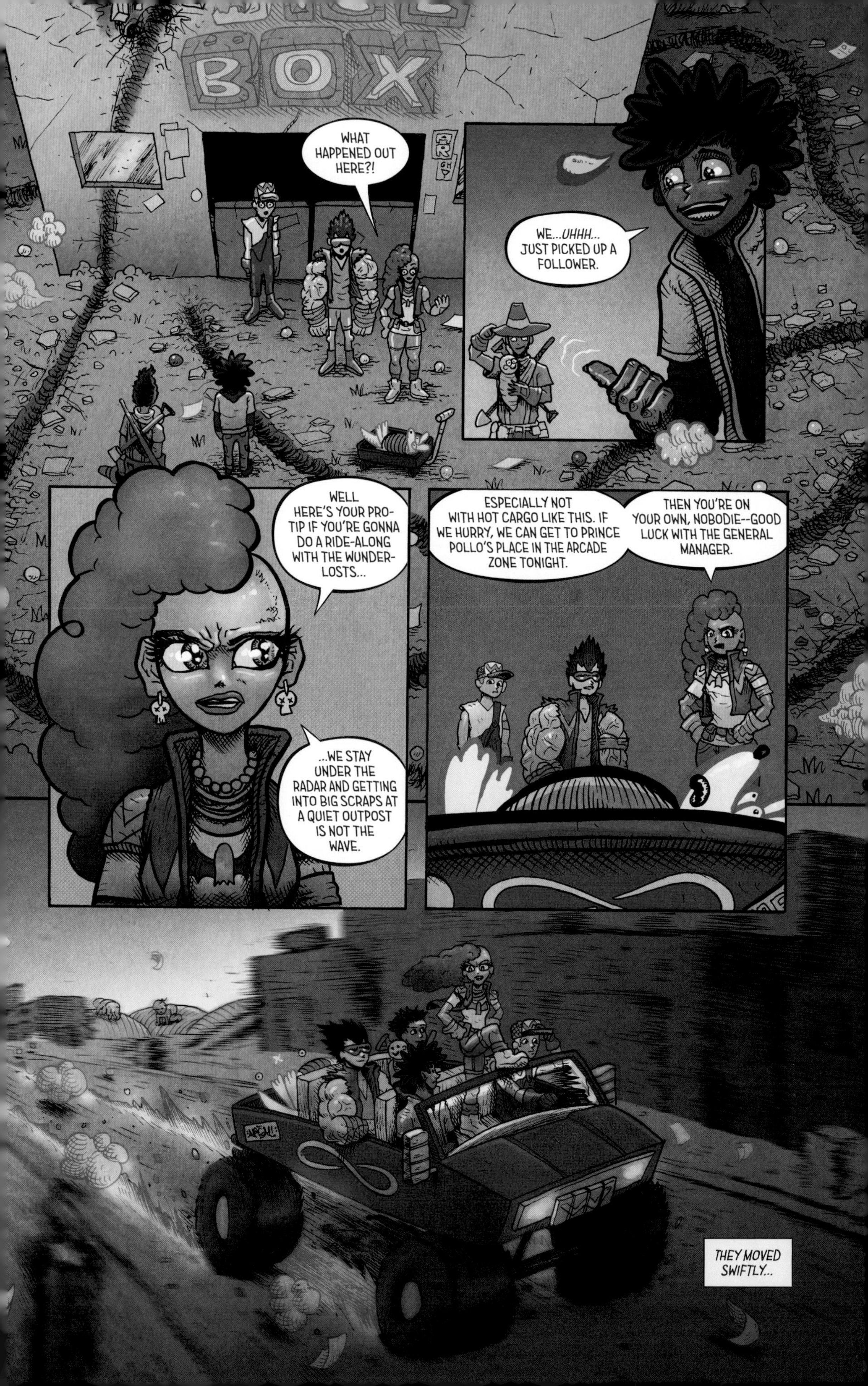
BOX
WHAT HAPPENED OUT HERE?!
WE...UHHH... JUST PICKED UP A FOLLOWER.
WELL HERE'S YOUR PRO-TIP IF YOU'RE GONNA DO A RIDE-ALONG WITH THE WUNDER-LOSTS...
...WE STAY UNDER THE RADAR AND GETTING INTO BIG SCRAPS AT A QUIET OUTPOST IS NOT THE WAVE.
ESPECIALLY NOT WITH HOT CARGO LIKE THIS. IF WE HURRY, WE CAN GET TO PRINCE POLLO'S PLACE IN THE ARCADE ZONE TONIGHT.
THEN YOU'RE ON YOUR OWN, NOBODIE--GOOD LUCK WITH THE GENERAL MANAGER.
THEY MOVED SWIFTLY...

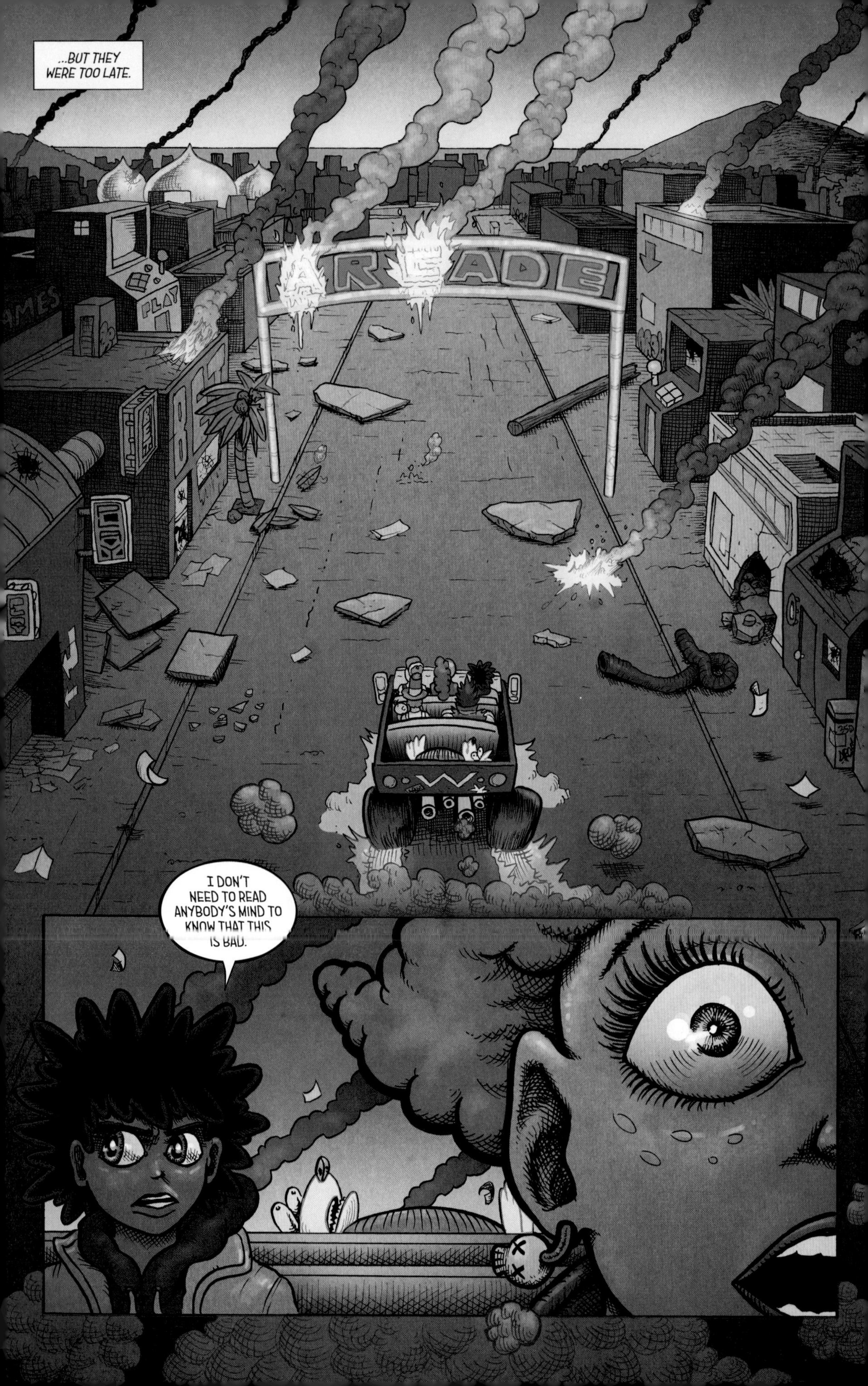
...BUT THEY WERE TOO LATE.
ARCADE
GAMES
PLAY
I DON'T NEED TO READ ANYBODY'S MIND TO KNOW THAT THIS IS BAD.

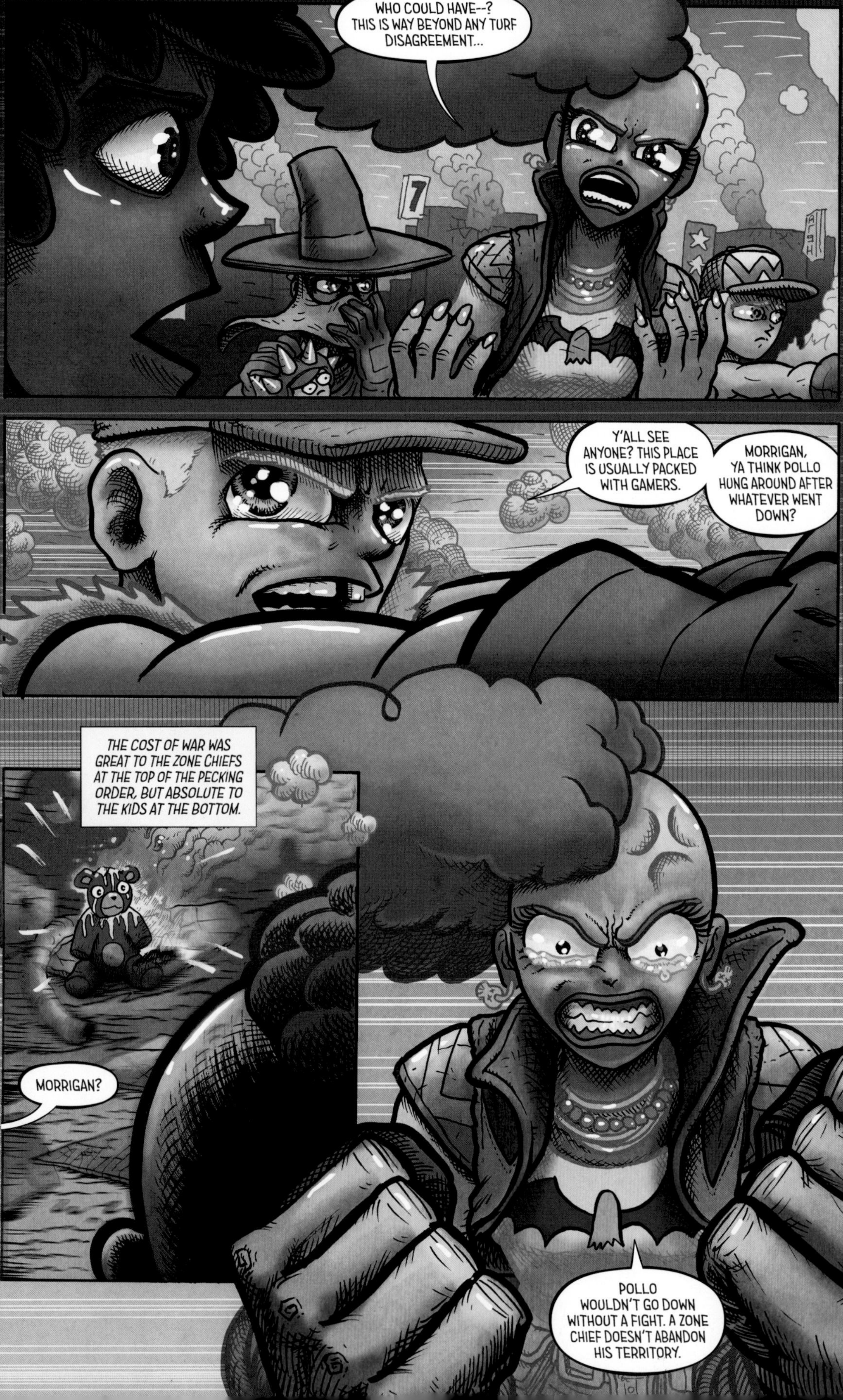
WHO COULD HAVE--? THIS IS WAY BEYOND ANY TURF DISAGREEMENT...
7
Y'ALL SEE ANYONE? THIS PLACE IS USUALLY PACKED WITH GAMERS.
MORRIGAN, YA THINK POLLO HUNG AROUND AFTER WHATEVER WENT DOWN?
THE COST OF WAR WAS GREAT TO THE ZONE CHIEFS AT THE TOP OF THE PECKING ORDER, BUT ABSOLUTE TO THE KIDS AT THE BOTTOM.
MORRIGAN?
POLLO WOULDN'T GO DOWN WITHOUT A FIGHT. A ZONE CHIEF DOESN'T ABANDON HIS TERRITORY.

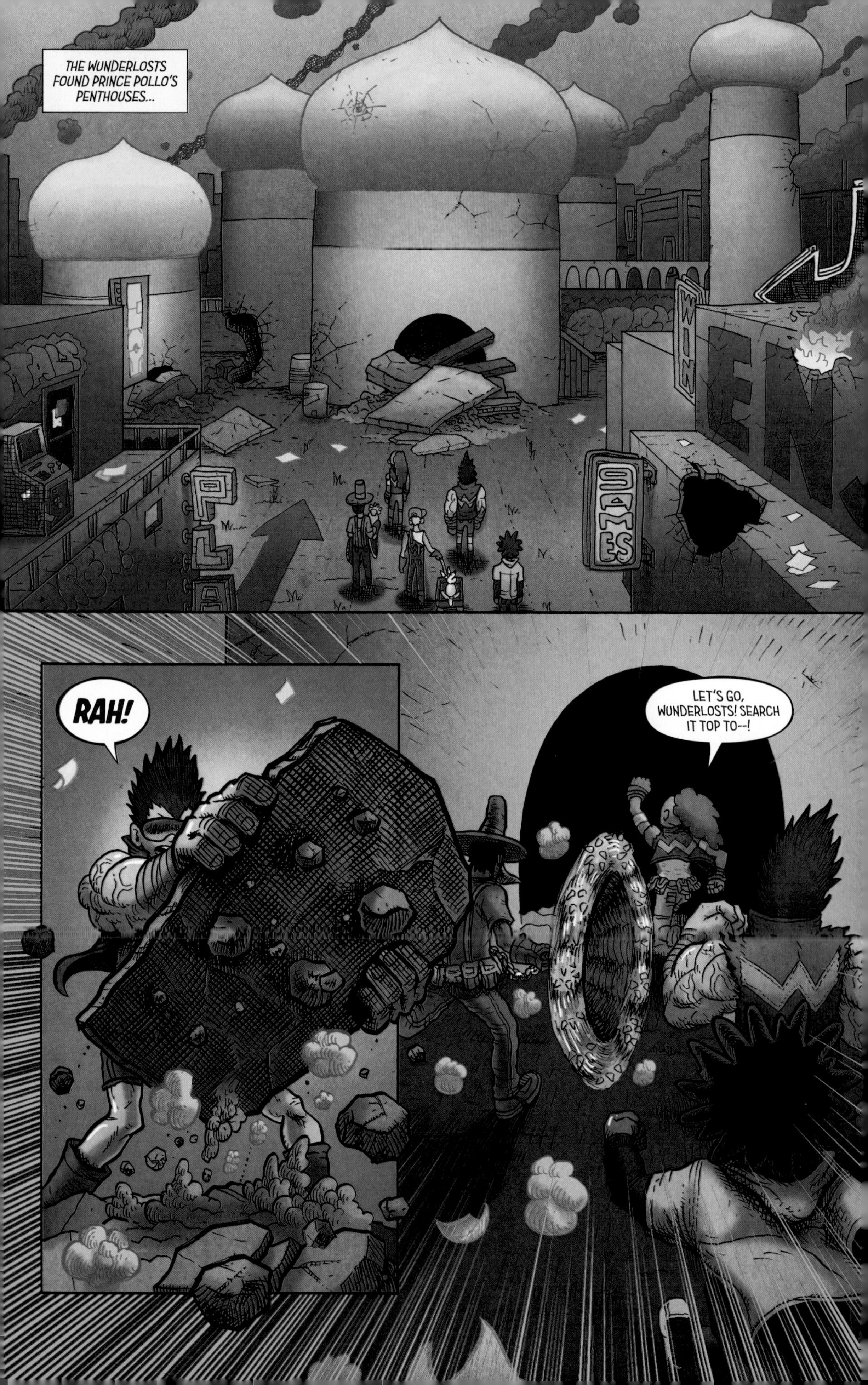
THE WUNDERLOSTS FOUND PRINCE POLLO'S PENTHOUSES...
RAH!
LET'S GO, WUNDERLOSTS! SEARCH IT TOP TO--!

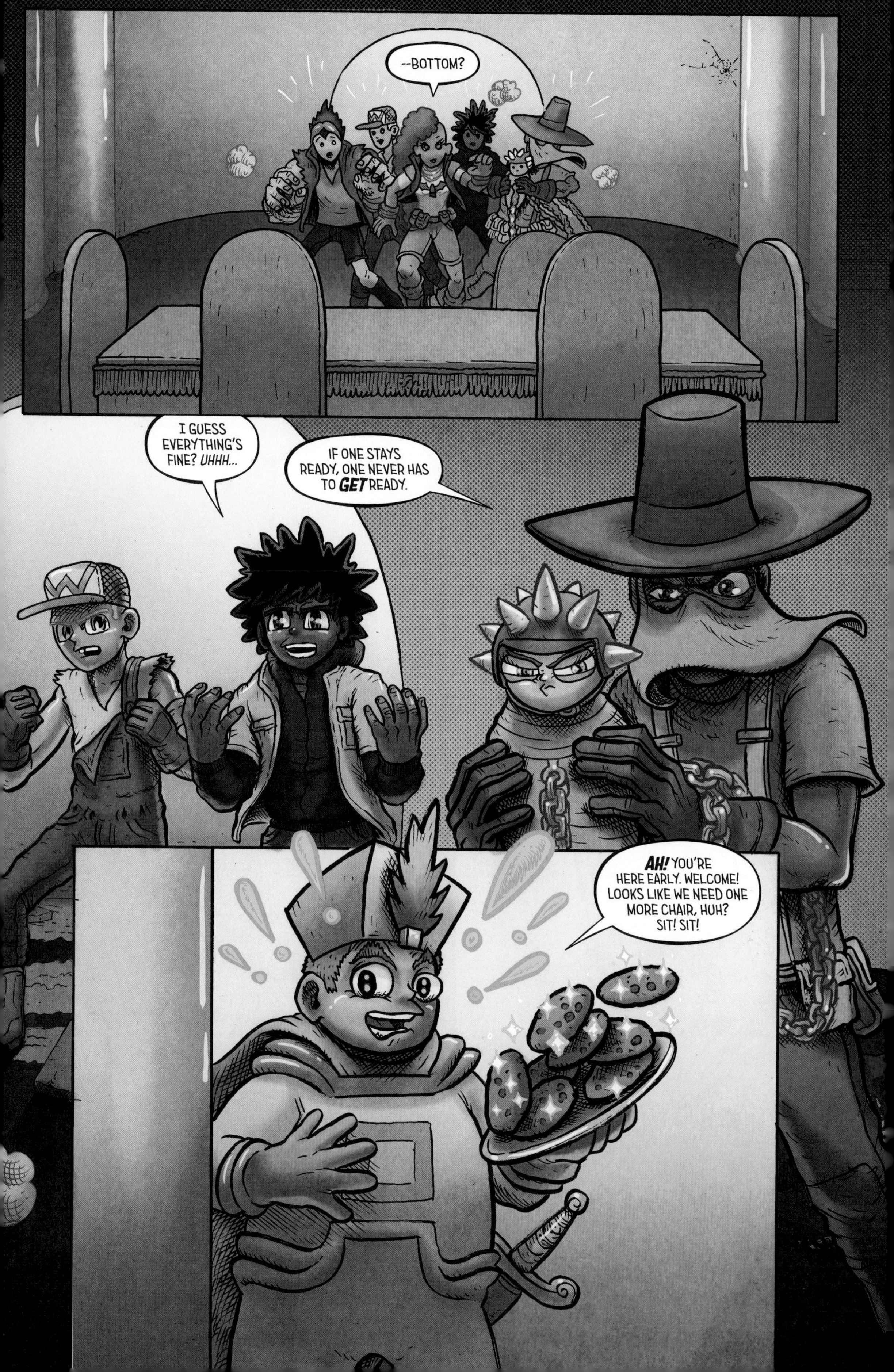
--BOTTOM?
I GUESS EVERYTHING'S FINE? *UHHH...*
IF ONE STAYS READY, ONE NEVER HAS TO ***GET*** READY.
AH! YOU'RE HERE EARLY. WELCOME! LOOKS LIKE WE NEED ONE MORE CHAIR, HUH? SIT! SIT!

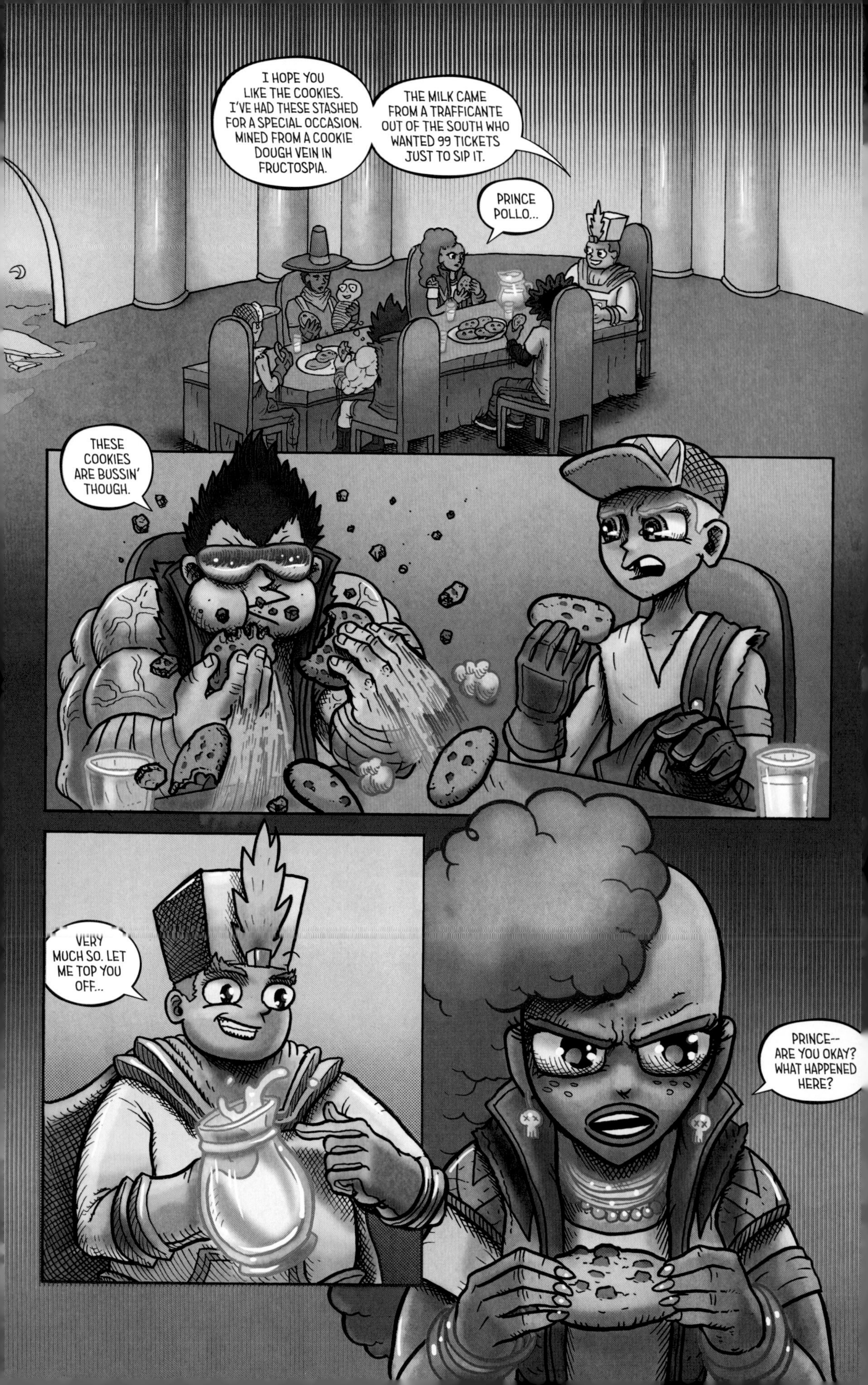
I HOPE YOU LIKE THE COOKIES. I'VE HAD THESE STASHED FOR A SPECIAL OCCASION. MINED FROM A COOKIE DOUGH VEIN IN FRUCTOSPIA.
THE MILK CAME FROM A TRAFFICANTE OUT OF THE SOUTH WHO WANTED 99 TICKETS JUST TO SIP IT.
PRINCE POLLO...
THESE COOKIES ARE BUSSIN' THOUGH.
VERY MUCH SO. LET ME TOP YOU OFF...
PRINCE-- ARE YOU OKAY? WHAT HAPPENED HERE?

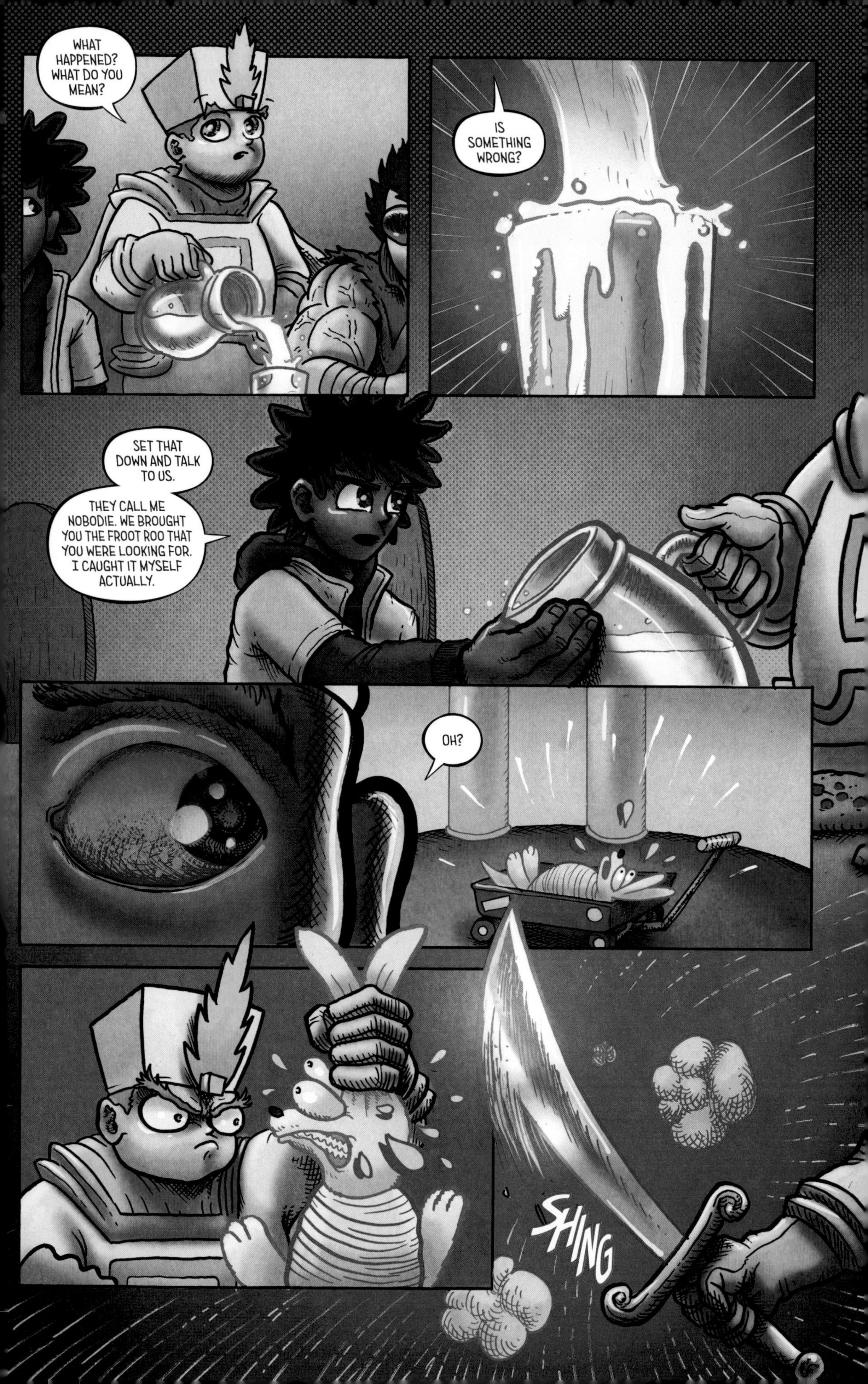
WHAT HAPPENED? WHAT DO YOU MEAN?
IS SOMETHING WRONG?
SET THAT DOWN AND TALK TO US.
THEY CALL ME NOBODIE. WE BROUGHT YOU THE FROOT ROO THAT YOU WERE LOOKING FOR. I CAUGHT IT MYSELF ACTUALLY.
OH?
SHING

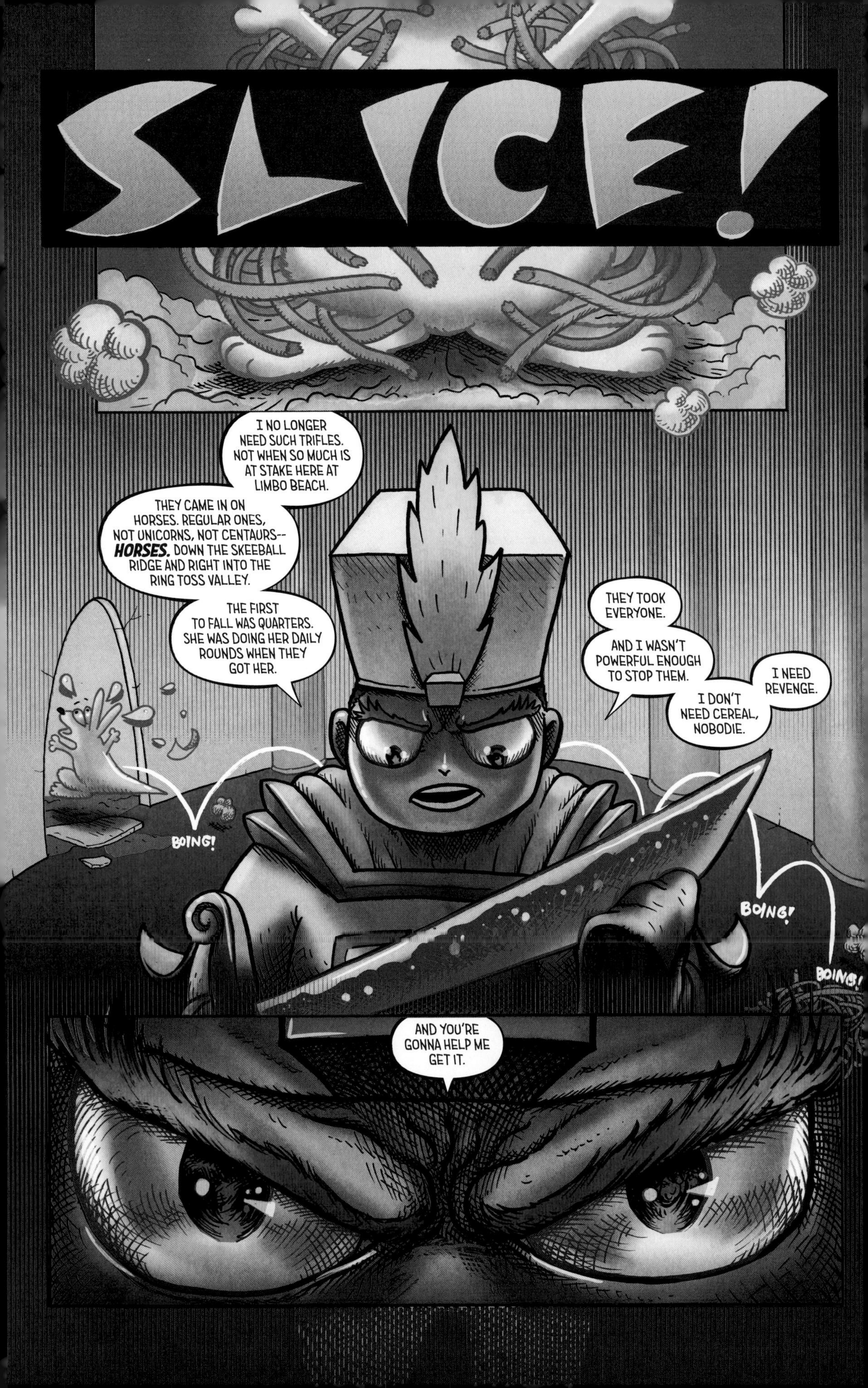
SLICE!
I NO LONGER NEED SUCH TRIFLES. NOT WHEN SO MUCH IS AT STAKE HERE AT LIMBO BEACH.
THEY CAME IN ON HORSES. REGULAR ONES, NOT UNICORNS, NOT CENTAURS-- HORSES. DOWN THE SKEEBALL RIDGE AND RIGHT INTO THE RING TOSS VALLEY.
THE FIRST TO FALL WAS QUARTERS. SHE WAS DOING HER DAILY ROUNDS WHEN THEY GOT HER.
THEY TOOK EVERYONE.
AND I WASN'T POWERFUL ENOUGH TO STOP THEM.
I DON'T NEED CEREAL, NOBODIE.
I NEED REVENGE.
BOING!
BOING!
BOING!
AND YOU'RE GONNA HELP ME GET IT.

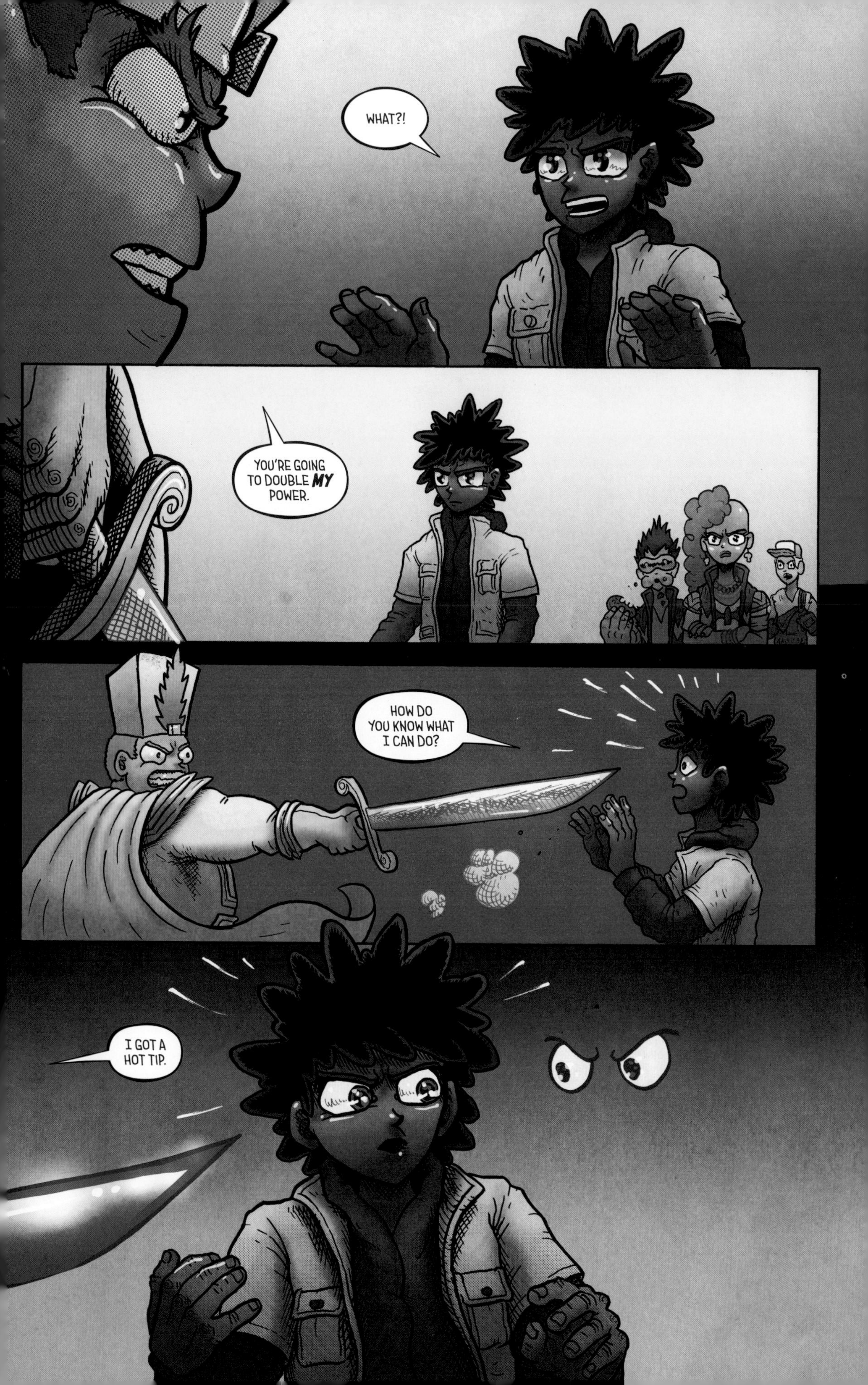
WHAT?!
YOU'RE GOING TO DOUBLE MY POWER.
HOW DO YOU KNOW WHAT I CAN DO?
I GOT A HOT TIP.

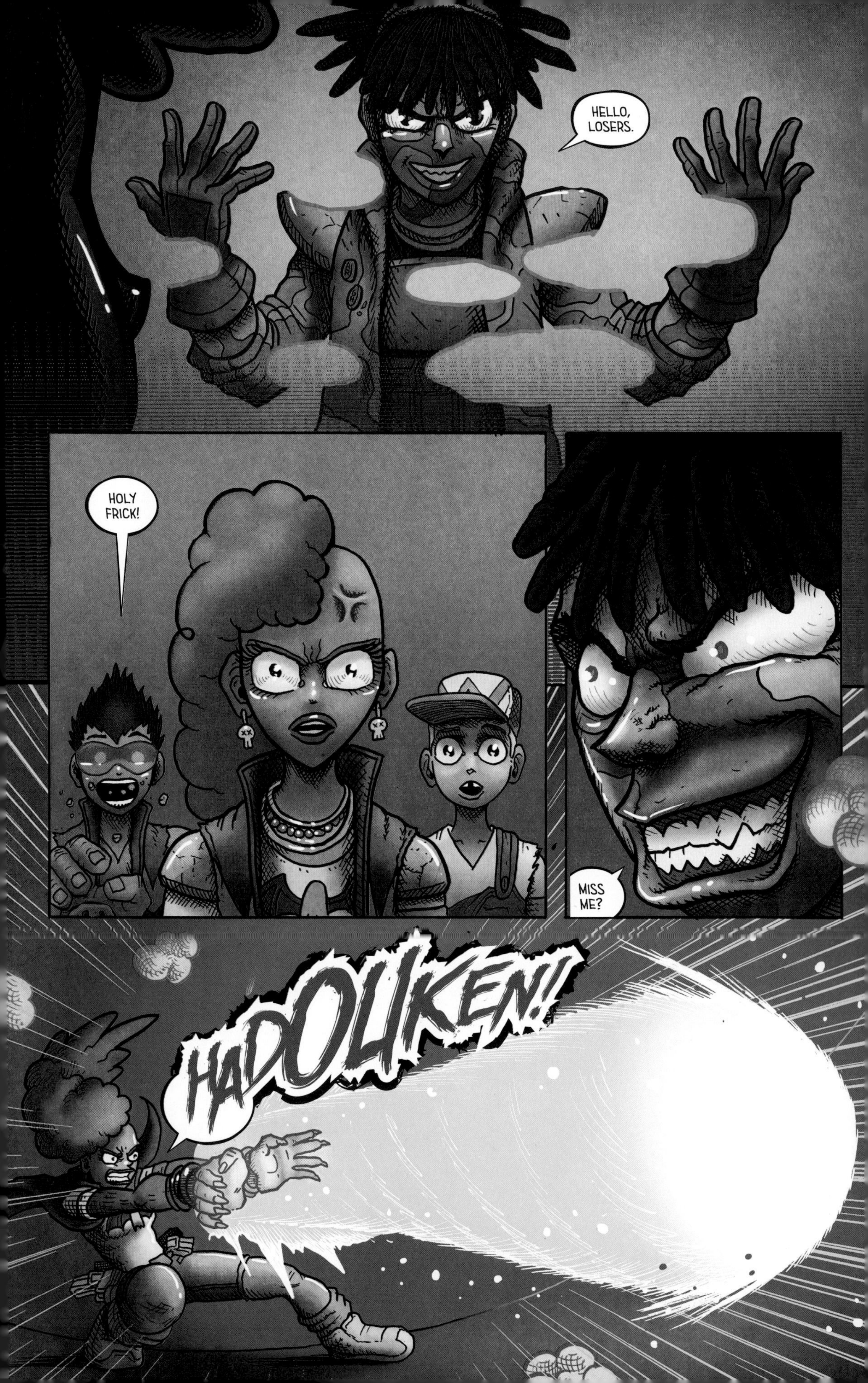
HELLO, LOSERS.
HOLY FRICK!
MISS ME?
HADOUKEN!

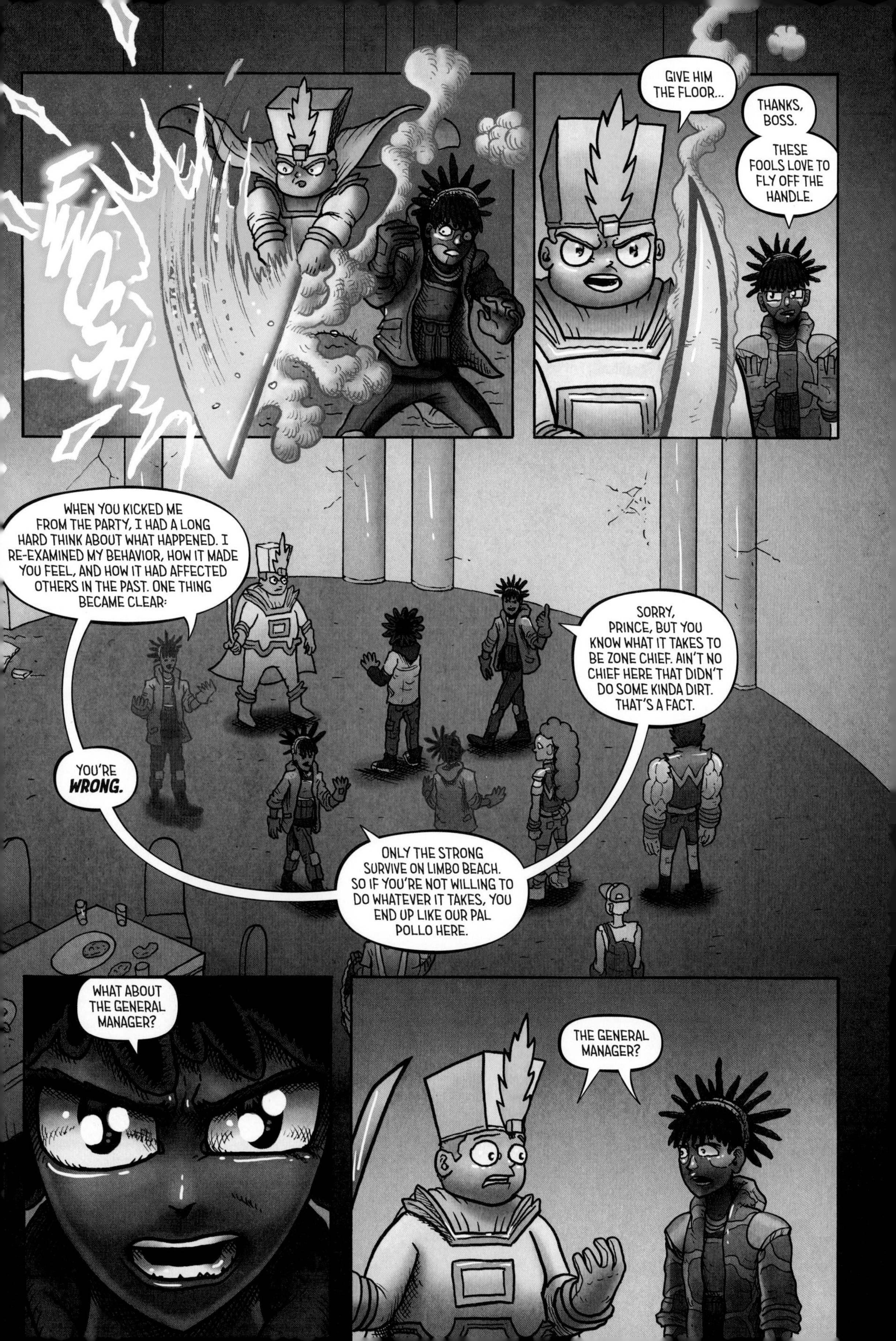
FWOOSH
GIVE HIM THE FLOOR...
THANKS, BOSS.
THESE FOOLS LOVE TO FLY OFF THE HANDLE.
WHEN YOU KICKED ME FROM THE PARTY, I HAD A LONG HARD THINK ABOUT WHAT HAPPENED. I RE-EXAMINED MY BEHAVIOR, HOW IT MADE YOU FEEL, AND HOW IT HAD AFFECTED OTHERS IN THE PAST. ONE THING BECAME CLEAR:
YOU'RE **WRONG.**
SORRY, PRINCE, BUT YOU KNOW WHAT IT TAKES TO BE ZONE CHIEF. AIN'T NO CHIEF HERE THAT DIDN'T DO SOME KINDA DIRT. THAT'S A FACT.
ONLY THE STRONG SURVIVE ON LIMBO BEACH. SO IF YOU'RE NOT WILLING TO DO WHATEVER IT TAKES, YOU END UP LIKE OUR PAL POLLO HERE.
WHAT ABOUT THE GENERAL MANAGER?
THE GENERAL MANAGER?

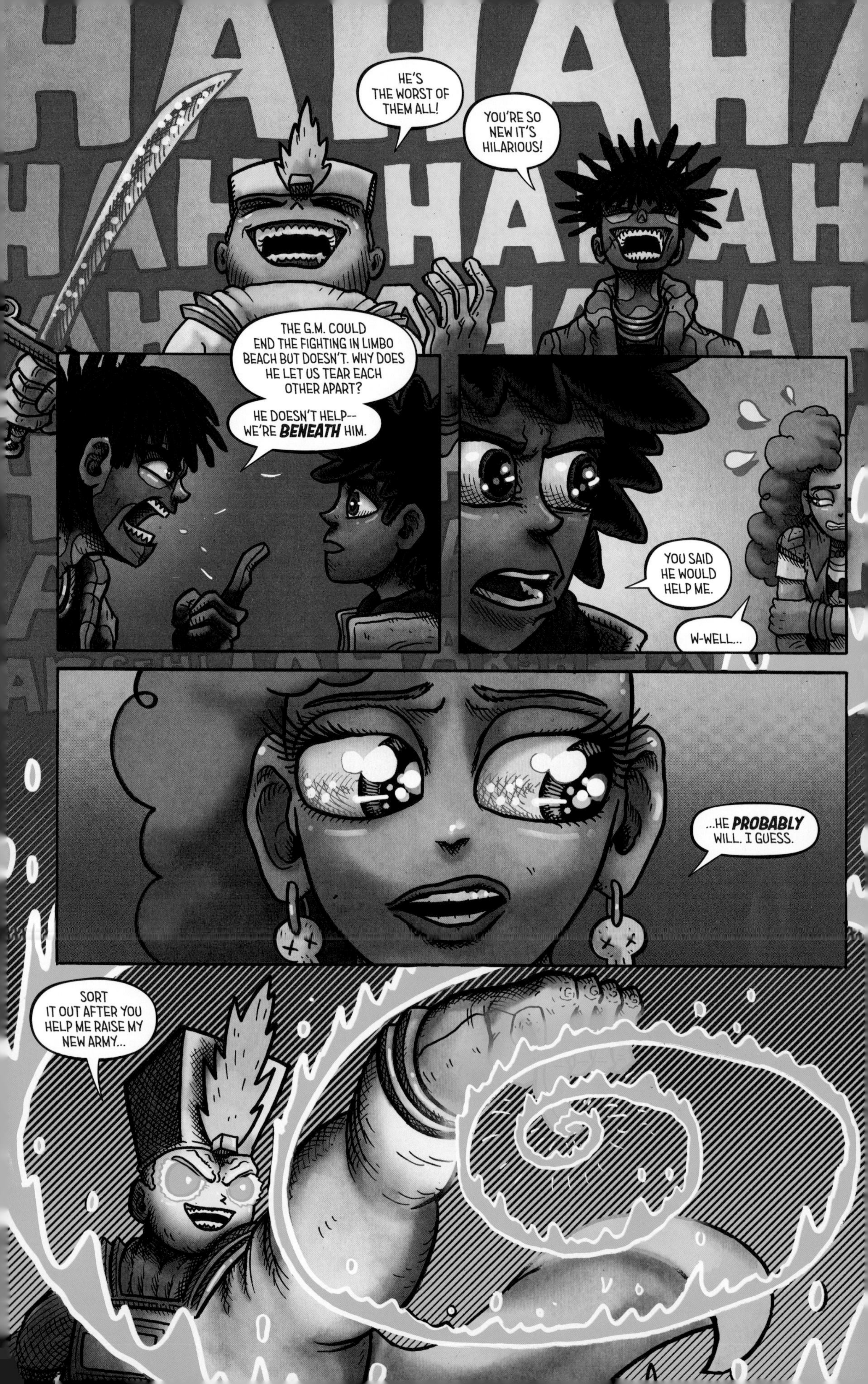
HAHAHAHAHAHAHAHAHA
HE'S THE WORST OF THEM ALL!
YOU'RE SO NEW IT'S HILARIOUS!
THE G.M. COULD END THE FIGHTING IN LIMBO BEACH BUT DOESN'T. WHY DOES HE LET US TEAR EACH OTHER APART?
HE DOESN'T HELP-- WE'RE **BENEATH** HIM.
YOU SAID HE WOULD HELP ME.
W-WELL...
...HE **PROBABLY** WILL. I GUESS.
SORT IT OUT AFTER YOU HELP ME RAISE MY NEW ARMY...

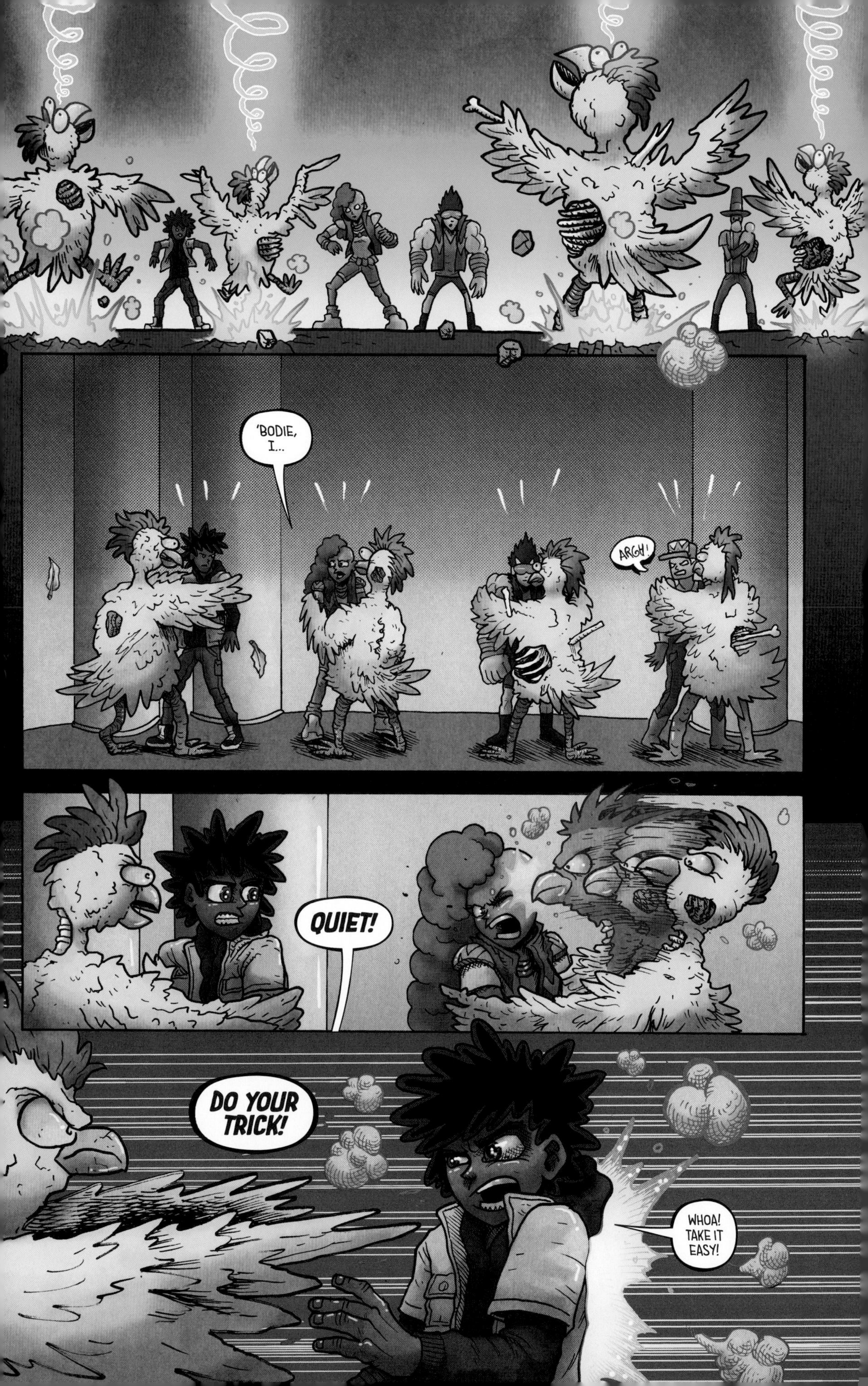
'BODIE, I...
ARGH!
QUIET!
DO YOUR TRICK!
WHOA! TAKE IT EASY!

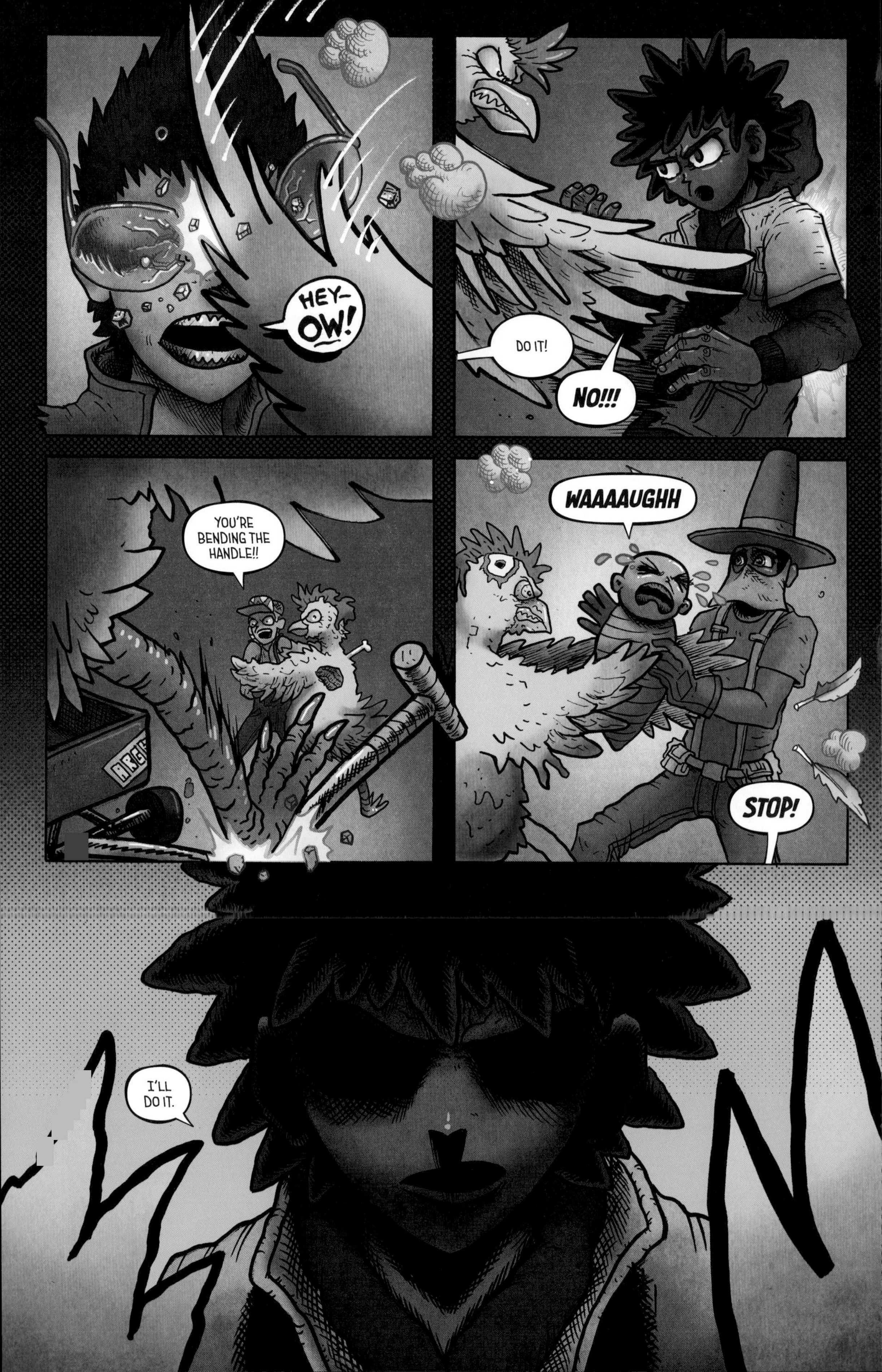
HEY-OW!
DO IT!
NO!!!
YOU'RE BENDING THE HANDLE!!
WAAAAUGHH
STOP!
I'LL DO IT.

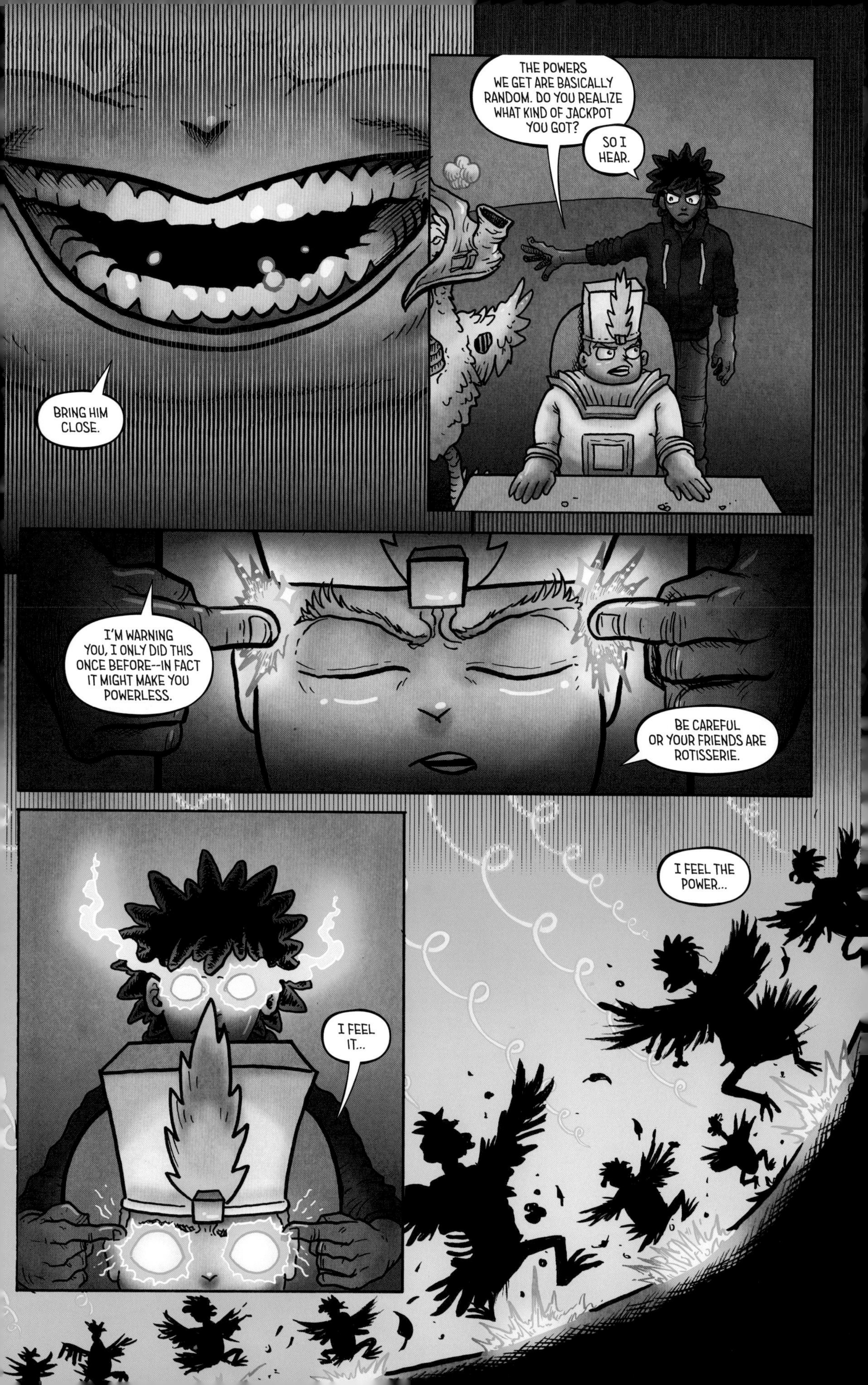
BRING HIM CLOSE.
THE POWERS WE GET ARE BASICALLY RANDOM. DO YOU REALIZE WHAT KIND OF JACKPOT YOU GOT?
SO I HEAR.
I'M WARNING YOU, I ONLY DID THIS ONCE BEFORE--IN FACT IT MIGHT MAKE YOU POWERLESS.
BE CAREFUL OR YOUR FRIENDS ARE ROTISSERIE.
I FEEL IT...
I FEEL THE POWER...

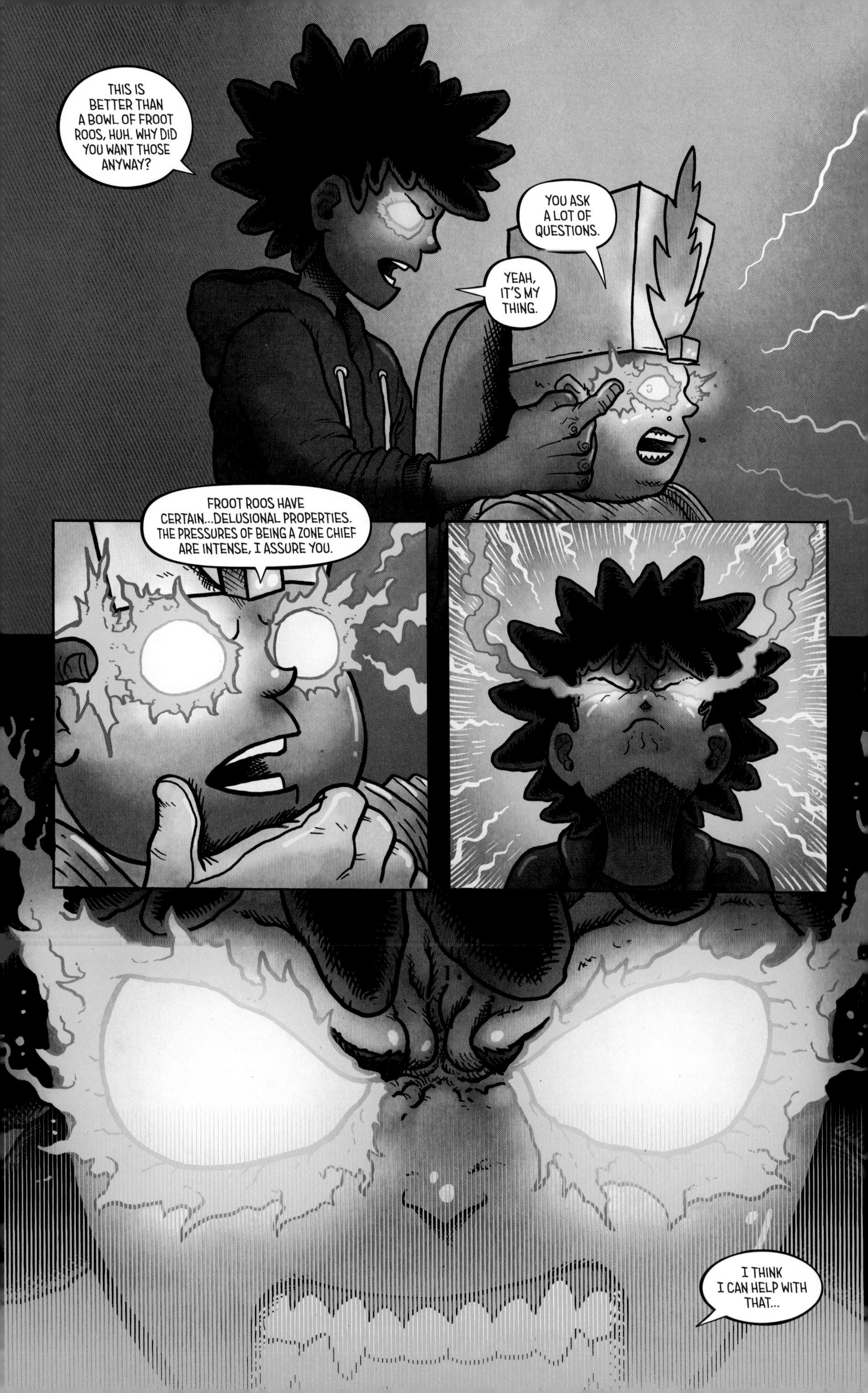
THIS IS BETTER THAN A BOWL OF FROOT ROOS, HUH. WHY DID YOU WANT THOSE ANYWAY?
YOU ASK A LOT OF QUESTIONS.
YEAH, IT'S MY THING.
FROOT ROOS HAVE CERTAIN...DELUSIONAL PROPERTIES. THE PRESSURES OF BEING A ZONE CHIEF ARE INTENSE, I ASSURE YOU.
I THINK I CAN HELP WITH THAT...

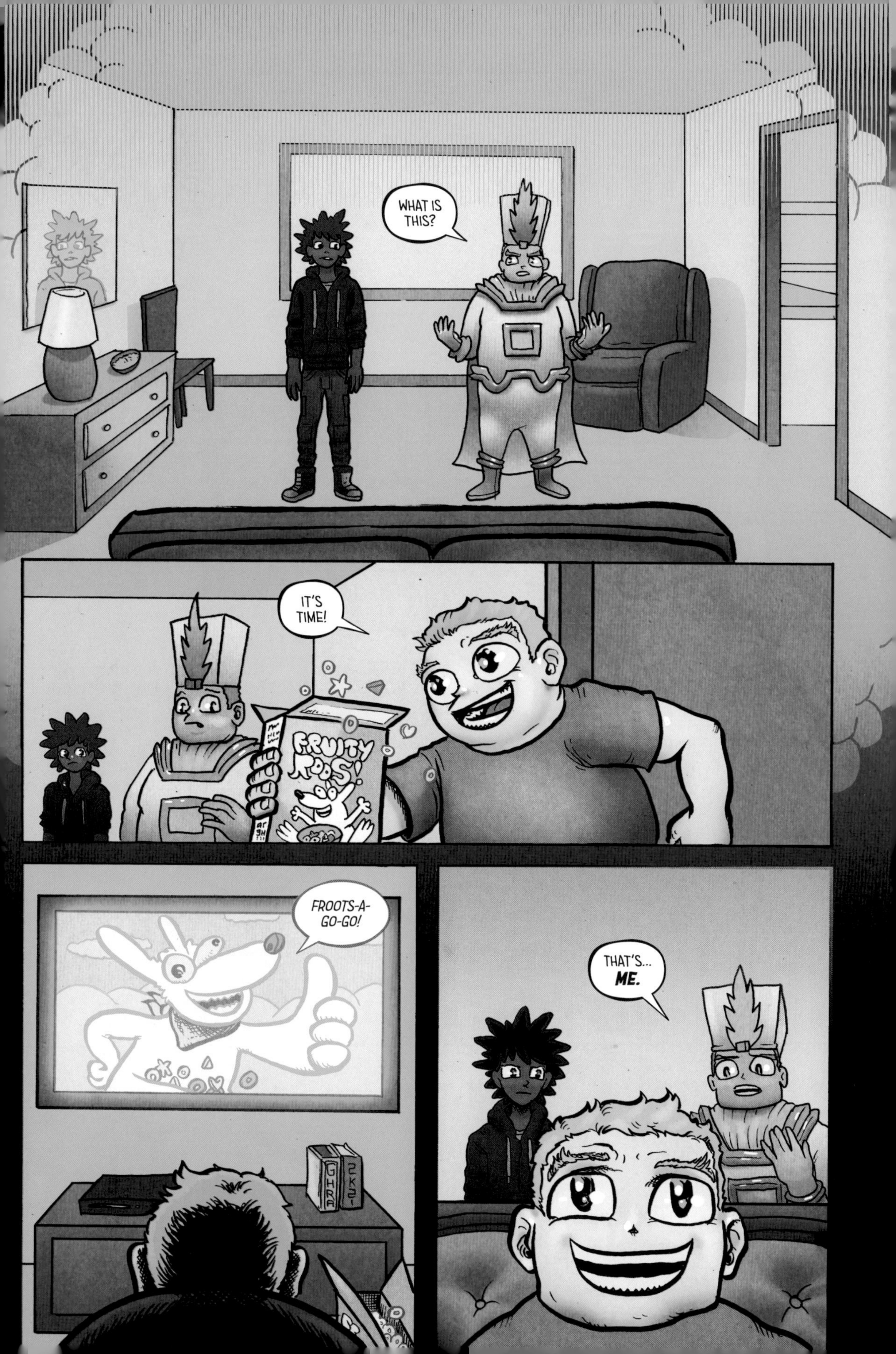
WHAT IS THIS?
IT'S TIME!
FRUITY ROOS!
FROOTS-A-GO-GO!
THAT'S... **ME.**

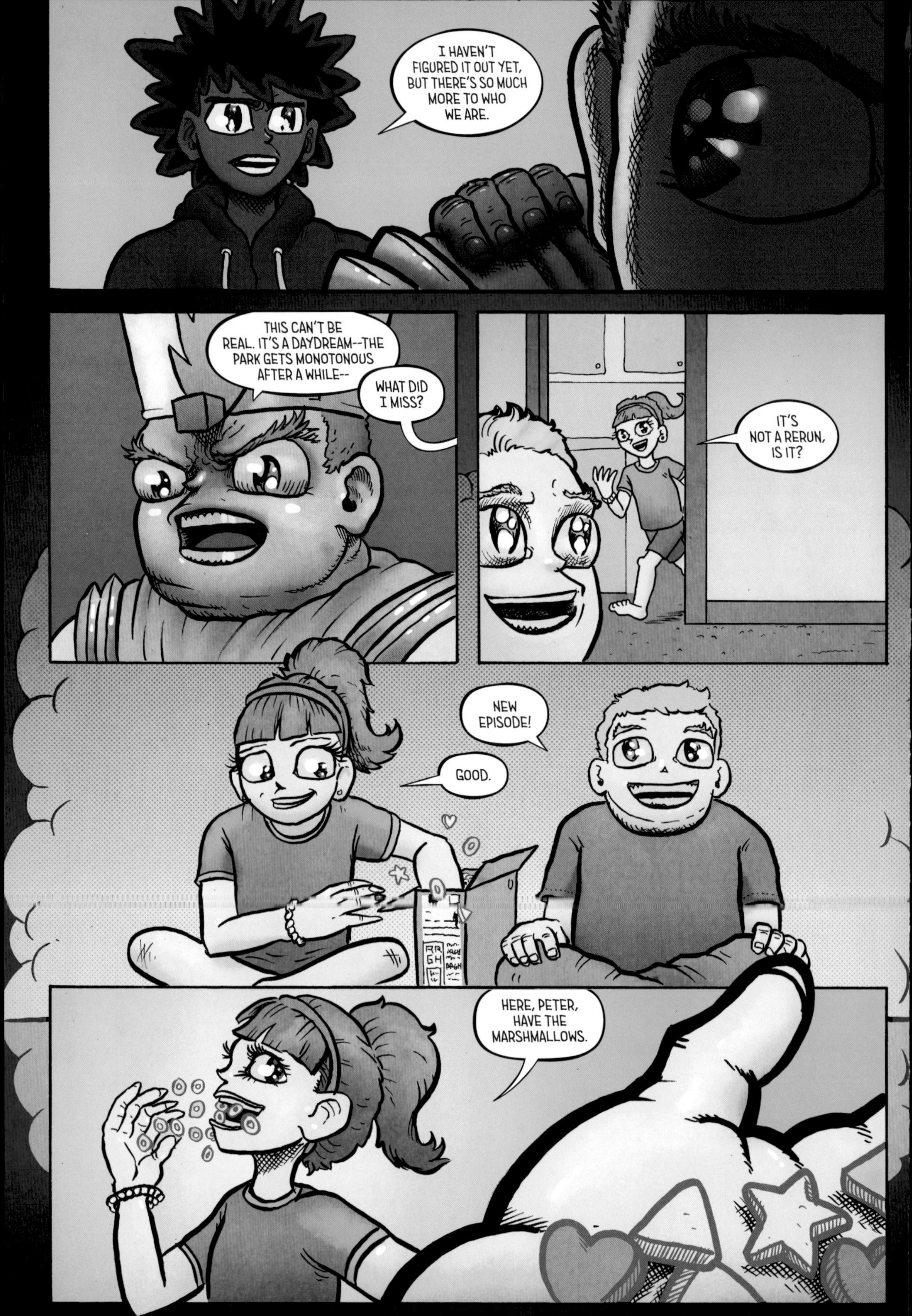
I HAVEN'T FIGURED IT OUT YET, BUT THERE'S SO MUCH MORE TO WHO WE ARE.
THIS CAN'T BE REAL. IT'S A DAYDREAM--THE PARK GETS MONOTONOUS AFTER A WHILE--
WHAT DID I MISS?
IT'S NOT A RERUN, IS IT?
NEW EPISODE!
GOOD.
HERE, PETER, HAVE THE MARSHMALLOWS.

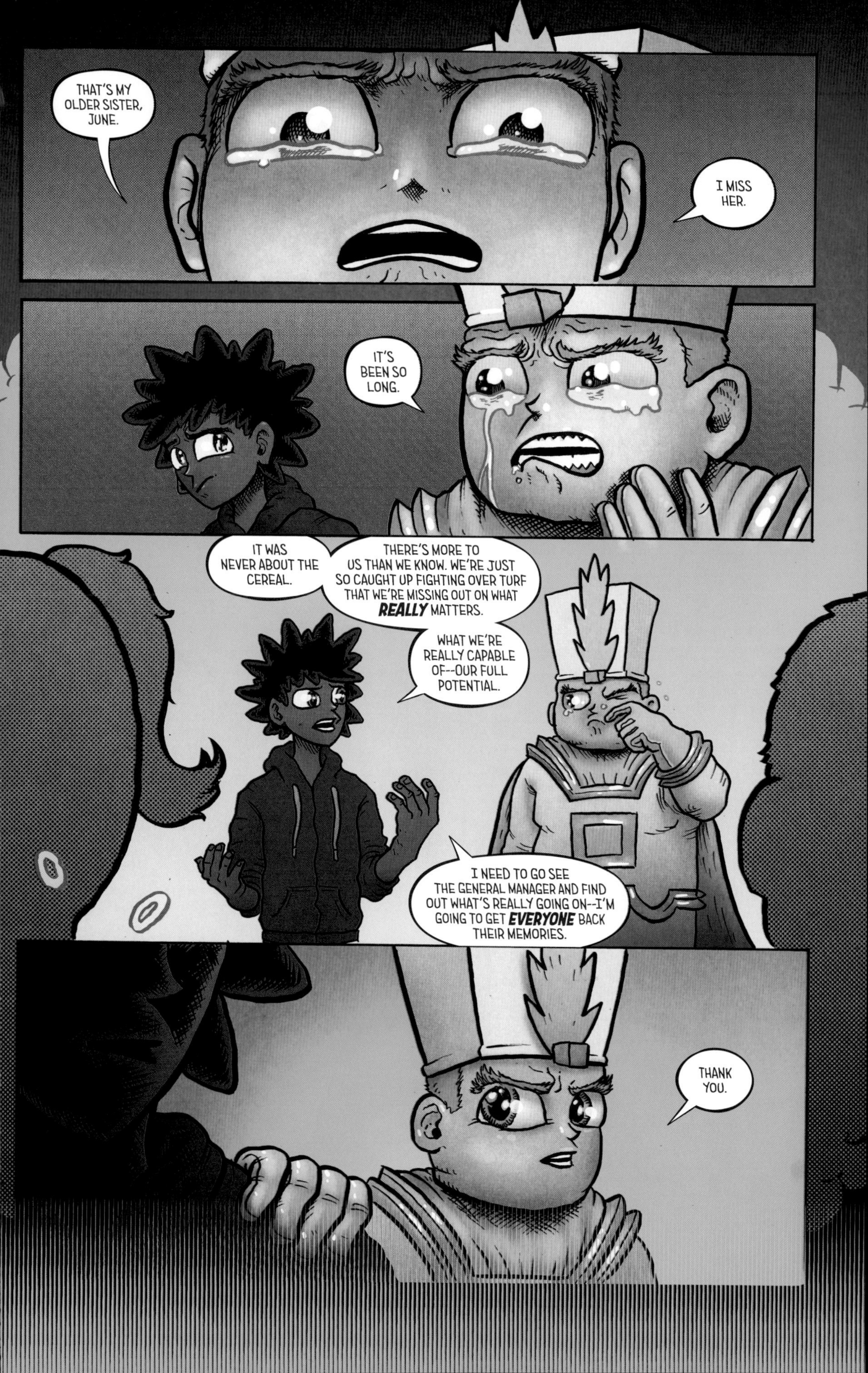
THAT'S MY OLDER SISTER, JUNE.
I MISS HER.
IT'S BEEN SO LONG.
IT WAS NEVER ABOUT THE CEREAL.
THERE'S MORE TO US THAN WE KNOW. WE'RE JUST SO CAUGHT UP FIGHTING OVER TURF THAT WE'RE MISSING OUT ON WHAT **REALLY** MATTERS.
WHAT WE'RE REALLY CAPABLE OF--OUR FULL POTENTIAL.
I NEED TO GO SEE THE GENERAL MANAGER AND FIND OUT WHAT'S REALLY GOING ON--I'M GOING TO GET **EVERYONE** BACK THEIR MEMORIES.
THANK YOU.

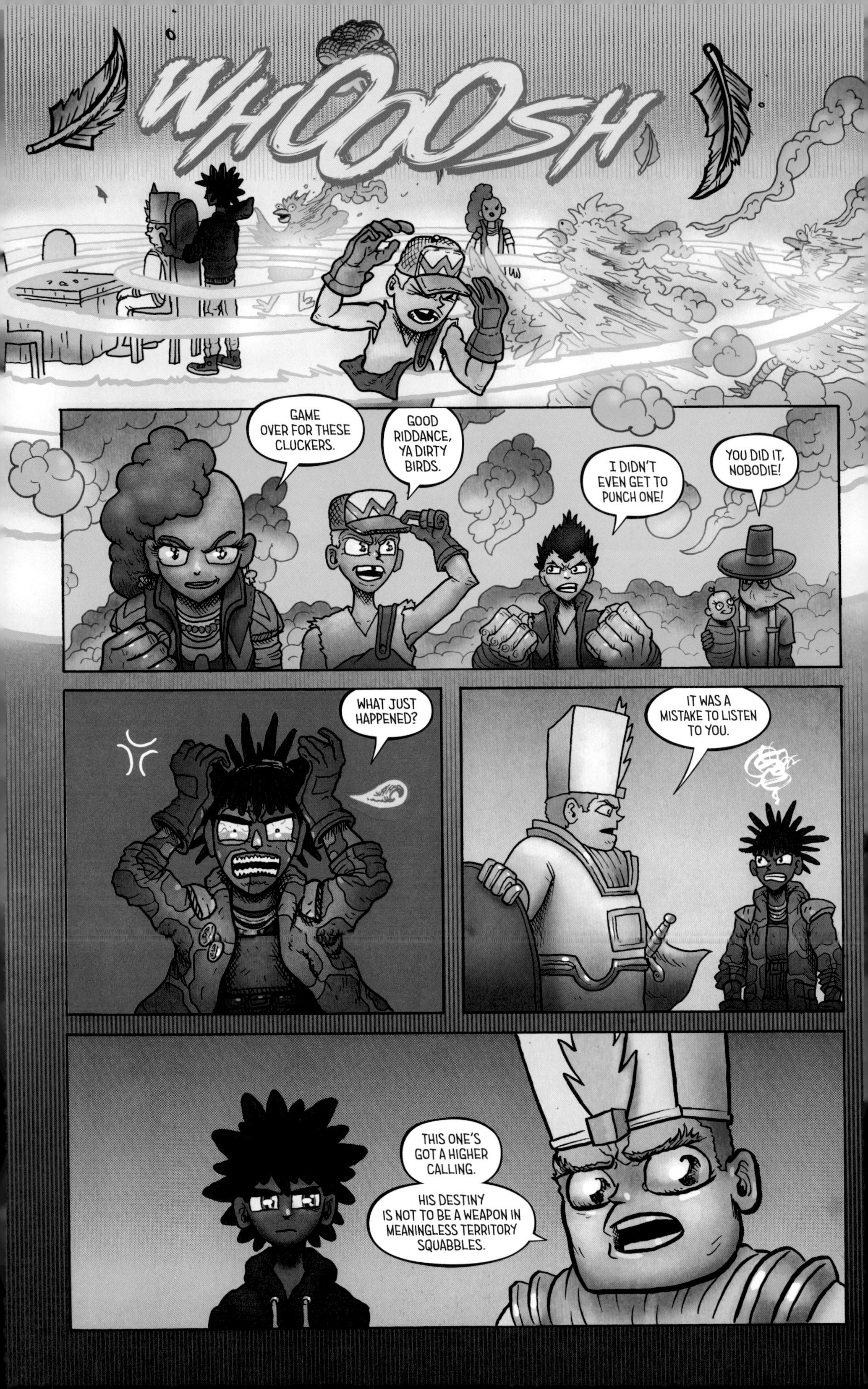
WHOOOSH
GAME OVER FOR THESE CLUCKERS.
GOOD RIDDANCE, YA DIRTY BIRDS.
I DIDN'T EVEN GET TO PUNCH ONE!
YOU DID IT, NOBODIE!
WHAT JUST HAPPENED?
IT WAS A MISTAKE TO LISTEN TO YOU.
THIS ONE'S GOT A HIGHER CALLING.
HIS DESTINY IS NOT TO BE A WEAPON IN MEANINGLESS TERRITORY SQUABBLES.

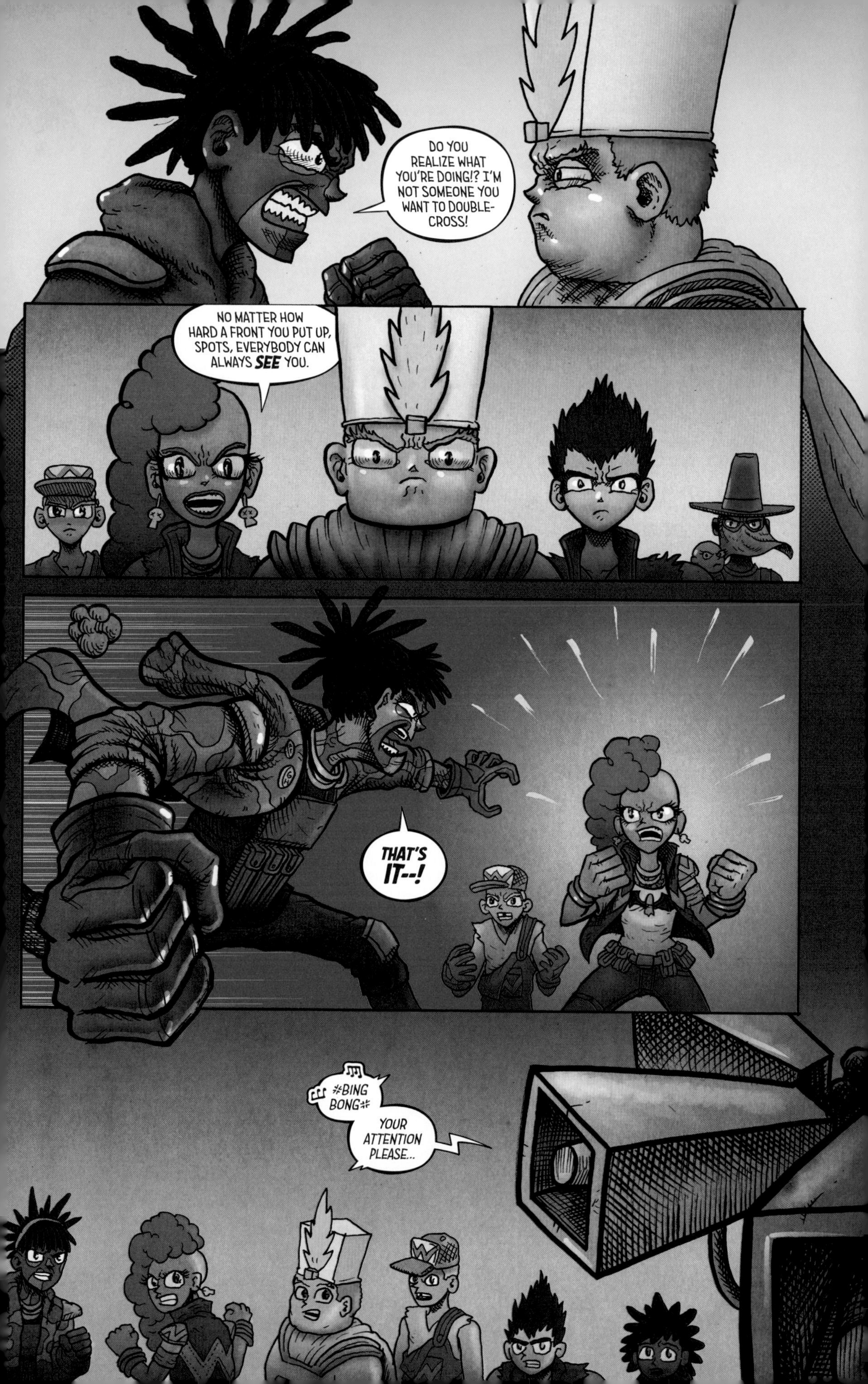
DO YOU REALIZE WHAT YOU'RE DOING!? I'M NOT SOMEONE YOU WANT TO DOUBLE-CROSS!
NO MATTER HOW HARD A FRONT YOU PUT UP, SPOTS, EVERYBODY CAN ALWAYS SEE YOU.
THAT'S IT--!
♯BING BONG♯
YOUR ATTENTION PLEASE...

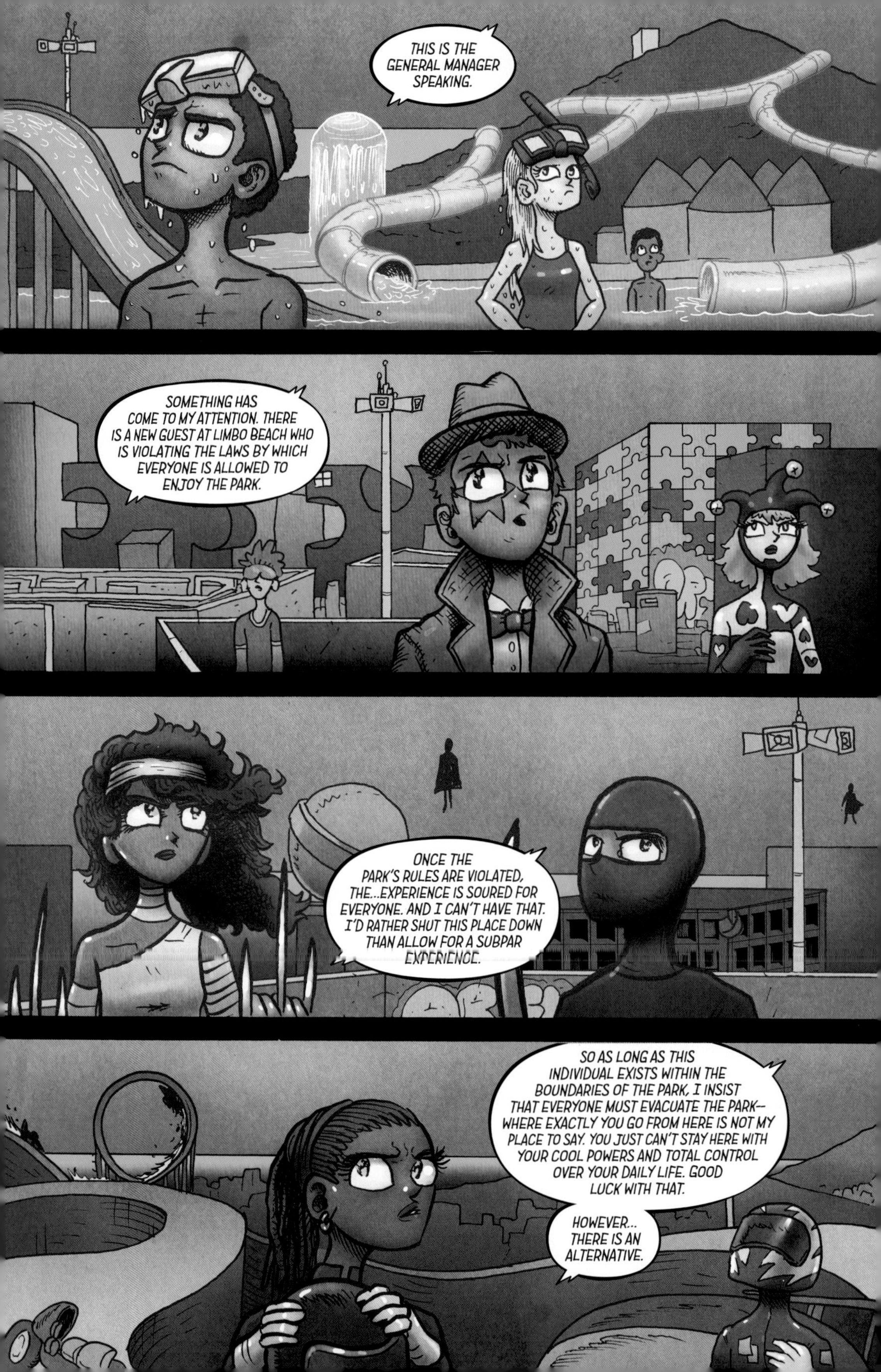
THIS IS THE GENERAL MANAGER SPEAKING.
SOMETHING HAS COME TO MY ATTENTION. THERE IS A NEW GUEST AT LIMBO BEACH WHO IS VIOLATING THE LAWS BY WHICH EVERYONE IS ALLOWED TO ENJOY THE PARK.
ONCE THE PARK'S RULES ARE VIOLATED, THE...EXPERIENCE IS SOURED FOR EVERYONE. AND I CAN'T HAVE THAT. I'D RATHER SHUT THIS PLACE DOWN THAN ALLOW FOR A SUBPAR EXPERIENCE.
SO AS LONG AS THIS INDIVIDUAL EXISTS WITHIN THE BOUNDARIES OF THE PARK, I INSIST THAT EVERYONE MUST EVACUATE THE PARK— WHERE EXACTLY YOU GO FROM HERE IS NOT MY PLACE TO SAY. YOU JUST CAN'T STAY HERE WITH YOUR COOL POWERS AND TOTAL CONTROL OVER YOUR DAILY LIFE. GOOD LUCK WITH THAT.
HOWEVER... THERE IS AN ALTERNATIVE.

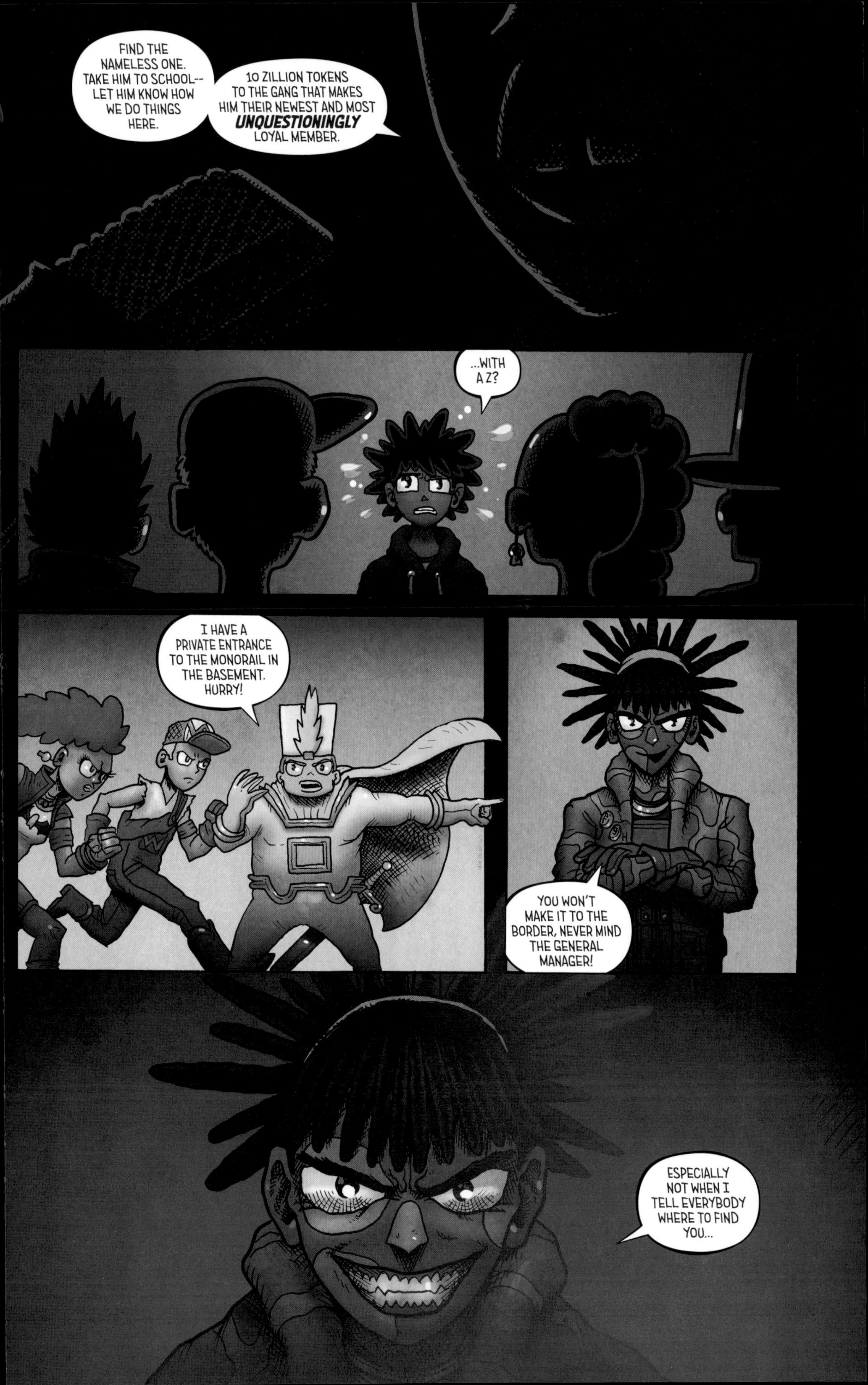
FIND THE NAMELESS ONE. TAKE HIM TO SCHOOL-- LET HIM KNOW HOW WE DO THINGS HERE.
10 ZILLION TOKENS TO THE GANG THAT MAKES HIM THEIR NEWEST AND MOST **UNQUESTIONINGLY** LOYAL MEMBER.
...WITH A Z?
I HAVE A PRIVATE ENTRANCE TO THE MONORAIL IN THE BASEMENT. HURRY!
YOU WON'T MAKE IT TO THE BORDER, NEVER MIND THE GENERAL MANAGER!
ESPECIALLY NOT WHEN I TELL EVERYBODY WHERE TO FIND YOU...

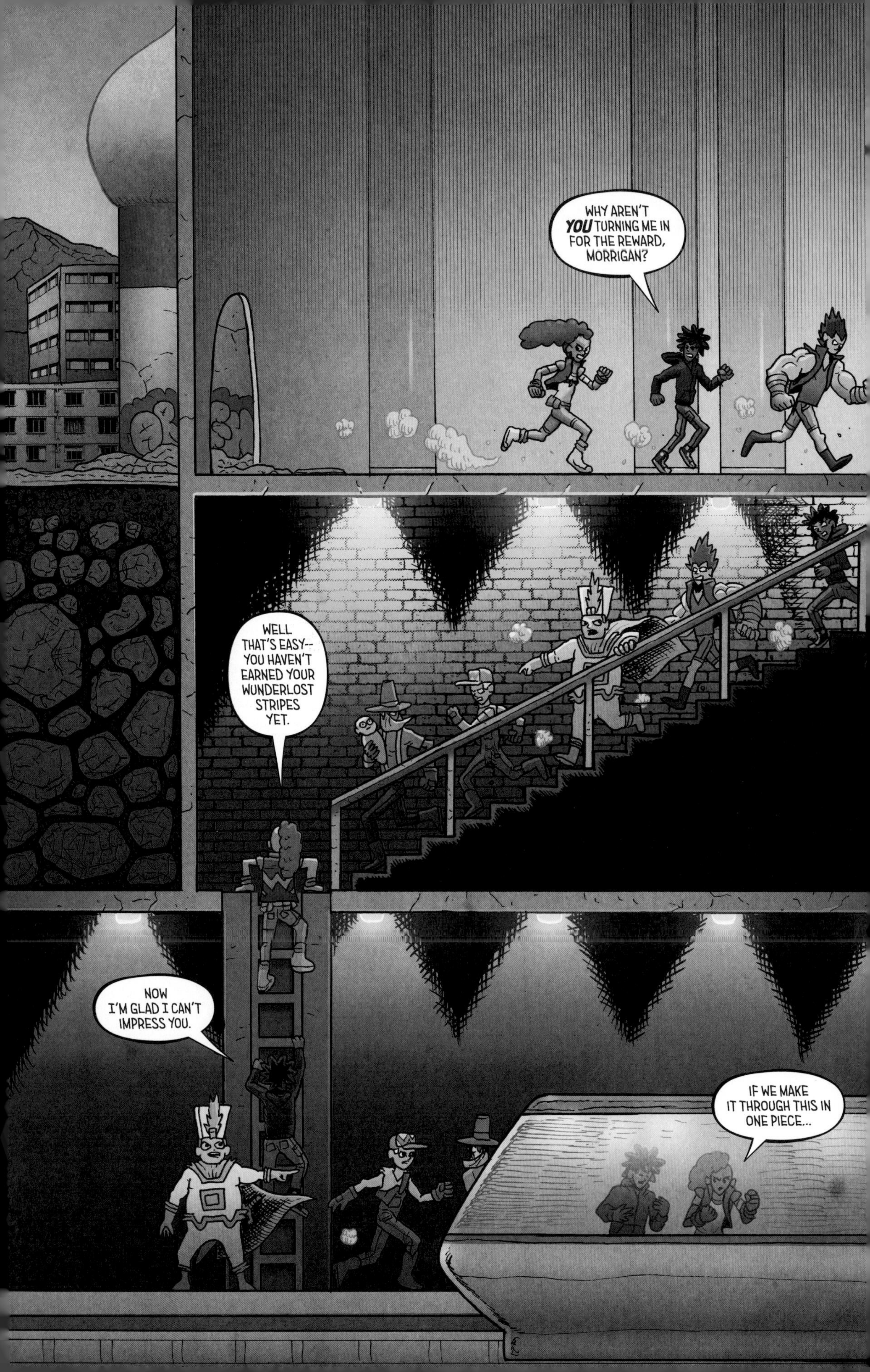
WHY AREN'T YOU TURNING ME IN FOR THE REWARD, MORRIGAN?
WELL THAT'S EASY-- YOU HAVEN'T EARNED YOUR WUNDERLOST STRIPES YET.
NOW I'M GLAD I CAN'T IMPRESS YOU.
IF WE MAKE IT THROUGH THIS IN ONE PIECE...

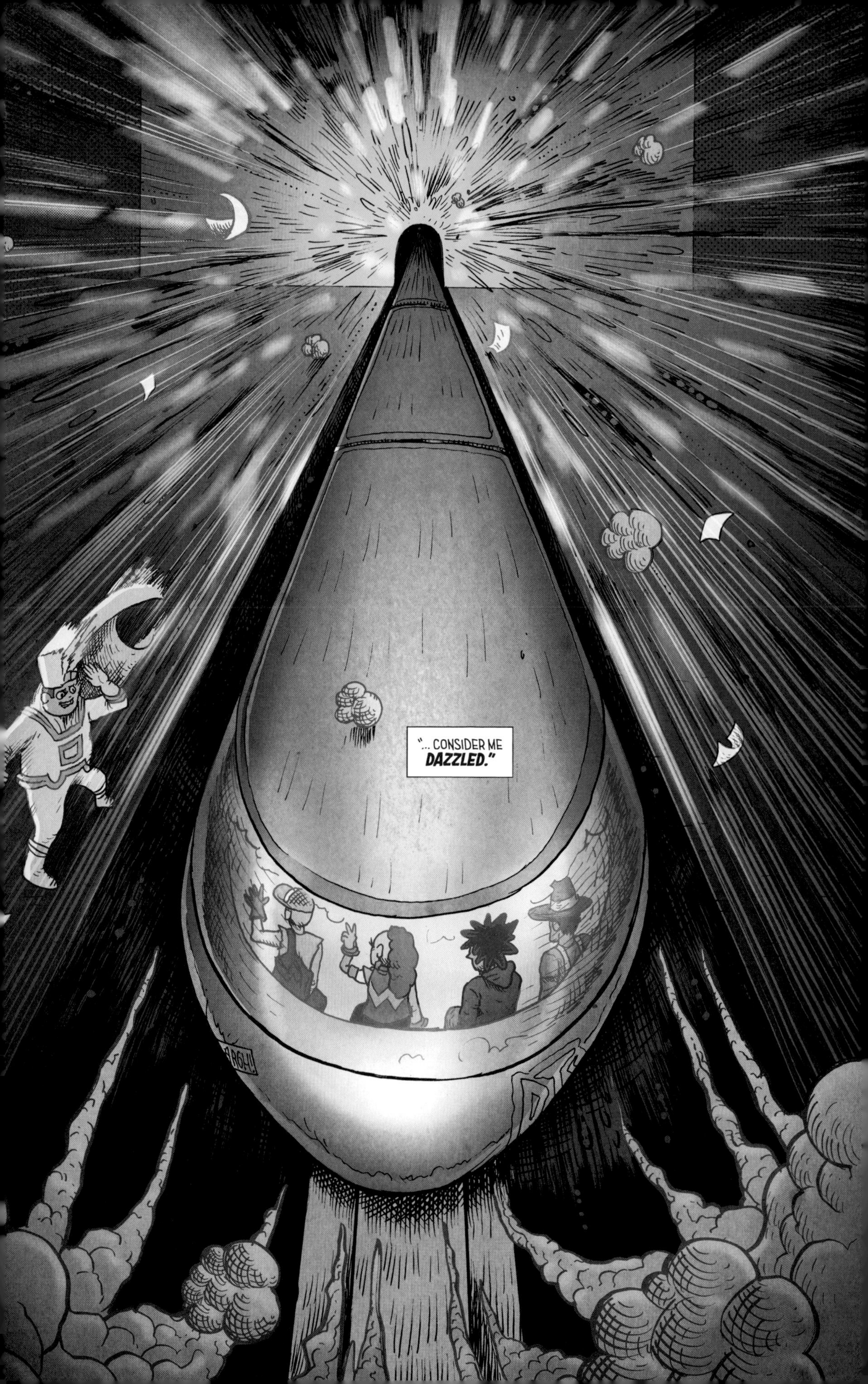
"... CONSIDER ME DAZZLED."

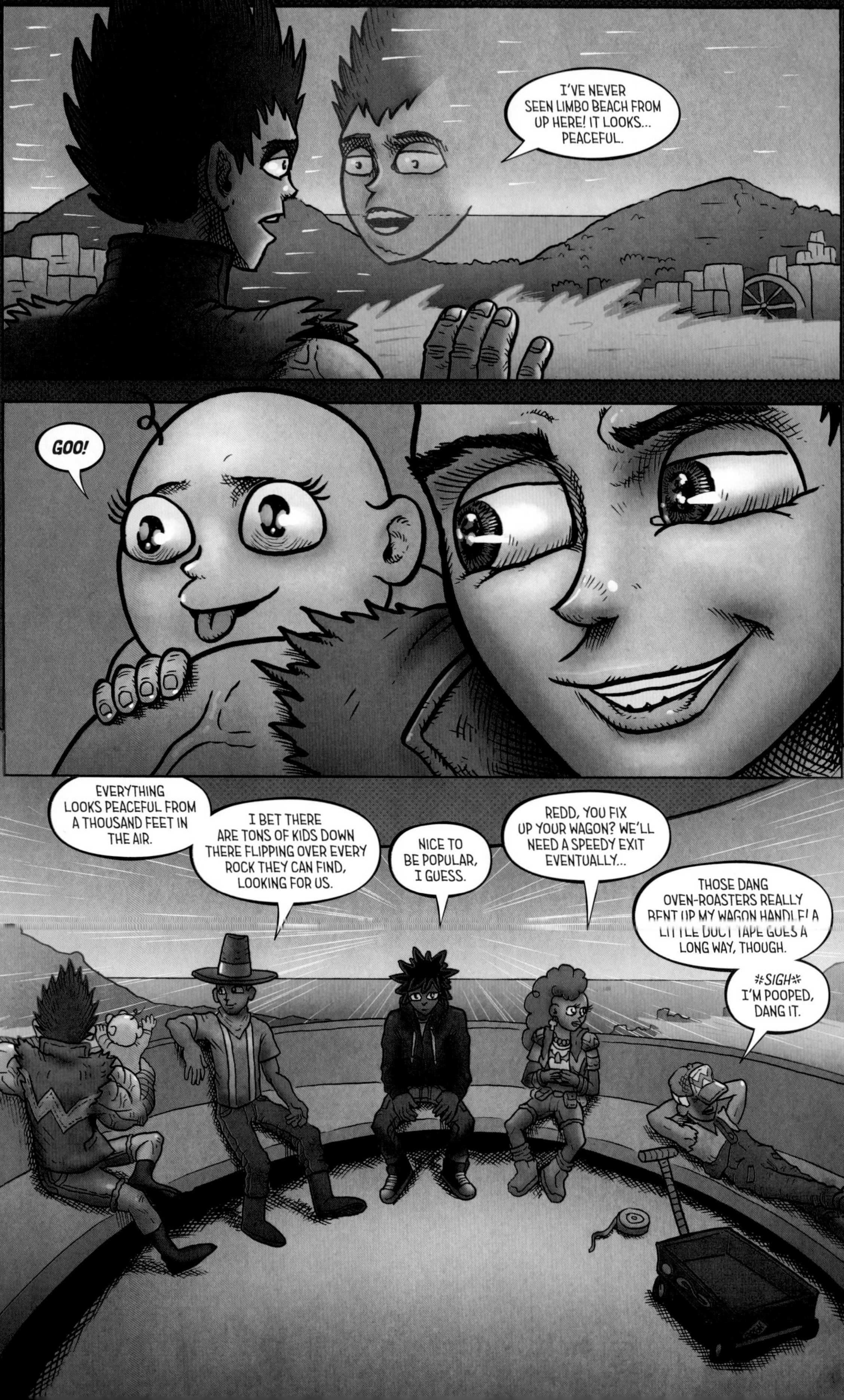
I'VE NEVER SEEN LIMBO BEACH FROM UP HERE! IT LOOKS... PEACEFUL.
GOO!
EVERYTHING LOOKS PEACEFUL FROM A THOUSAND FEET IN THE AIR.
I BET THERE ARE TONS OF KIDS DOWN THERE FLIPPING OVER EVERY ROCK THEY CAN FIND, LOOKING FOR US.
NICE TO BE POPULAR, I GUESS.
REDD, YOU FIX UP YOUR WAGON? WE'LL NEED A SPEEDY EXIT EVENTUALLY...
THOSE DANG OVEN-ROASTERS REALLY BENT UP MY WAGON HANDLE! A LITTLE DUCT TAPE GOES A LONG WAY, THOUGH.
SIGH I'M POOPED, DANG IT.

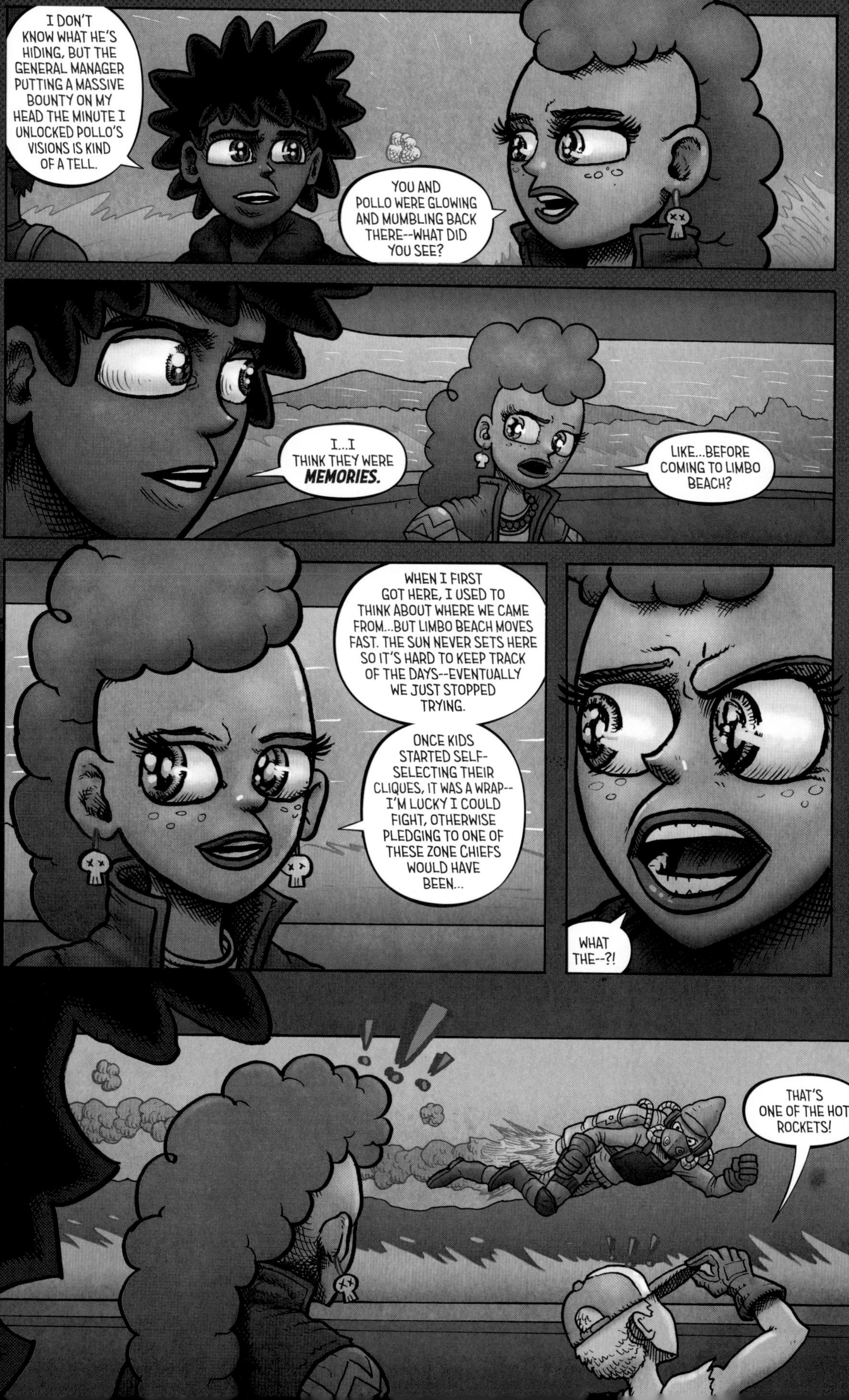
I DON'T KNOW WHAT HE'S HIDING, BUT THE GENERAL MANAGER PUTTING A MASSIVE BOUNTY ON MY HEAD THE MINUTE I UNLOCKED POLLO'S VISIONS IS KIND OF A TELL.
YOU AND POLLO WERE GLOWING AND MUMBLING BACK THERE--WHAT DID YOU SEE?
I...I THINK THEY WERE **MEMORIES.**
LIKE...BEFORE COMING TO LIMBO BEACH?
WHEN I FIRST GOT HERE, I USED TO THINK ABOUT WHERE WE CAME FROM...BUT LIMBO BEACH MOVES FAST. THE SUN NEVER SETS HERE SO IT'S HARD TO KEEP TRACK OF THE DAYS--EVENTUALLY WE JUST STOPPED TRYING.
ONCE KIDS STARTED SELF-SELECTING THEIR CLIQUES, IT WAS A WRAP--I'M LUCKY I COULD FIGHT, OTHERWISE PLEDGING TO ONE OF THESE ZONE CHIEFS WOULD HAVE BEEN...
WHAT THE--?!
THAT'S ONE OF THE HOT ROCKETS!

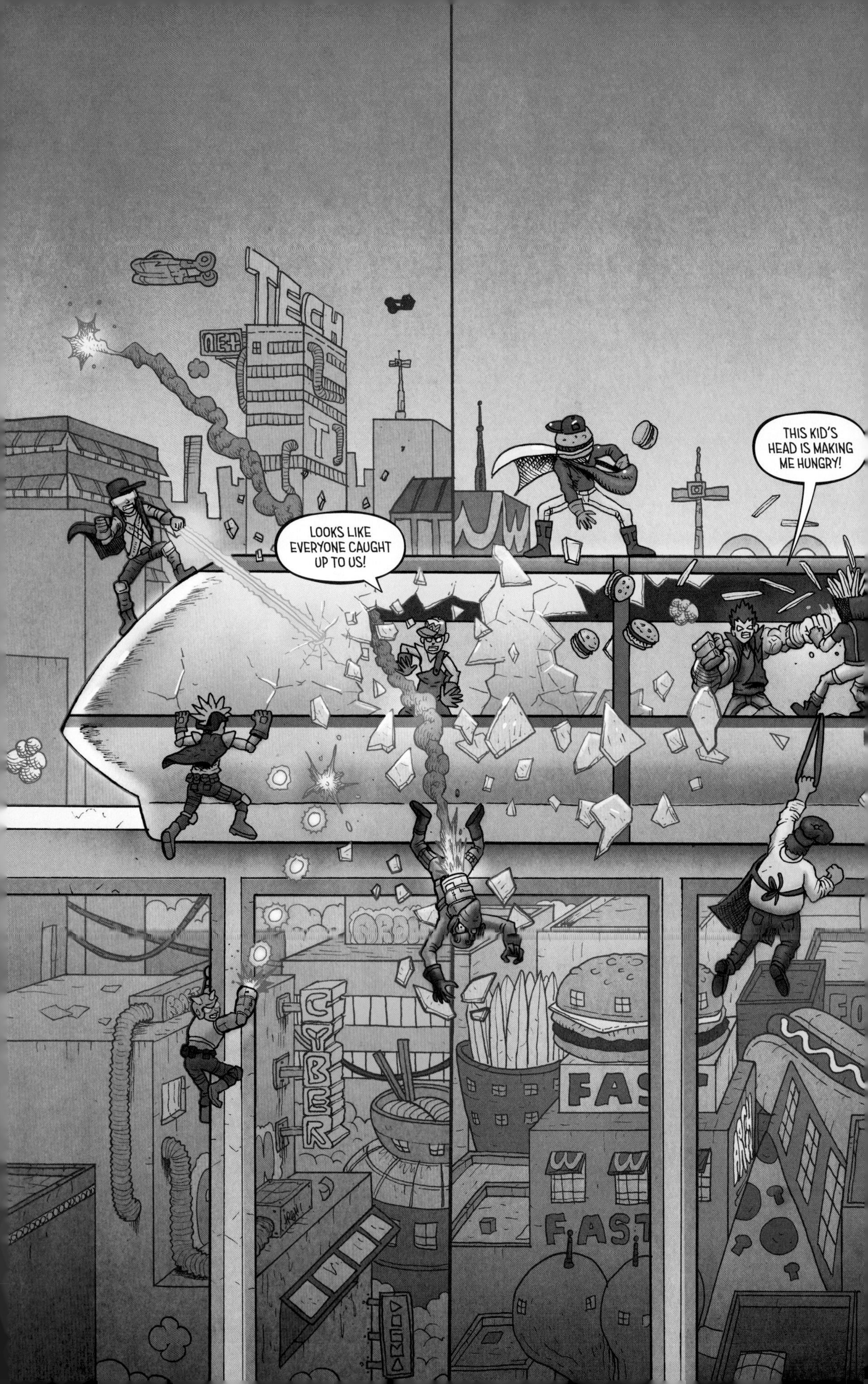
LOOKS LIKE EVERYONE CAUGHT UP TO US!
THIS KID'S HEAD IS MAKING ME HUNGRY!
TECH
CYBER
FAST
FAST

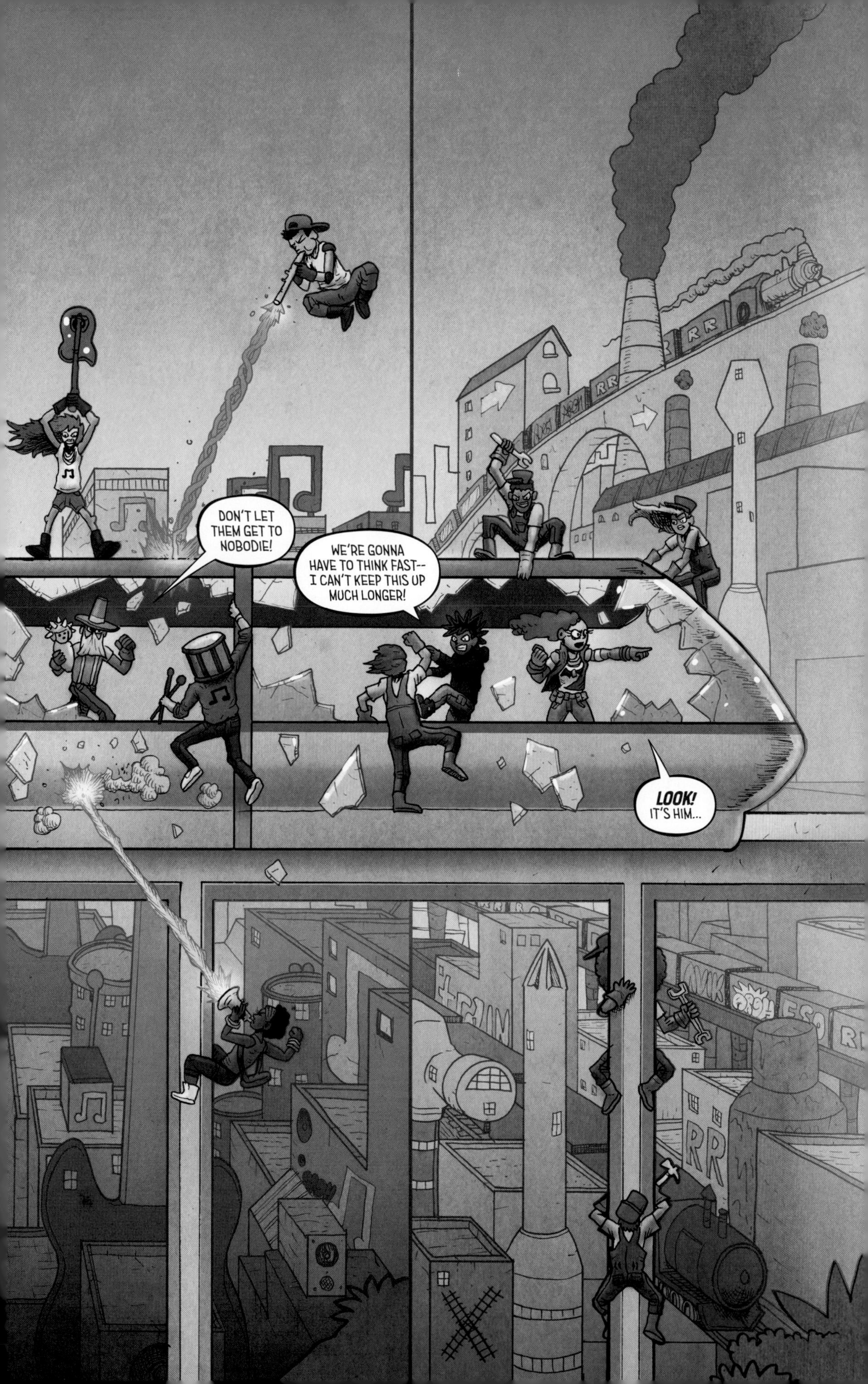

DON'T LET THEM GET TO NOBODIE!
WE'RE GONNA HAVE TO THINK FAST-- I CAN'T KEEP THIS UP MUCH LONGER!
LOOK! IT'S HIM...

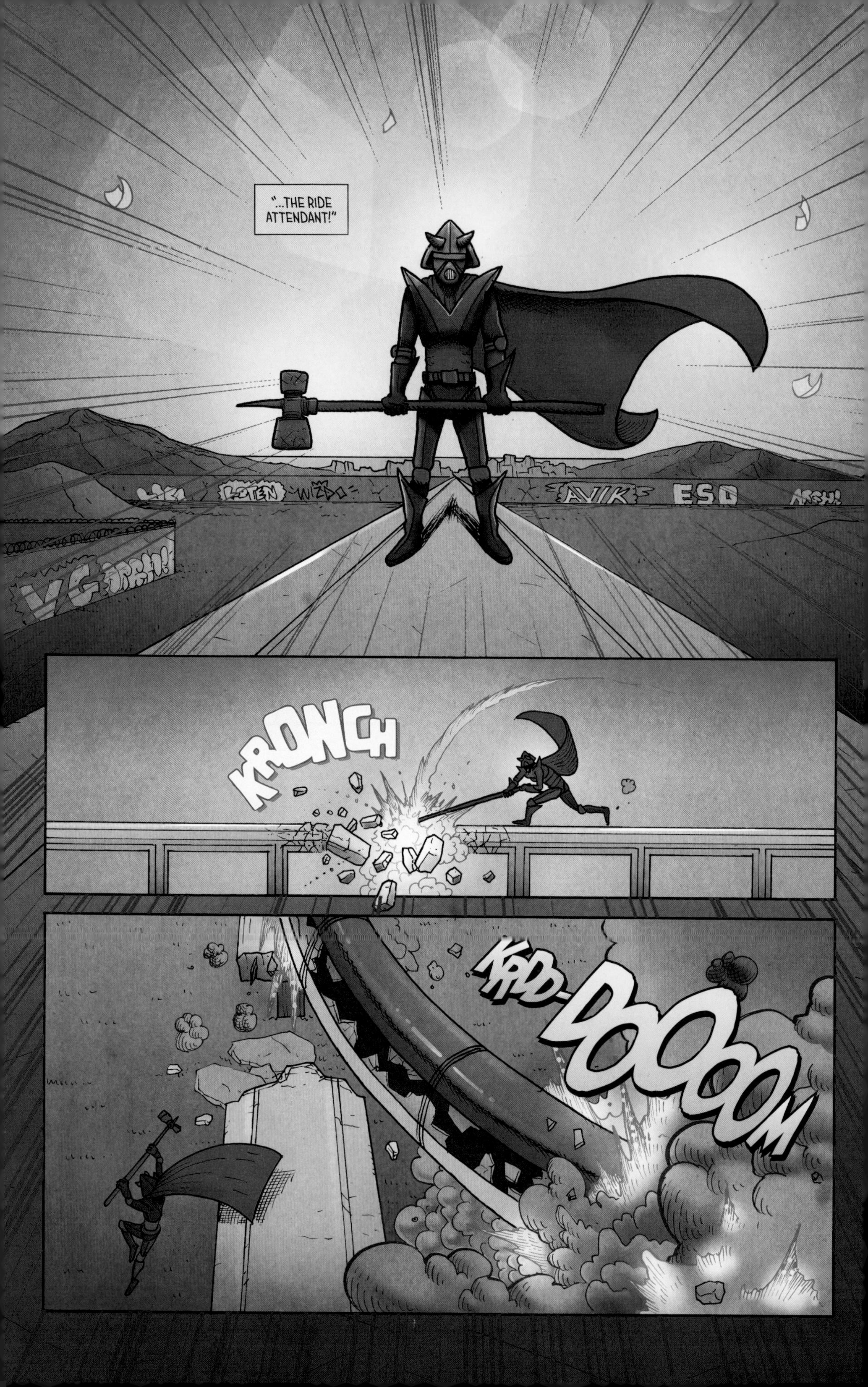
"...THE RIDE ATTENDANT!"
KRONCH
KRO-DOOOOM

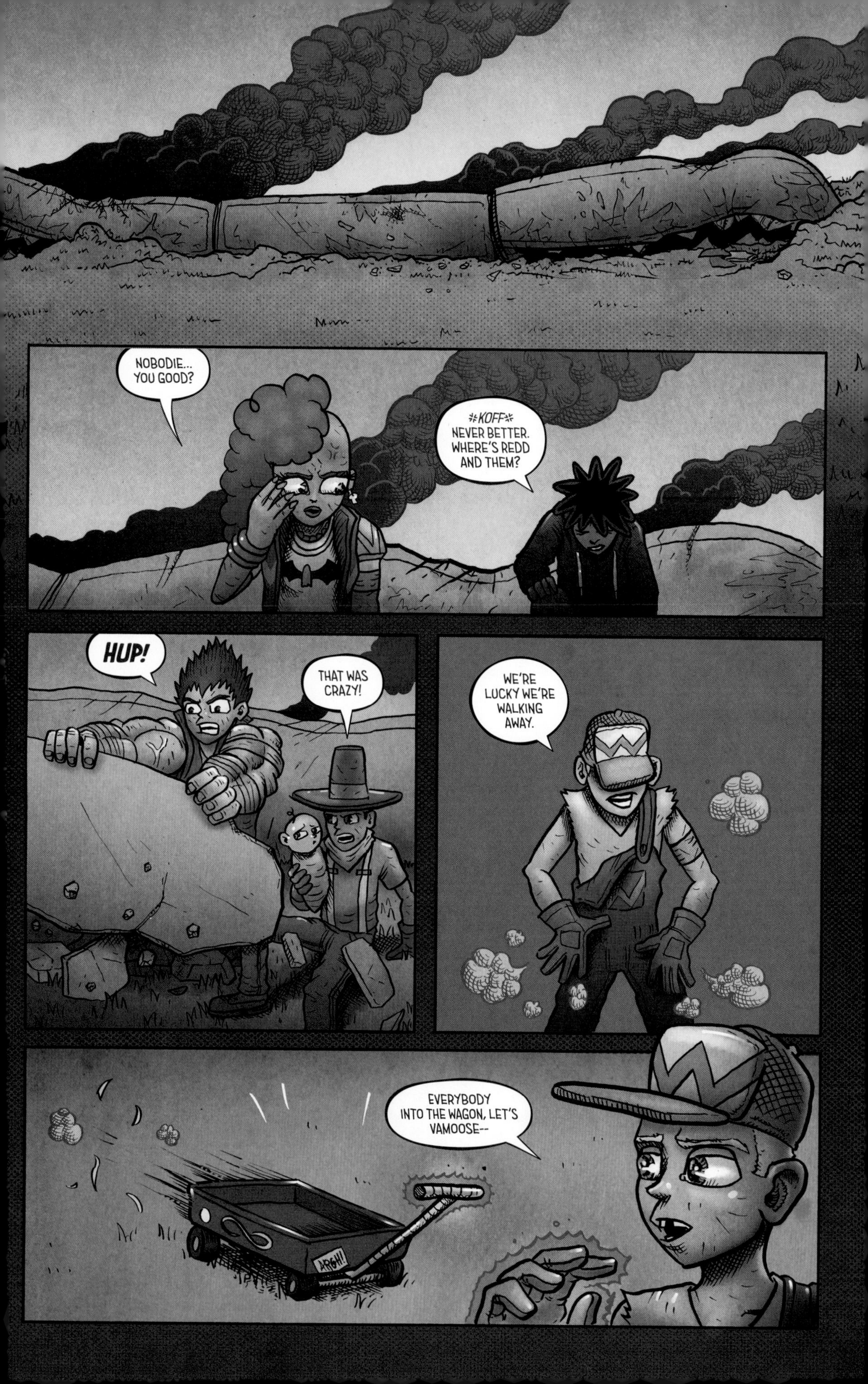
NOBODIE... YOU GOOD?
#KOFF# NEVER BETTER. WHERE'S REDD AND THEM?
HUP!
THAT WAS CRAZY!
WE'RE LUCKY WE'RE WALKING AWAY.
EVERYBODY INTO THE WAGON, LET'S VAMOOSE--
ARGH!

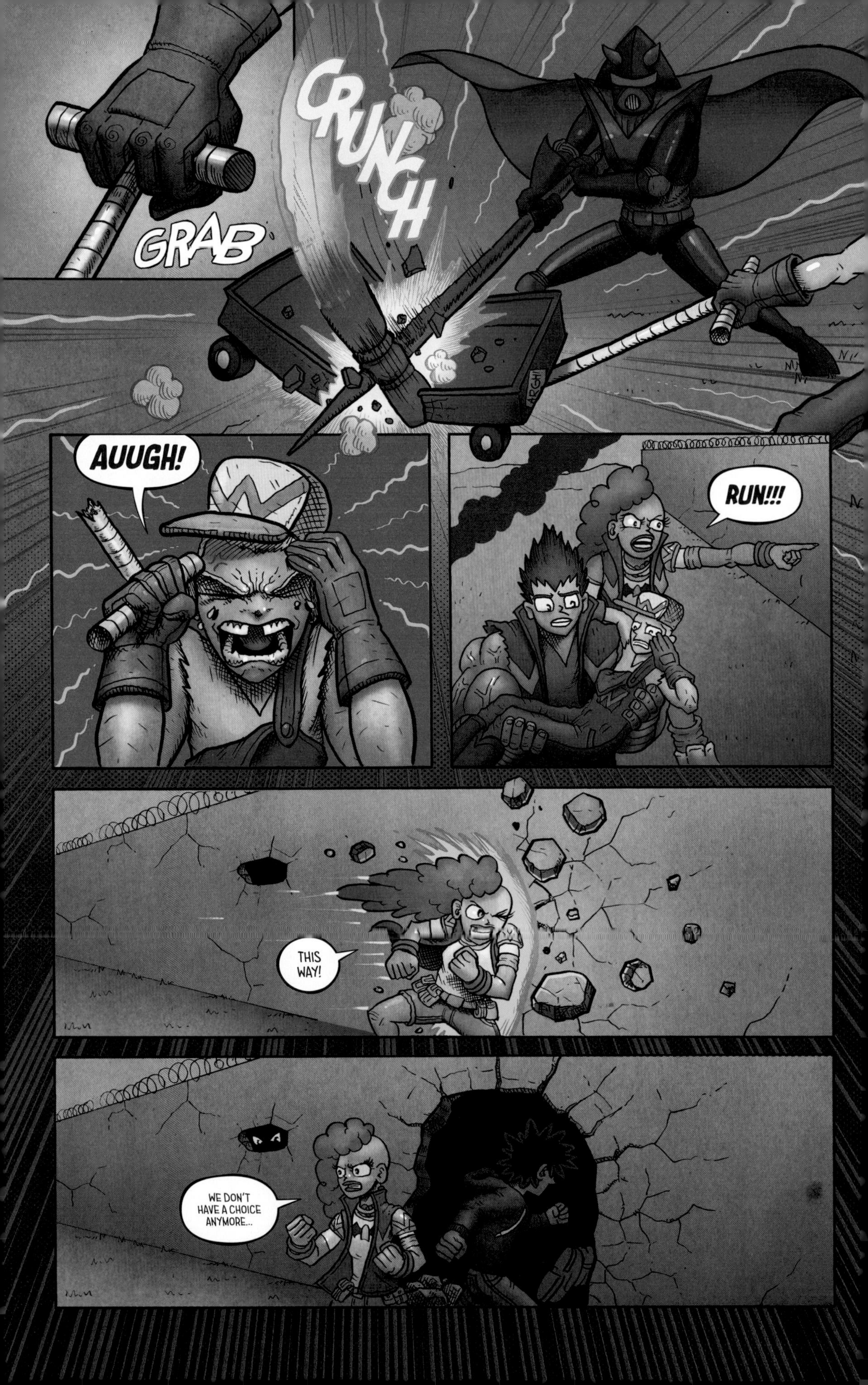
GRAB
CRUNCH
ARGH!
AUUGH!
RUN!!!
THIS WAY!
WE DON'T HAVE A CHOICE ANYMORE...

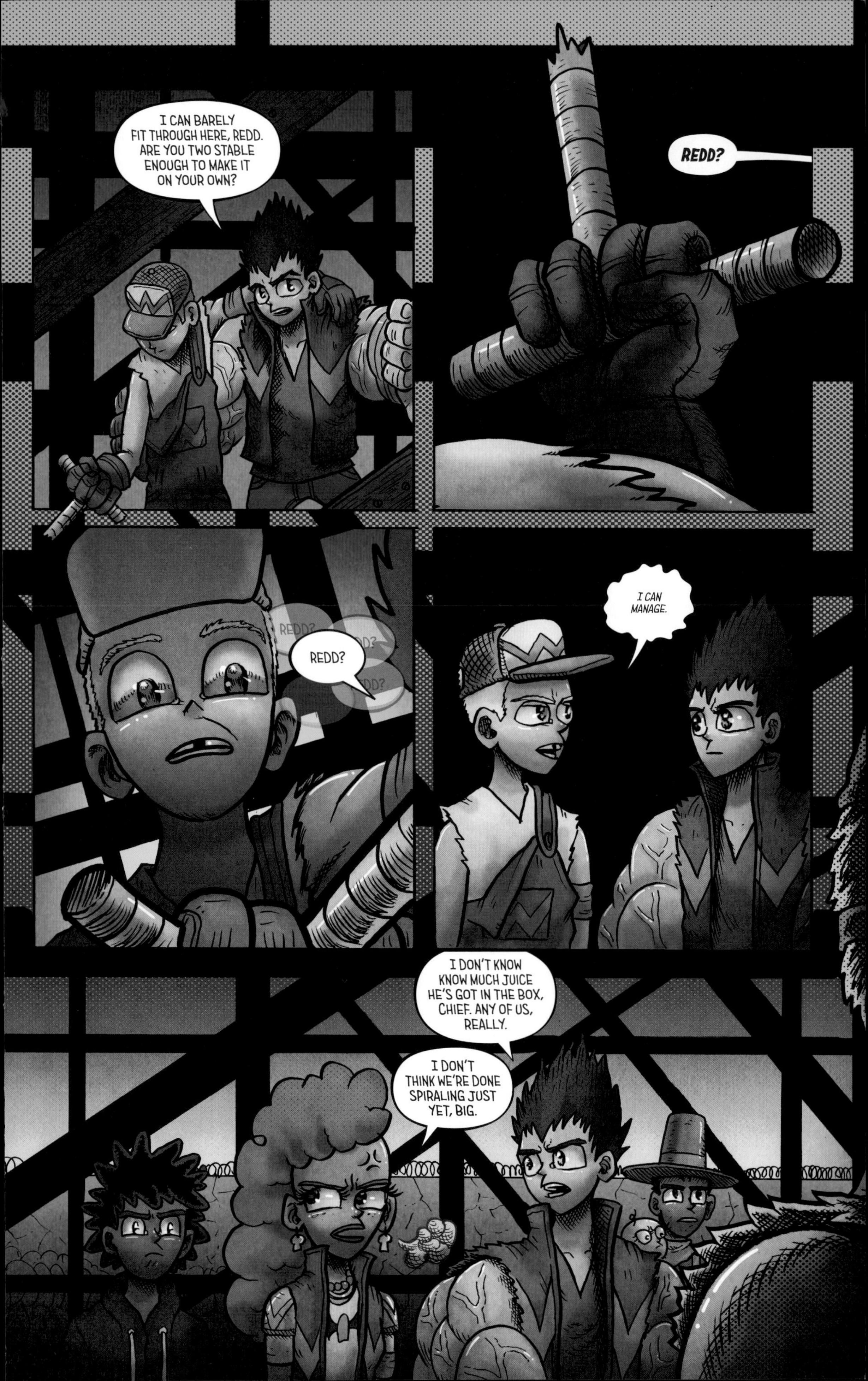

I CAN BARELY FIT THROUGH HERE, REDD. ARE YOU TWO STABLE ENOUGH TO MAKE IT ON YOUR OWN?
REDD?
REDD?
I CAN MANAGE.
I DON'T KNOW KNOW MUCH JUICE HE'S GOT IN THE BOX, CHIEF. ANY OF US, REALLY.
I DON'T THINK WE'RE DONE SPIRALING JUST YET, BIG.

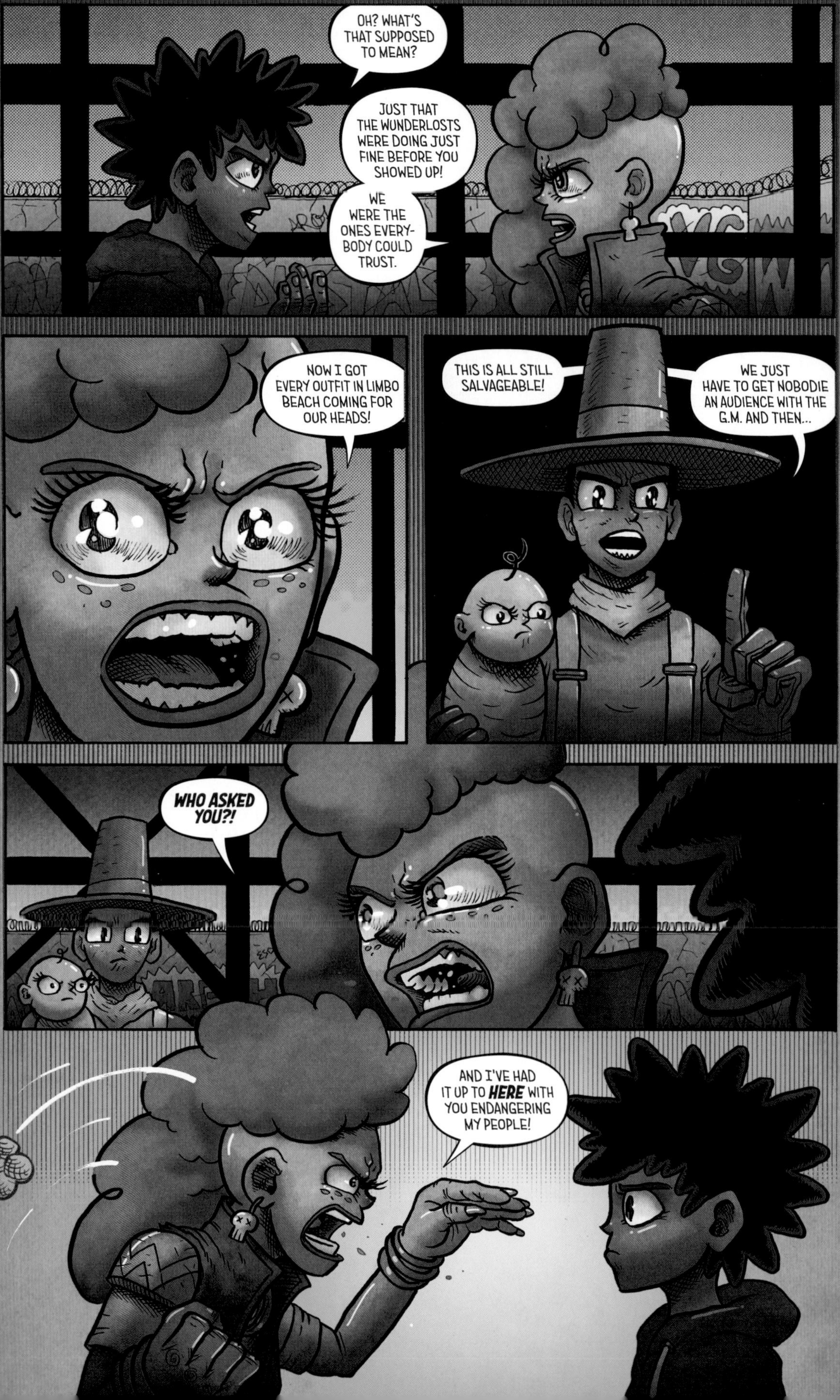
OH? WHAT'S THAT SUPPOSED TO MEAN?
JUST THAT THE WUNDERLOSTS WERE DOING JUST FINE BEFORE YOU SHOWED UP!
WE WERE THE ONES EVERY-BODY COULD TRUST.
NOW I GOT EVERY OUTFIT IN LIMBO BEACH COMING FOR OUR HEADS!
THIS IS ALL STILL SALVAGEABLE!
WE JUST HAVE TO GET NOBODIE AN AUDIENCE WITH THE G.M. AND THEN...
WHO ASKED YOU?!
AND I'VE HAD IT UP TO HERE WITH YOU ENDANGERING MY PEOPLE!

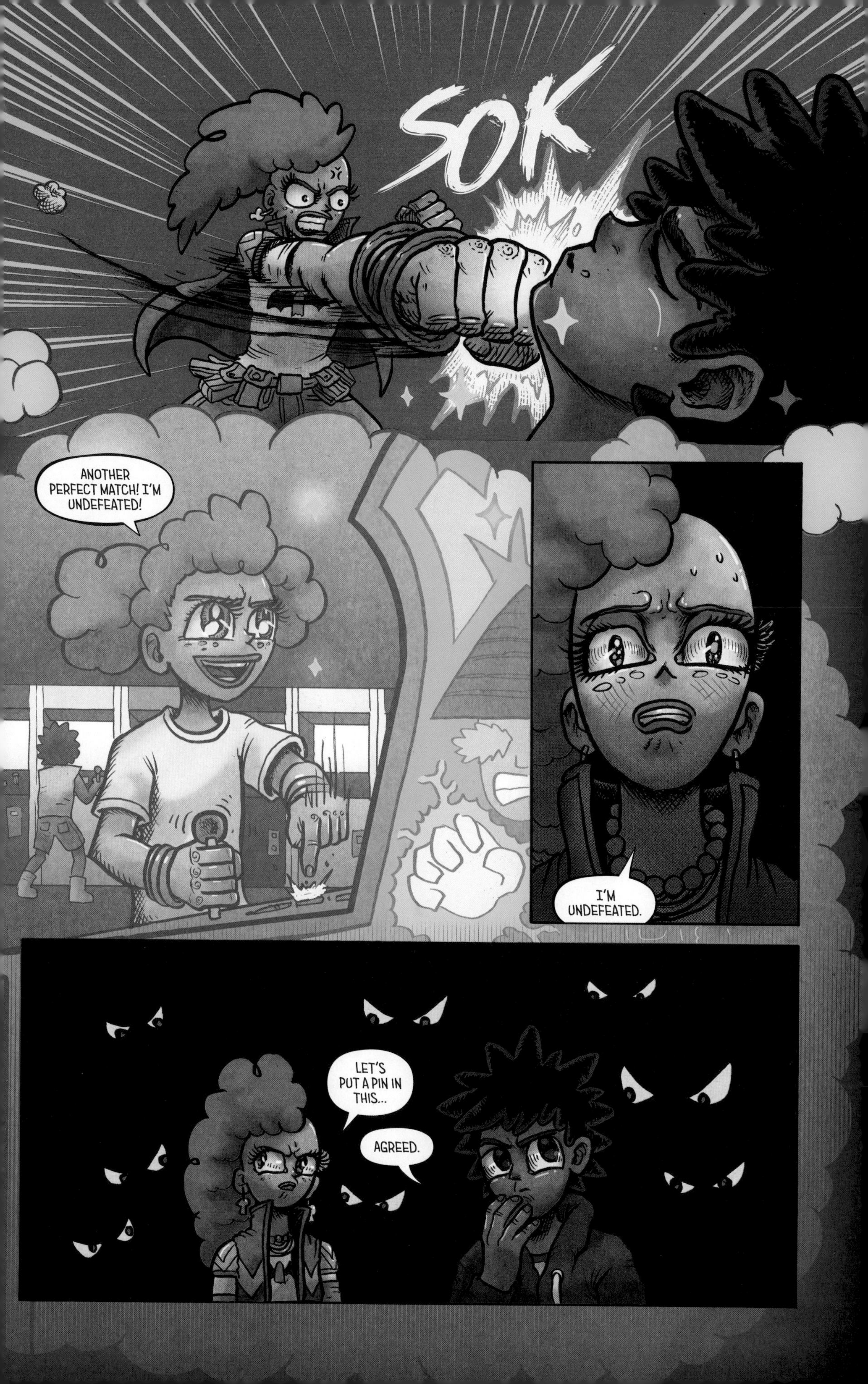
SOK
ANOTHER PERFECT MATCH! I'M UNDEFEATED!
I'M UNDEFEATED.
LET'S PUT A PIN IN THIS...
AGREED.

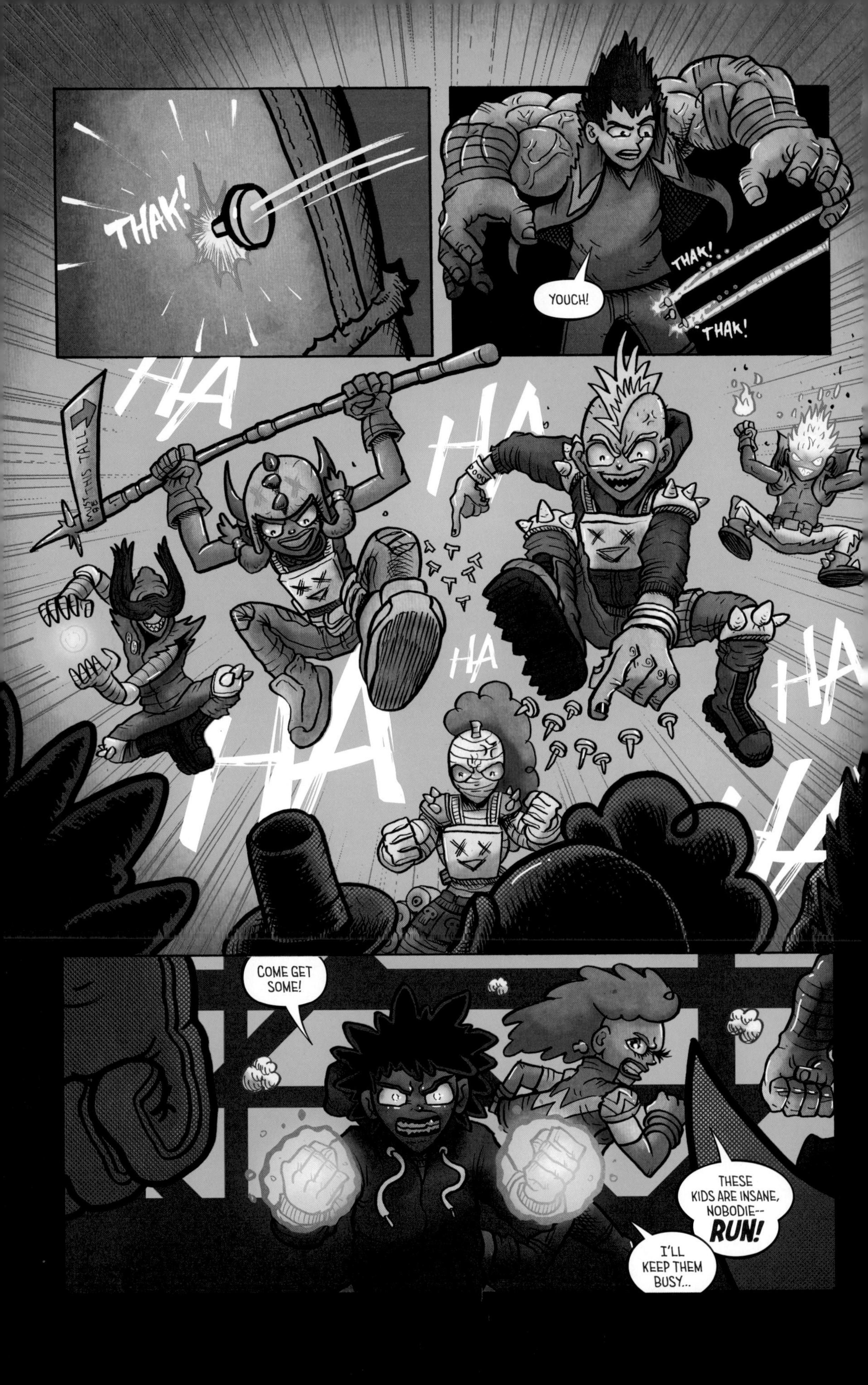
THAK!
YOUCH!
THAK!
THAK!
HA
HA
MUST BE THIS TALL
HA
HA
HA
HA
COME GET SOME!
THESE KIDS ARE INSANE, NOBODIE-- **RUN!**
I'LL KEEP THEM BUSY...

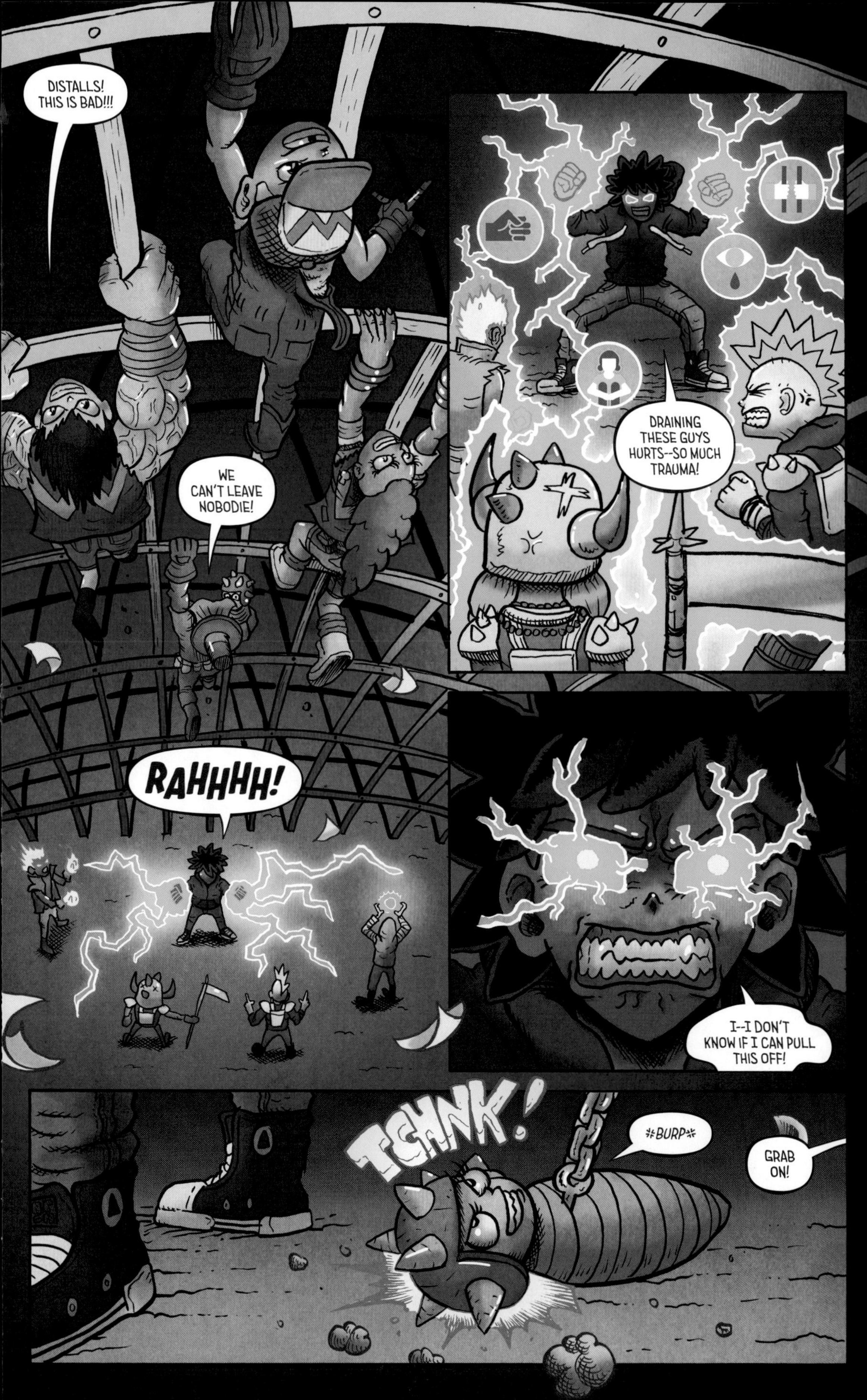
DISTALLS! THIS IS BAD!!!
DRAINING THESE GUYS HURTS--SO MUCH TRAUMA!
WE CAN'T LEAVE NOBODIE!
RAHHHH!
I--I DON'T KNOW IF I CAN PULL THIS OFF!
TCHNK!
BURP
GRAB ON!

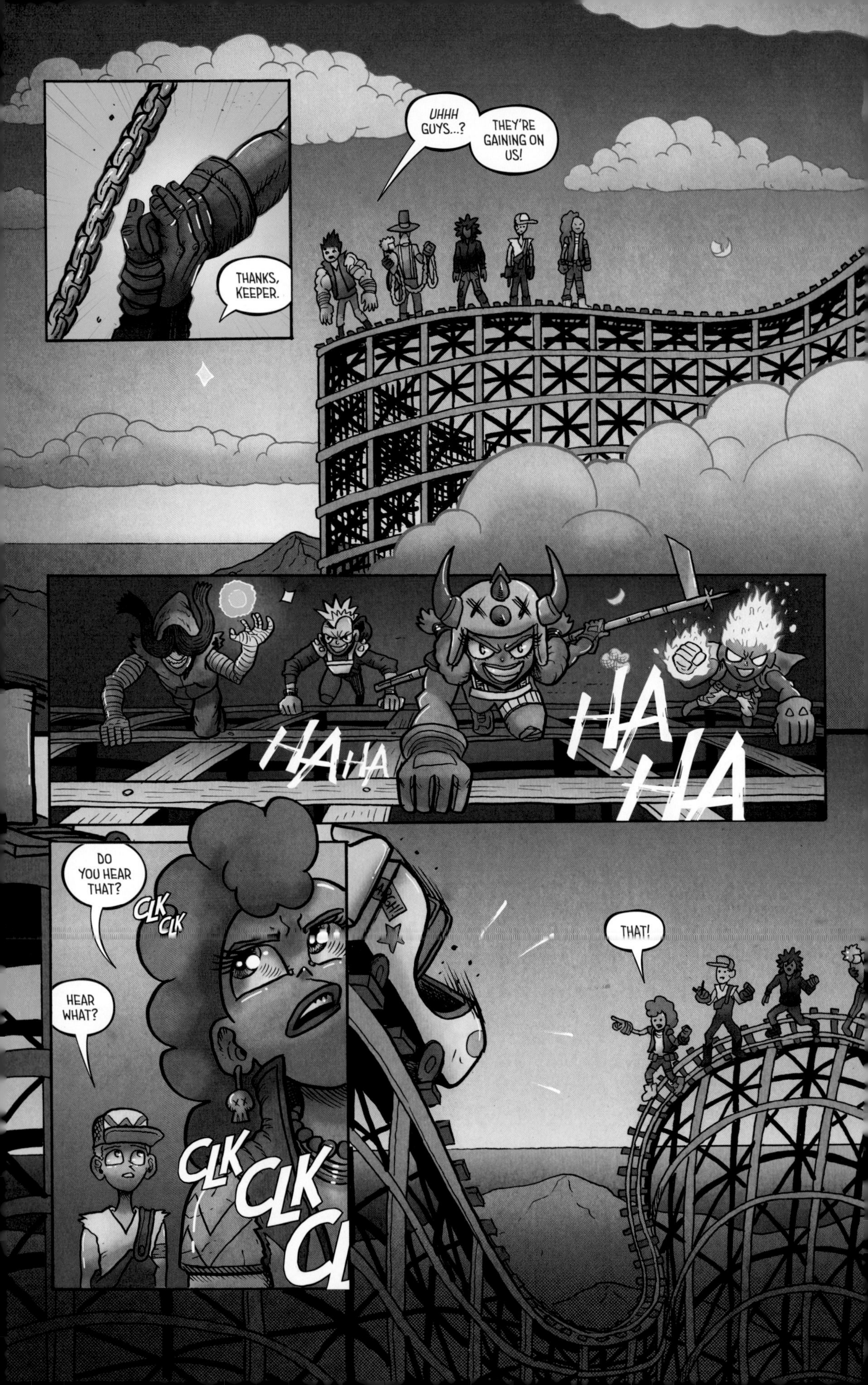
THANKS, KEEPER.
UHHH GUYS...?
THEY'RE GAINING ON US!
HAHAHA
HA HA
DO YOU HEAR THAT?
CLK CLK
HEAR WHAT?
CLK CLK CL
THAT!

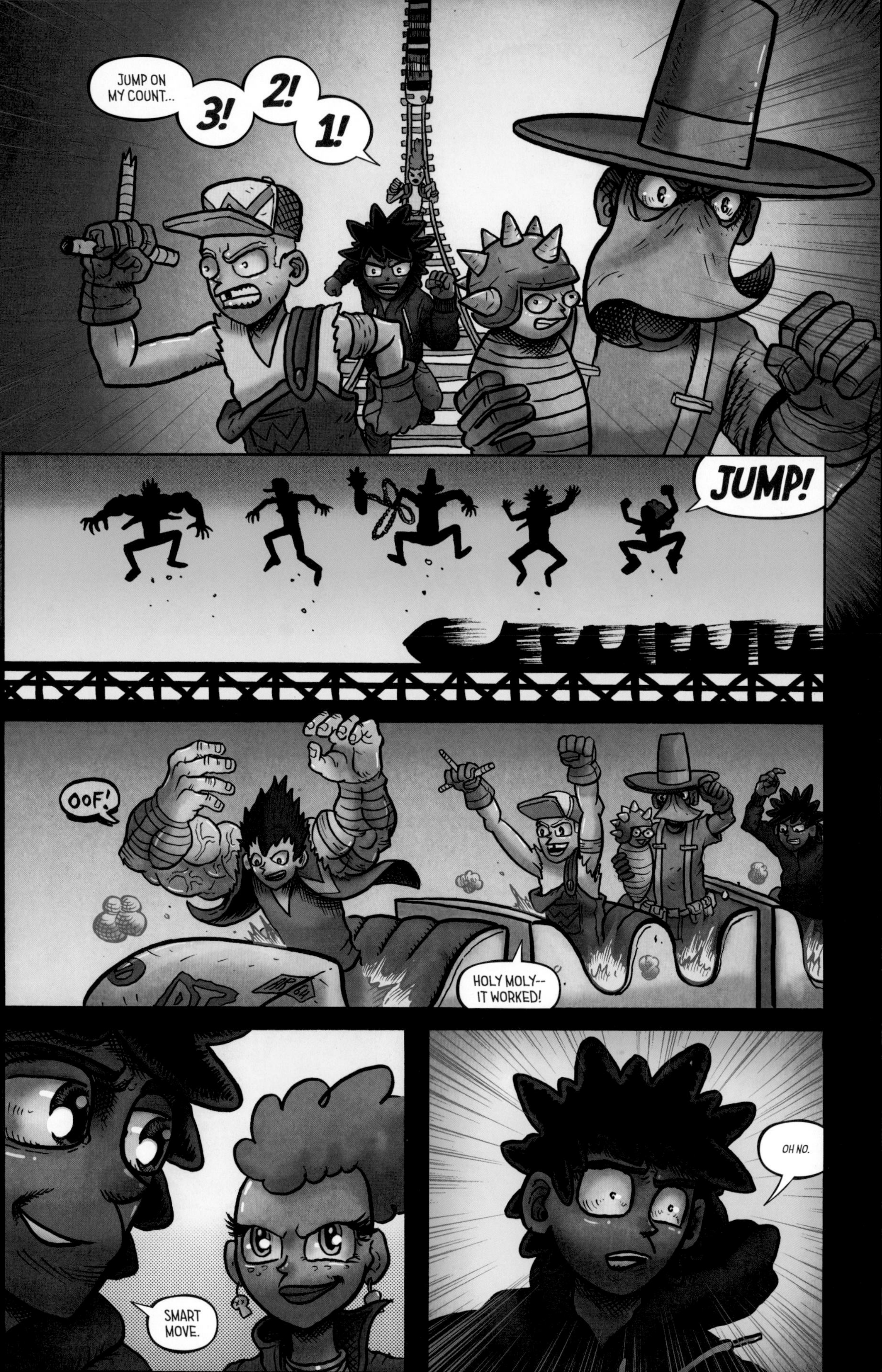
JUMP ON MY COUNT...
3!
2!
1!
JUMP!
OOF!
HOLY MOLY-- IT WORKED!
SMART MOVE.
OH NO.

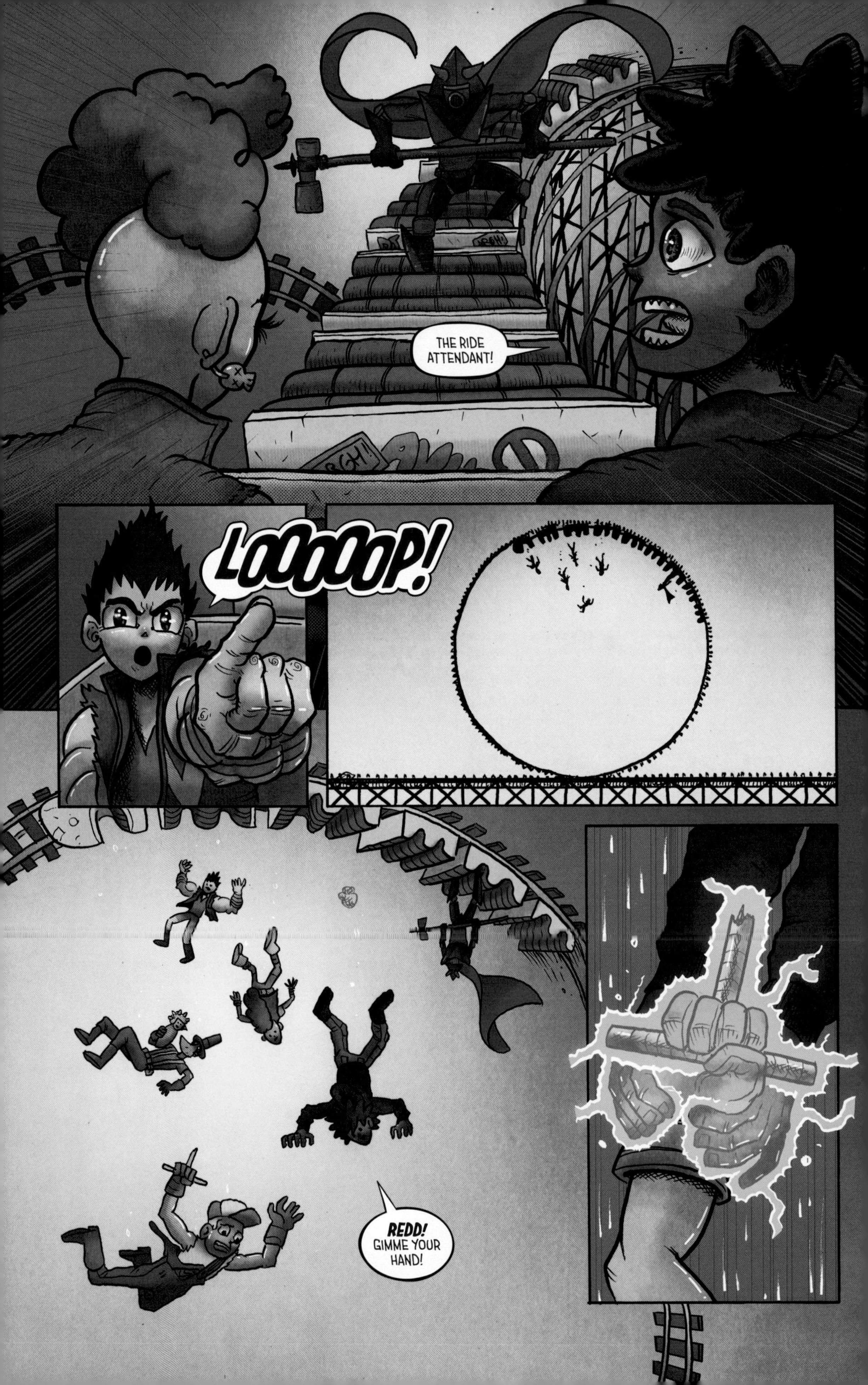
THE RIDE ATTENDANT!
LOOOOOOP!
REDD! GIMME YOUR HAND!

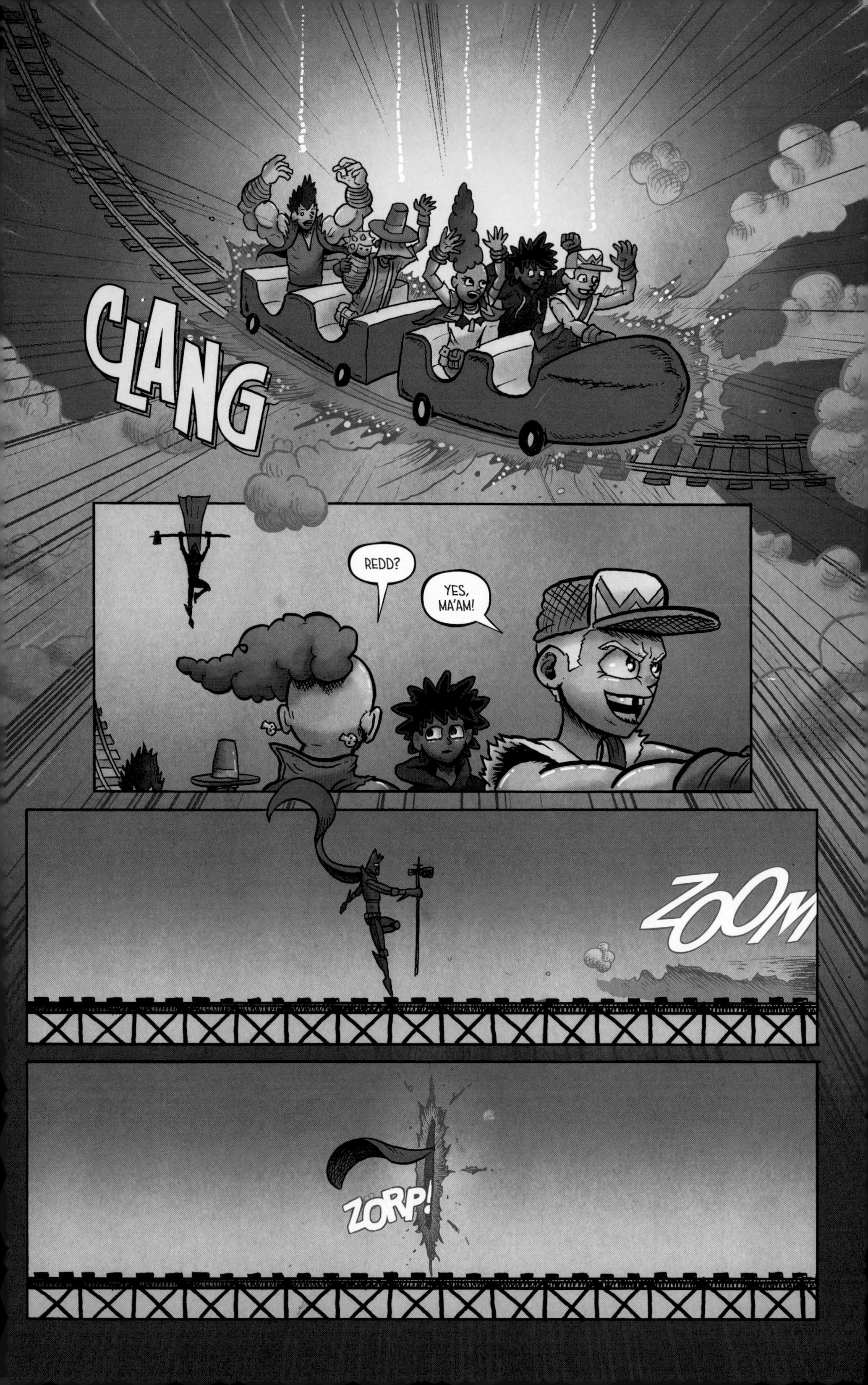
CLANG
REDD?
YES, MA'AM!
ZOOM
ZORP!

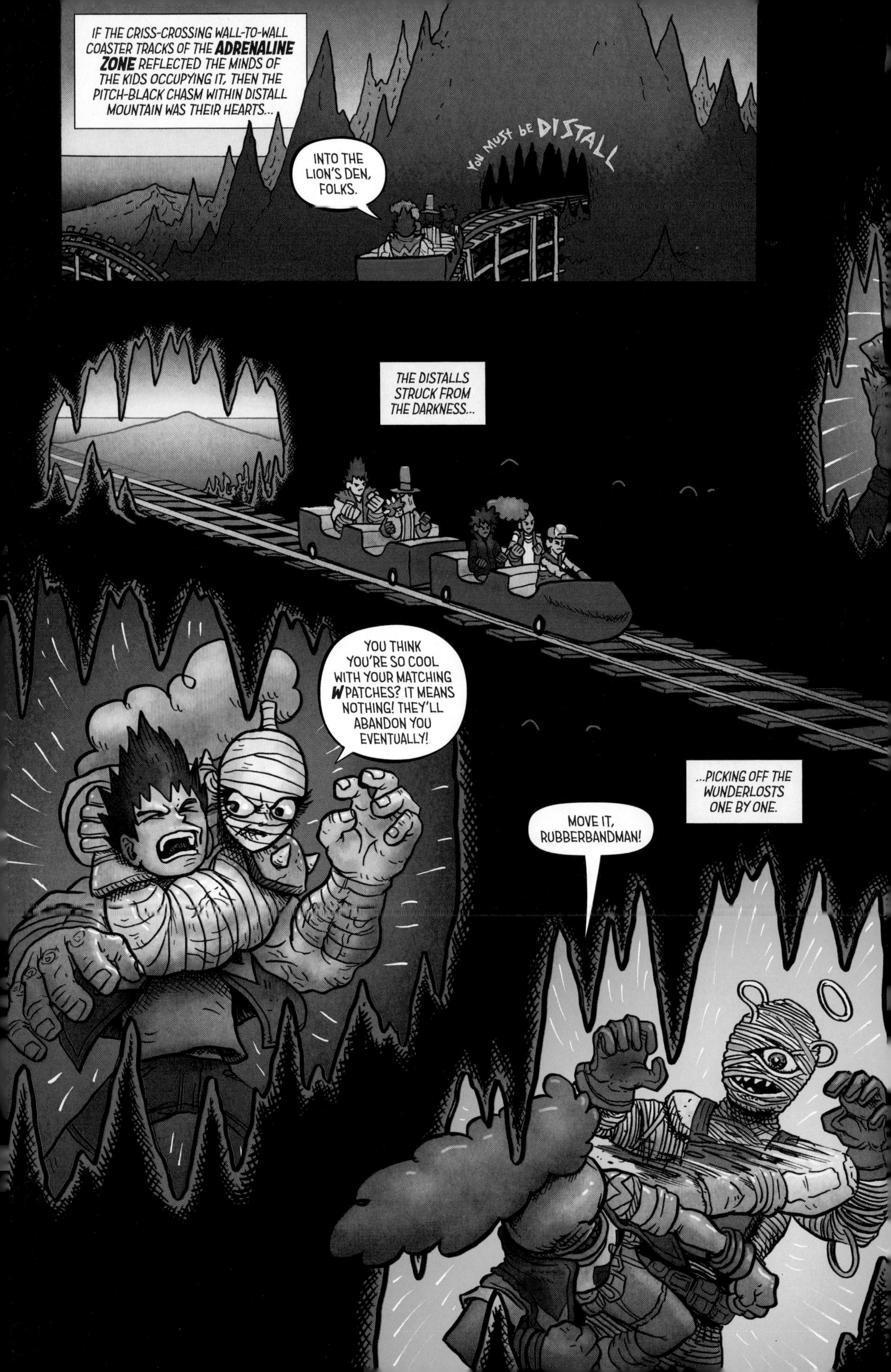
IF THE CRISS-CROSSING WALL-TO-WALL COASTER TRACKS OF THE **ADRENALINE ZONE** REFLECTED THE MINDS OF THE KIDS OCCUPYING IT, THEN THE PITCH-BLACK CHASM WITHIN DISTALL MOUNTAIN WAS THEIR HEARTS...
INTO THE LION'S DEN, FOLKS.
YOU MUST BE DISTALL
THE DISTALLS STRUCK FROM THE DARKNESS...
YOU THINK YOU'RE SO COOL WITH YOUR MATCHING **W** PATCHES? IT MEANS NOTHING! THEY'LL ABANDON YOU EVENTUALLY!
...PICKING OFF THE WUNDERLOSTS ONE BY ONE.
MOVE IT, RUBBERBANDMAN!

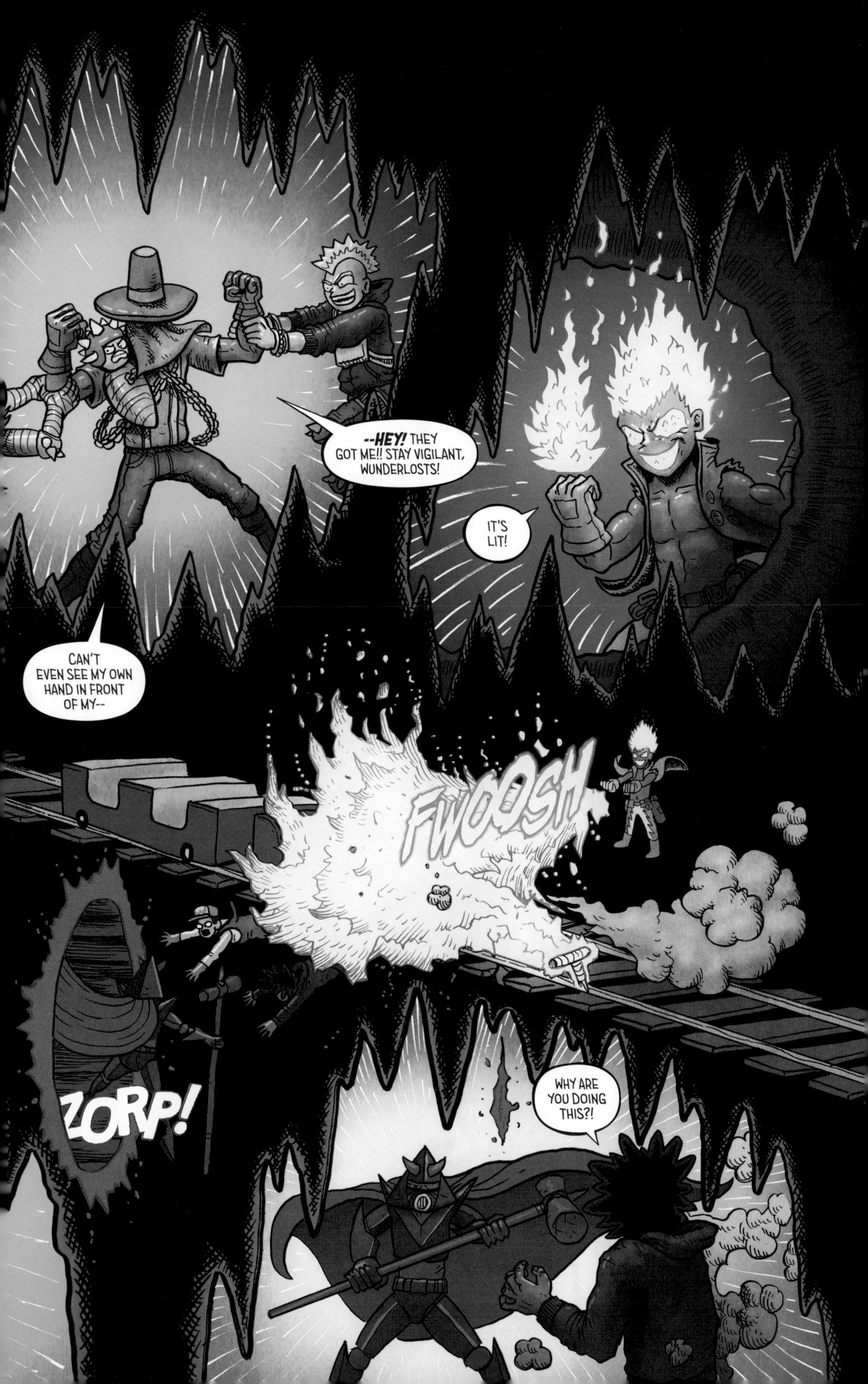
--HEY! THEY GOT ME!! STAY VIGILANT, WUNDERLOSTS!
IT'S LIT!
CAN'T EVEN SEE MY OWN HAND IN FRONT OF MY--
FWOOSH
ZORP!
WHY ARE YOU DOING THIS?!

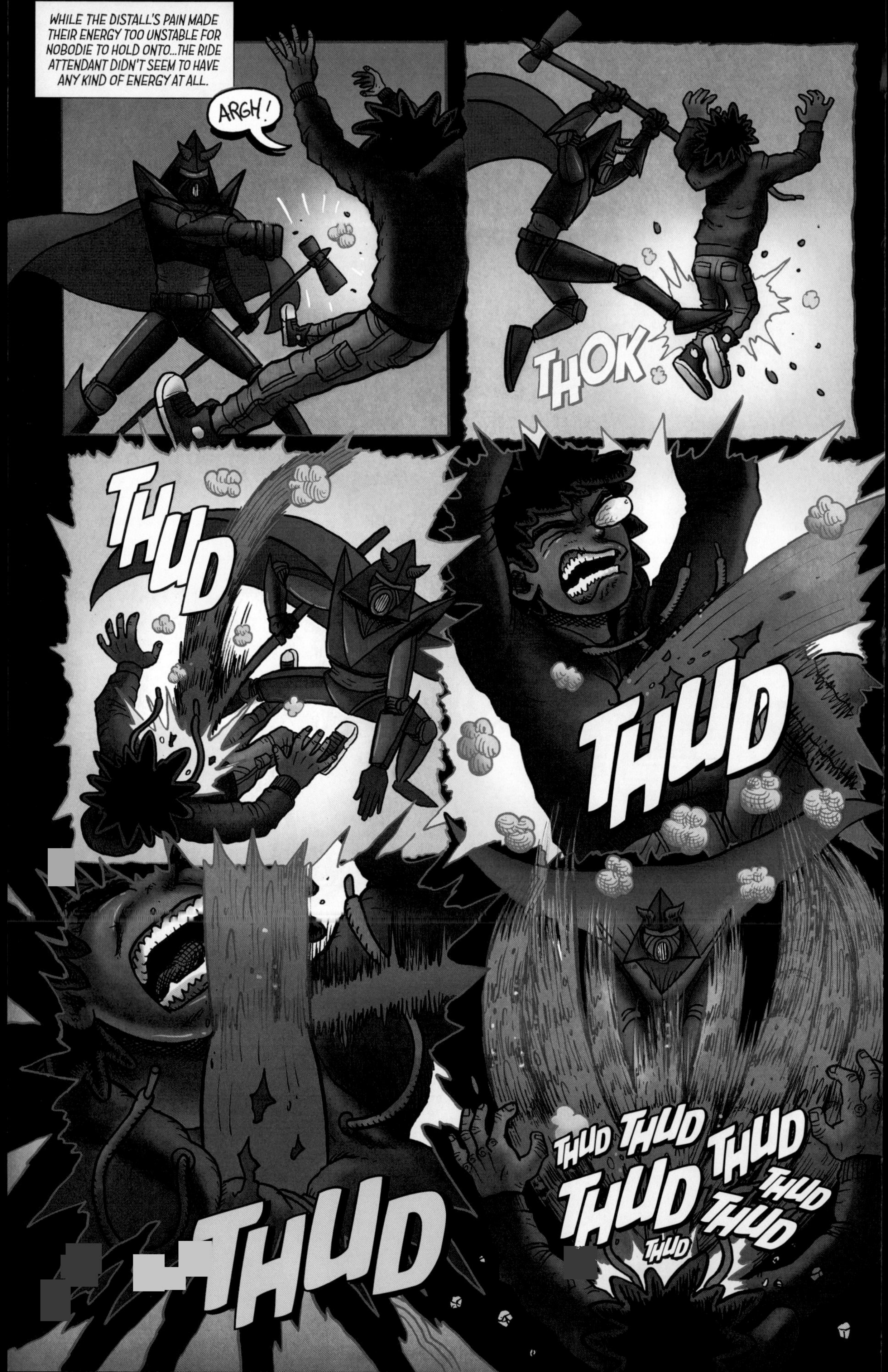

WHILE THE DISTALL'S PAIN MADE THEIR ENERGY TOO UNSTABLE FOR NOBODIE TO HOLD ONTO...THE RIDE ATTENDANT DIDN'T SEEM TO HAVE ANY KIND OF ENERGY AT ALL.
ARGH!
THOK
THUD
THUD
THUD
THUD THUD THUD
THUD THUD THUD THUD
THUD

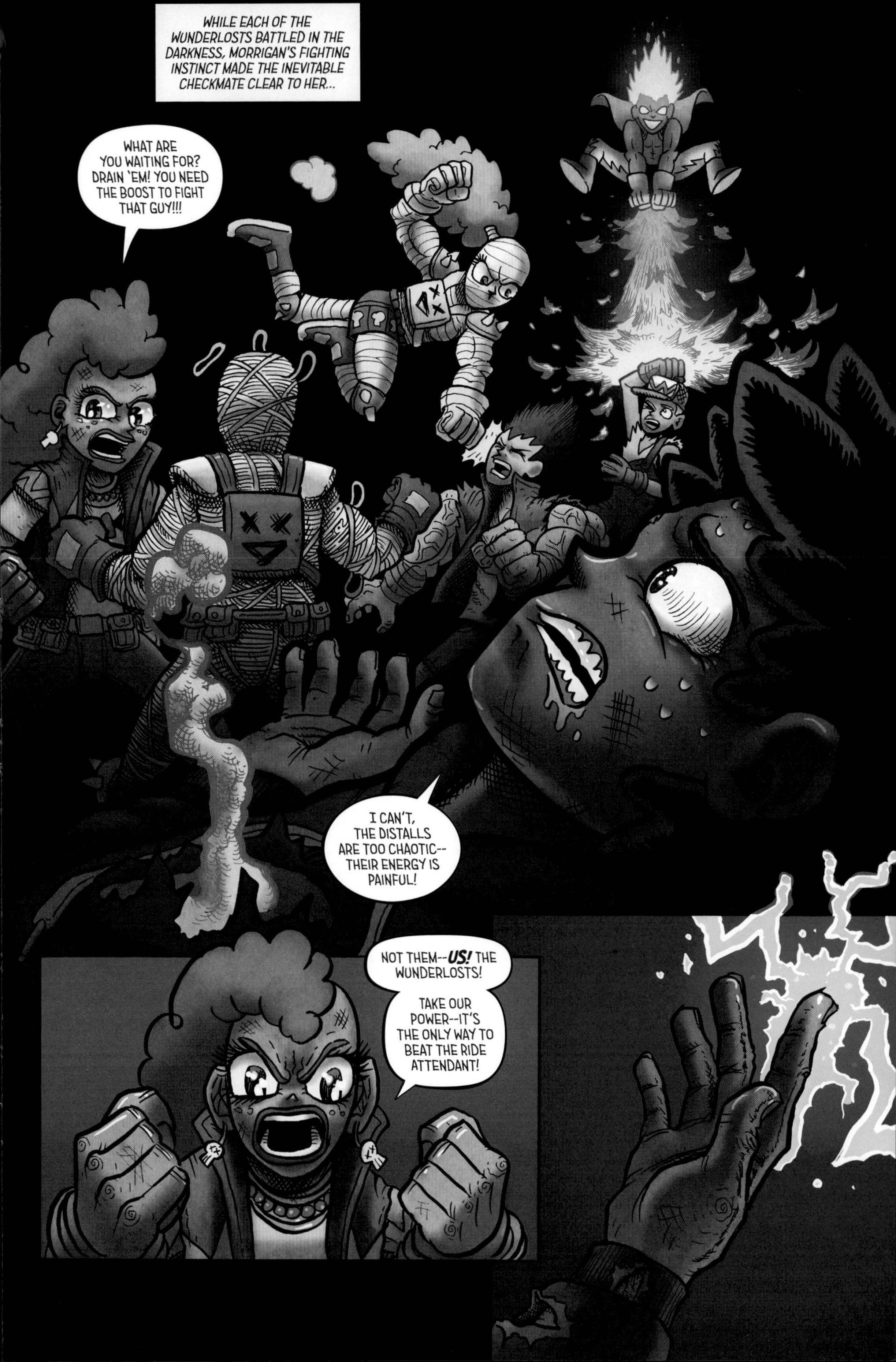
WHILE EACH OF THE WUNDERLOSTS BATTLED IN THE DARKNESS, MORRIGAN'S FIGHTING INSTINCT MADE THE INEVITABLE CHECKMATE CLEAR TO HER...
WHAT ARE YOU WAITING FOR? DRAIN 'EM! YOU NEED THE BOOST TO FIGHT THAT GUY!!!
I CAN'T, THE DISTALLS ARE TOO CHAOTIC-- THEIR ENERGY IS PAINFUL!
NOT THEM--US! THE WUNDERLOSTS!
TAKE OUR POWER--IT'S THE ONLY WAY TO BEAT THE RIDE ATTENDANT!

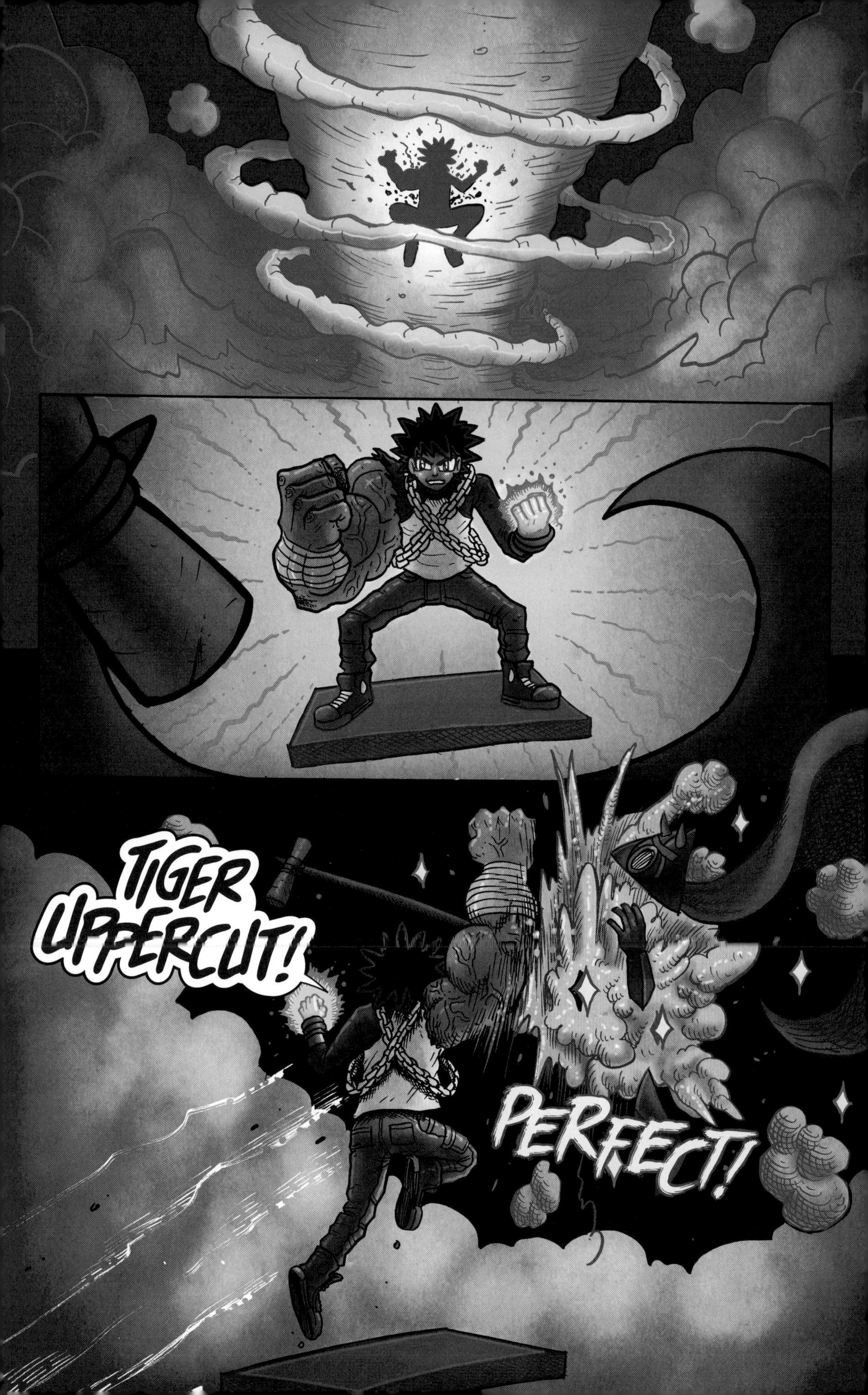
TIGER UPPERCUT!
PERFECT!

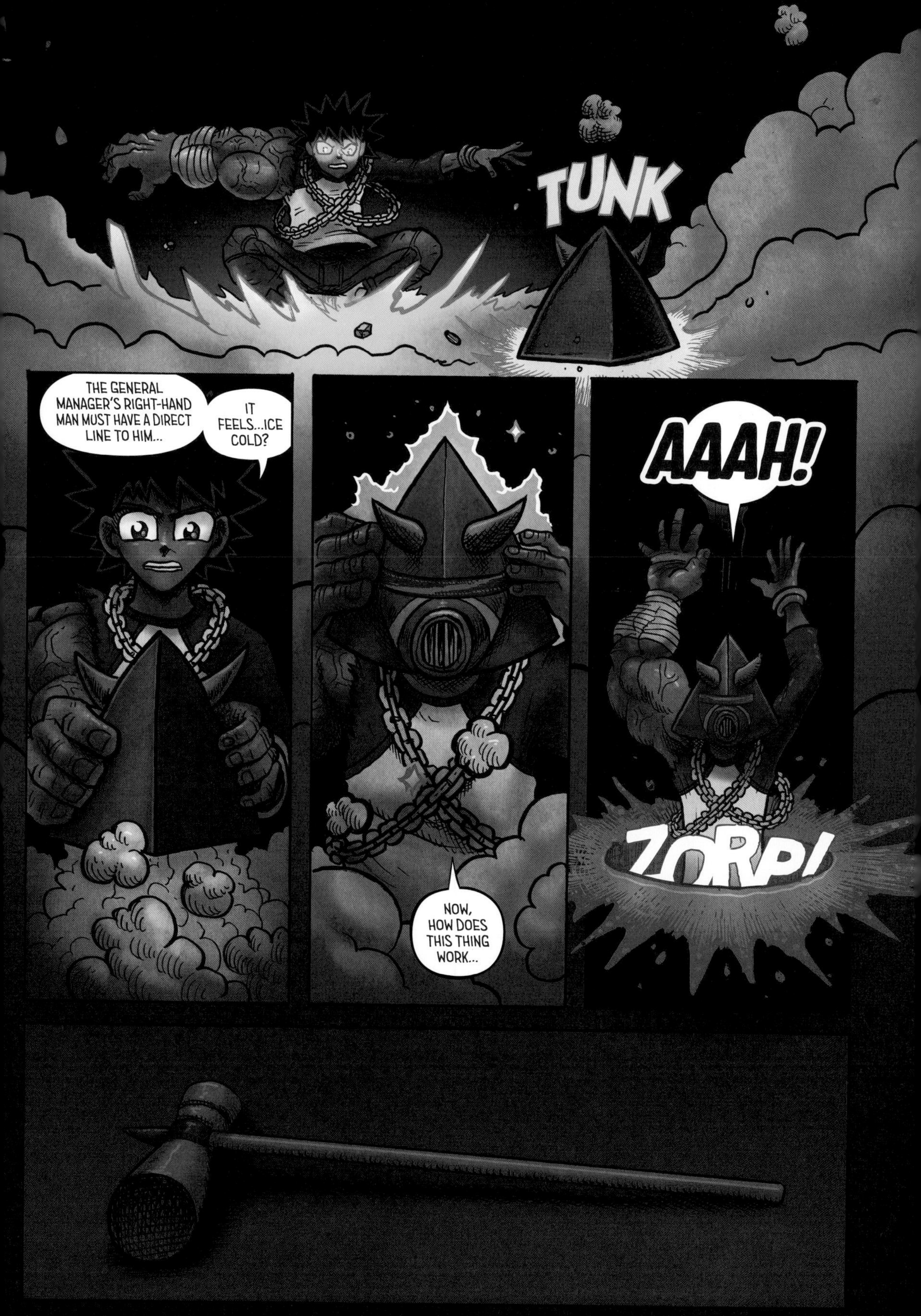
TUNK
THE GENERAL MANAGER'S RIGHT-HAND MAN MUST HAVE A DIRECT LINE TO HIM...
IT FEELS...ICE COLD?
NOW, HOW DOES THIS THING WORK...
AAAH!
ZORP!

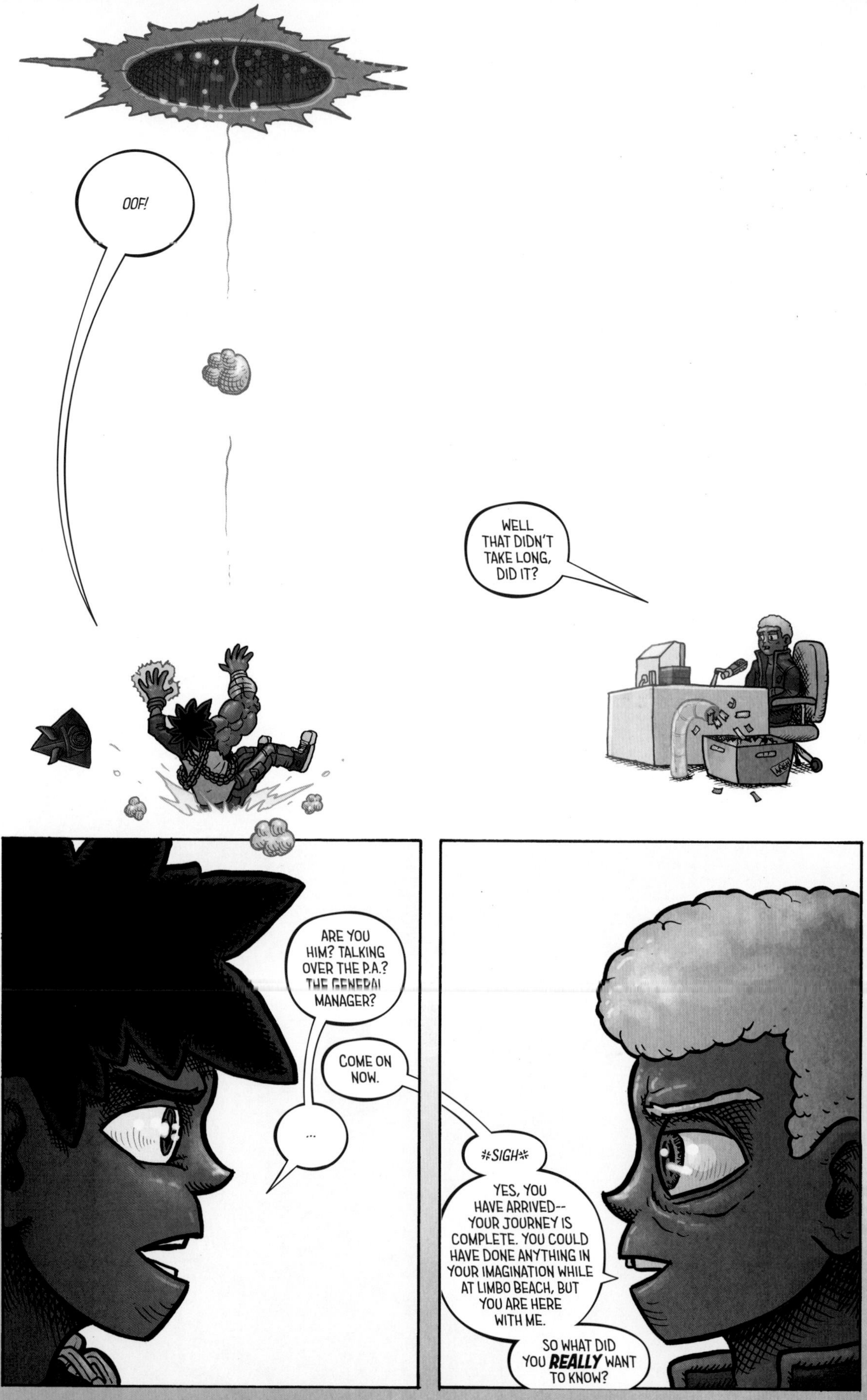
OOF!
WELL THAT DIDN'T TAKE LONG, DID IT?
ARE YOU HIM? TALKING OVER THE P.A.? THE GENERAL MANAGER?
COME ON NOW.
...
SIGH
YES, YOU HAVE ARRIVED-- YOUR JOURNEY IS COMPLETE. YOU COULD HAVE DONE ANYTHING IN YOUR IMAGINATION WHILE AT LIMBO BEACH, BUT YOU ARE HERE WITH ME.
SO WHAT DID YOU REALLY WANT TO KNOW?

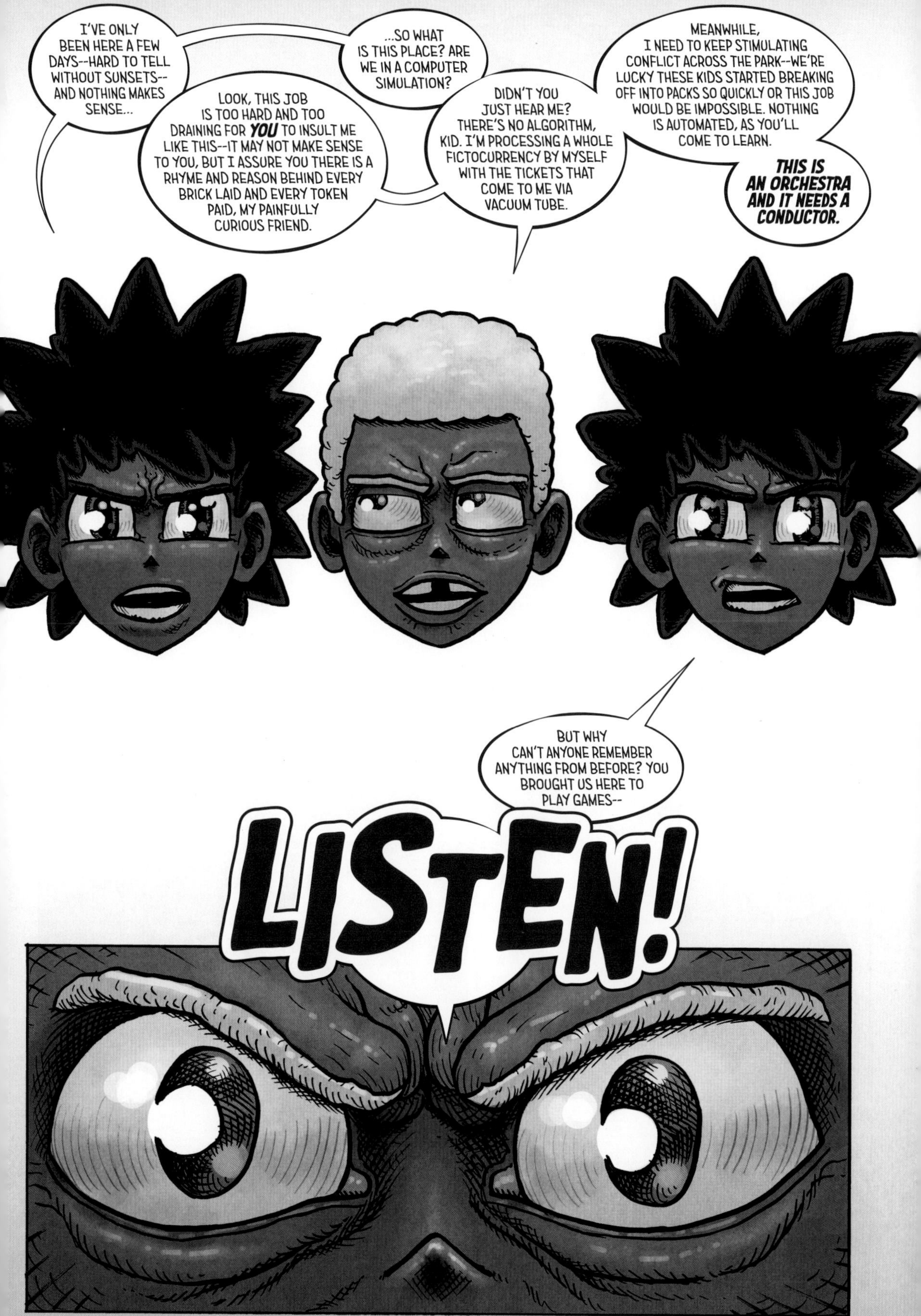
I'VE ONLY BEEN HERE A FEW DAYS--HARD TO TELL WITHOUT SUNSETS--AND NOTHING MAKES SENSE...
LOOK, THIS JOB IS TOO HARD AND TOO DRAINING FOR YOU TO INSULT ME LIKE THIS--IT MAY NOT MAKE SENSE TO YOU, BUT I ASSURE YOU THERE IS A RHYME AND REASON BEHIND EVERY BRICK LAID AND EVERY TOKEN PAID, MY PAINFULLY CURIOUS FRIEND.
...SO WHAT IS THIS PLACE? ARE WE IN A COMPUTER SIMULATION?
DIDN'T YOU JUST HEAR ME? THERE'S NO ALGORITHM, KID. I'M PROCESSING A WHOLE FICTOCURRENCY BY MYSELF WITH THE TICKETS THAT COME TO ME VIA VACUUM TUBE.
MEANWHILE, I NEED TO KEEP STIMULATING CONFLICT ACROSS THE PARK--WE'RE LUCKY THESE KIDS STARTED BREAKING OFF INTO PACKS SO QUICKLY OR THIS JOB WOULD BE IMPOSSIBLE. NOTHING IS AUTOMATED, AS YOU'LL COME TO LEARN.
THIS IS AN ORCHESTRA AND IT NEEDS A CONDUCTOR.
BUT WHY CAN'T ANYONE REMEMBER ANYTHING FROM BEFORE? YOU BROUGHT US HERE TO PLAY GAMES--
LISTEN!

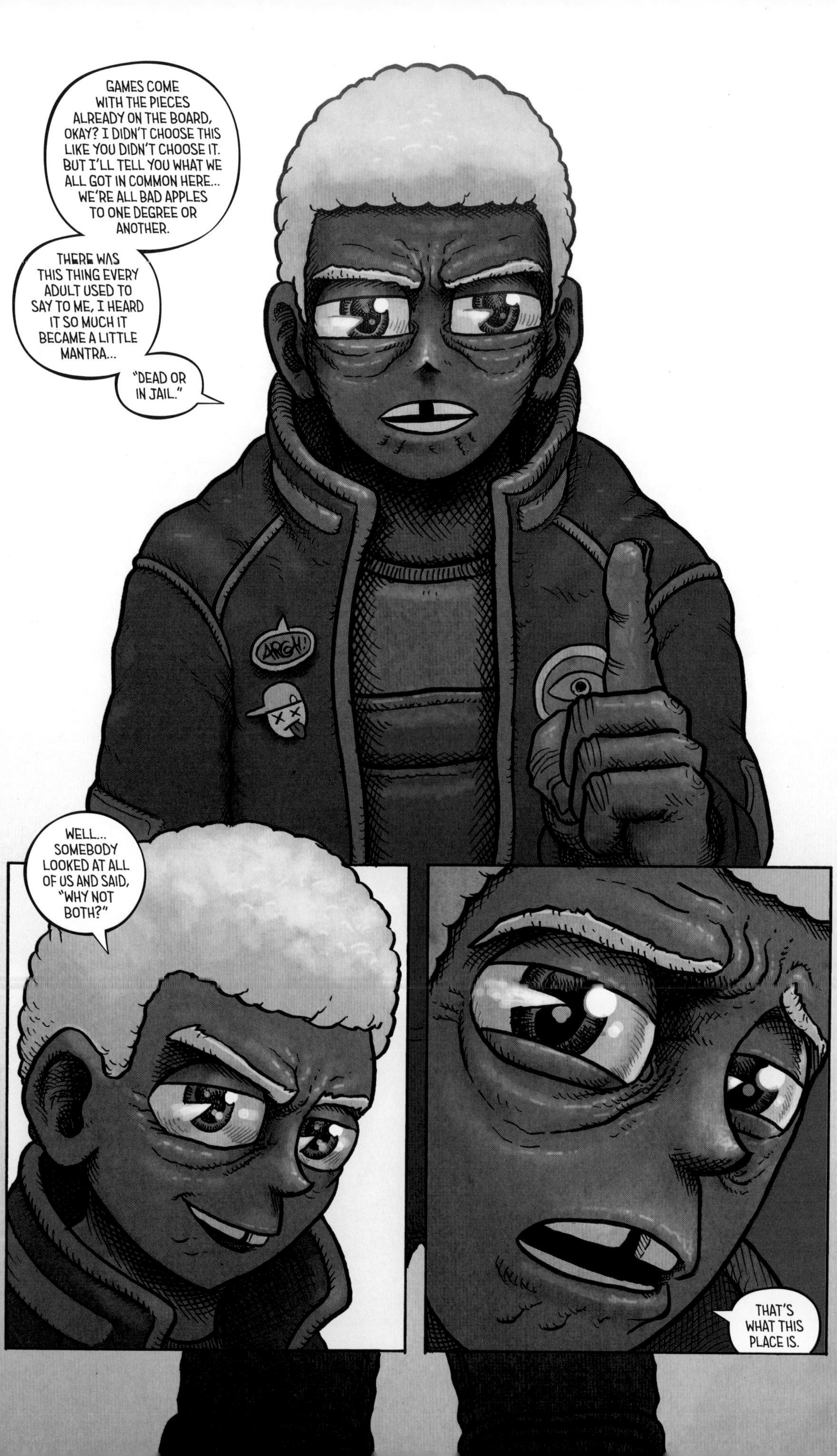
GAMES COME WITH THE PIECES ALREADY ON THE BOARD, OKAY? I DIDN'T CHOOSE THIS LIKE YOU DIDN'T CHOOSE IT. BUT I'LL TELL YOU WHAT WE ALL GOT IN COMMON HERE... WE'RE ALL BAD APPLES TO ONE DEGREE OR ANOTHER.
THERE WAS THIS THING EVERY ADULT USED TO SAY TO ME, I HEARD IT SO MUCH IT BECAME A LITTLE MANTRA...
"DEAD OR IN JAIL."
ARGH!
WELL... SOMEBODY LOOKED AT ALL OF US AND SAID, "WHY NOT BOTH?"
THAT'S WHAT THIS PLACE IS.

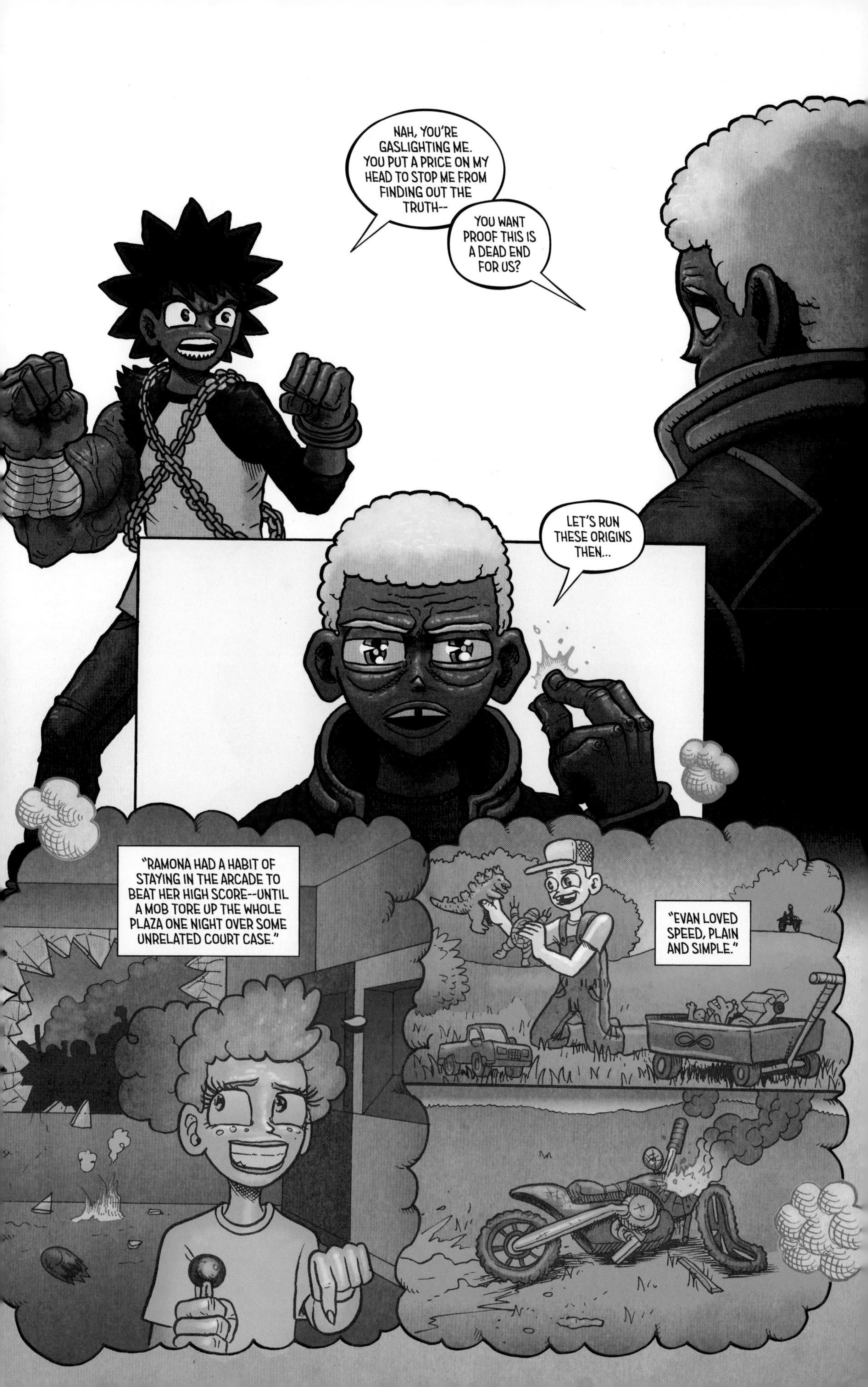
NAH, YOU'RE GASLIGHTING ME. YOU PUT A PRICE ON MY HEAD TO STOP ME FROM FINDING OUT THE TRUTH--
YOU WANT PROOF THIS IS A DEAD END FOR US?
LET'S RUN THESE ORIGINS THEN...
"RAMONA HAD A HABIT OF STAYING IN THE ARCADE TO BEAT HER HIGH SCORE--UNTIL A MOB TORE UP THE WHOLE PLAZA ONE NIGHT OVER SOME UNRELATED COURT CASE."
"EVAN LOVED SPEED, PLAIN AND SIMPLE."

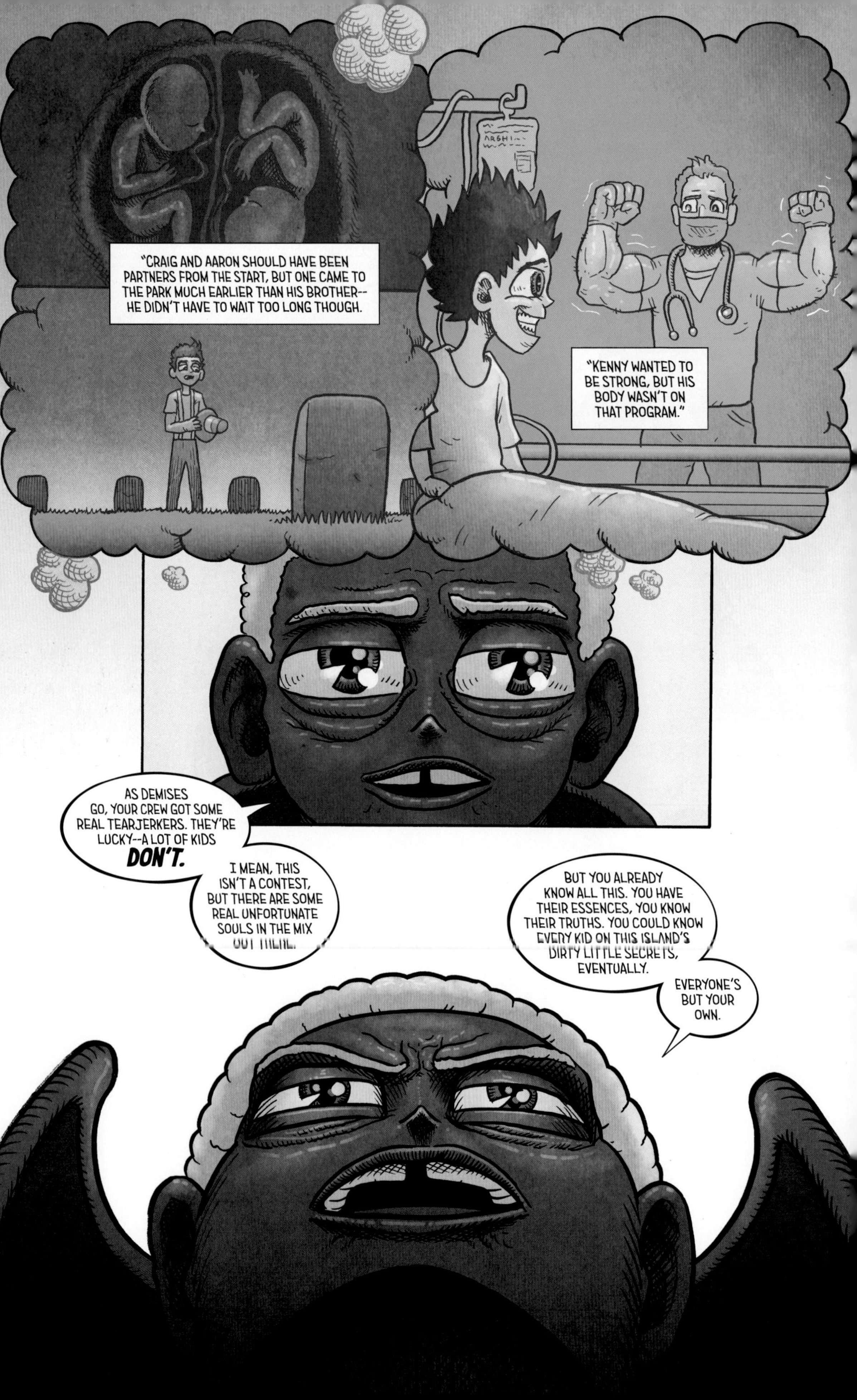
"CRAIG AND AARON SHOULD HAVE BEEN PARTNERS FROM THE START, BUT ONE CAME TO THE PARK MUCH EARLIER THAN HIS BROTHER-- HE DIDN'T HAVE TO WAIT TOO LONG THOUGH.
"KENNY WANTED TO BE STRONG, BUT HIS BODY WASN'T ON THAT PROGRAM."
AS DEMISES GO, YOUR CREW GOT SOME REAL TEARJERKERS. THEY'RE LUCKY--A LOT OF KIDS **DON'T.**
I MEAN, THIS ISN'T A CONTEST, BUT THERE ARE SOME REAL UNFORTUNATE SOULS IN THE MIX OUT THERE.
BUT YOU ALREADY KNOW ALL THIS. YOU HAVE THEIR ESSENCES, YOU KNOW THEIR TRUTHS. YOU COULD KNOW EVERY KID ON THIS ISLAND'S DIRTY LITTLE SECRETS, EVENTUALLY.
EVERYONE'S BUT YOUR OWN.

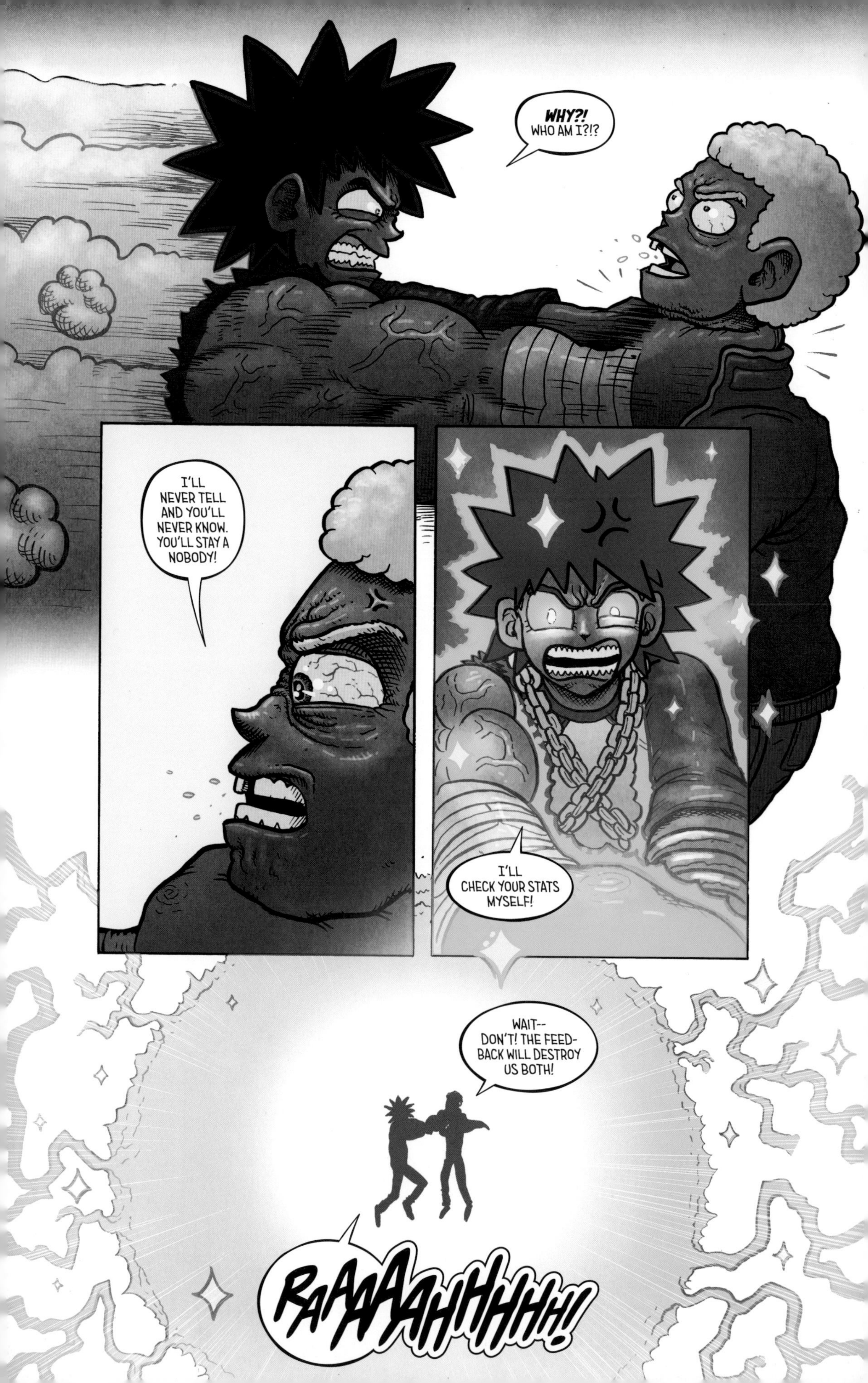
WHY?! WHO AM I?!?
I'LL NEVER TELL AND YOU'LL NEVER KNOW. YOU'LL STAY A NOBODY!
I'LL CHECK YOUR STATS MYSELF!
WAIT-- DON'T! THE FEED-BACK WILL DESTROY US BOTH!
RAAAAAHHHHHH!

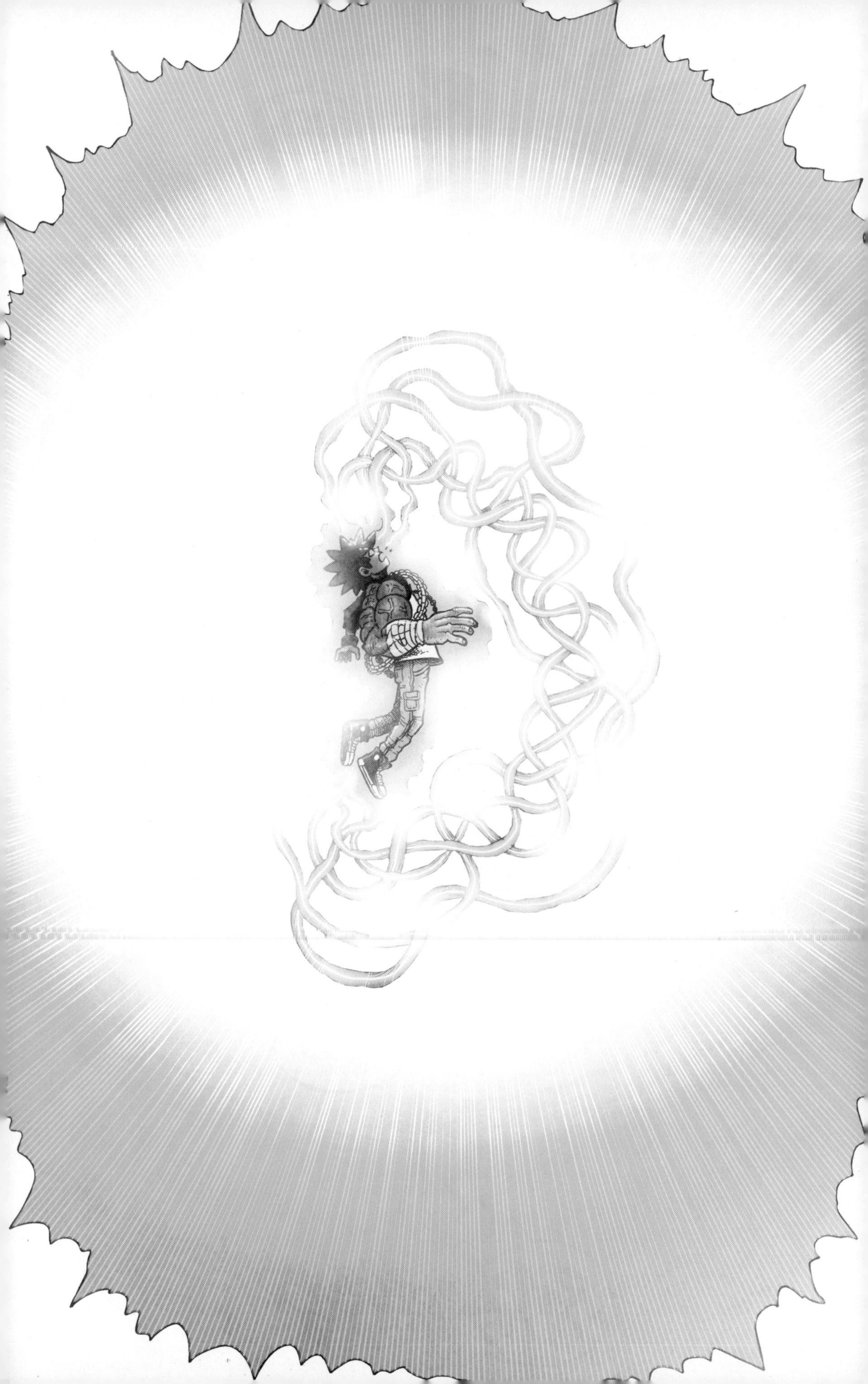

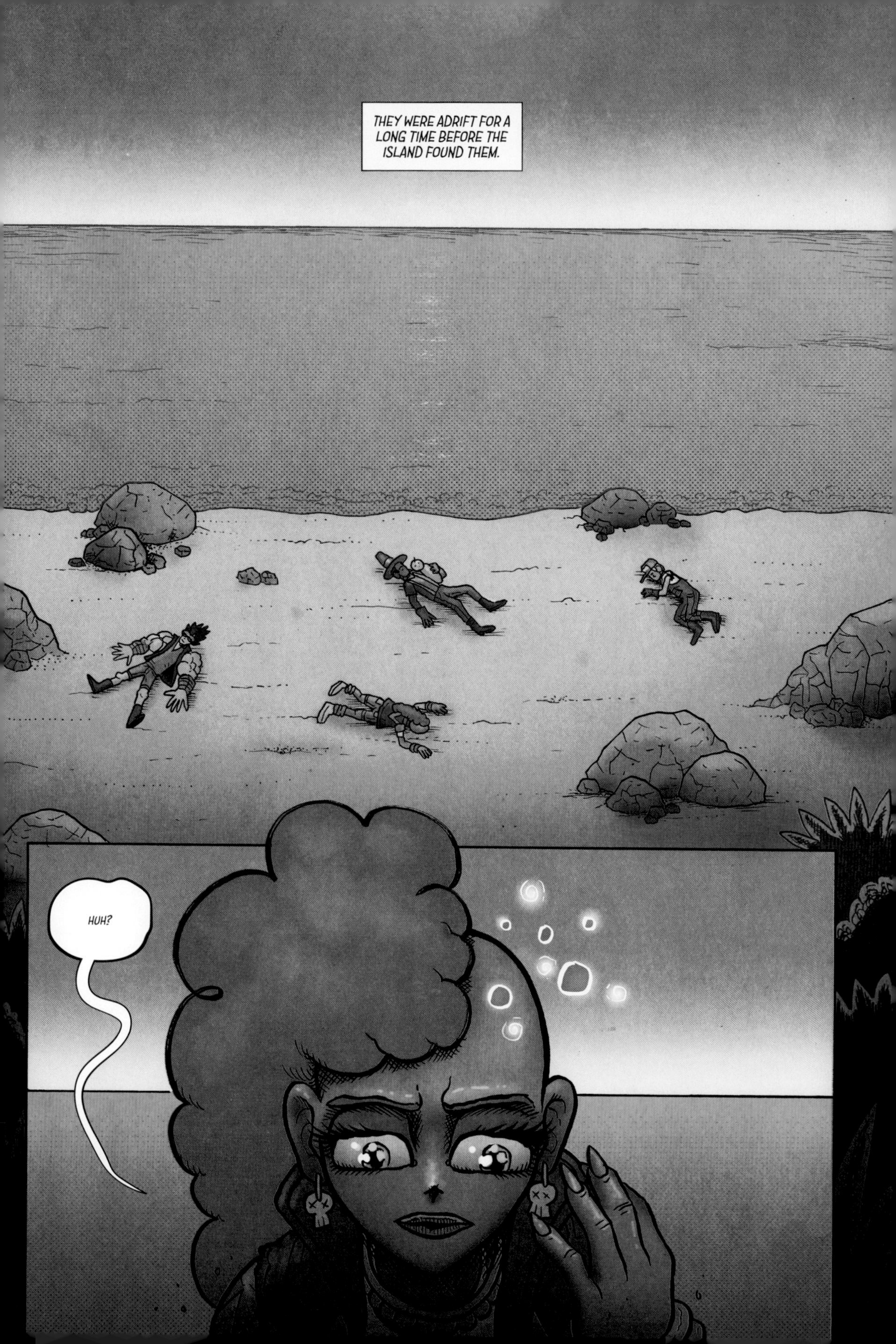
THEY WERE ADRIFT FOR A LONG TIME BEFORE THE ISLAND FOUND THEM.
HUH?

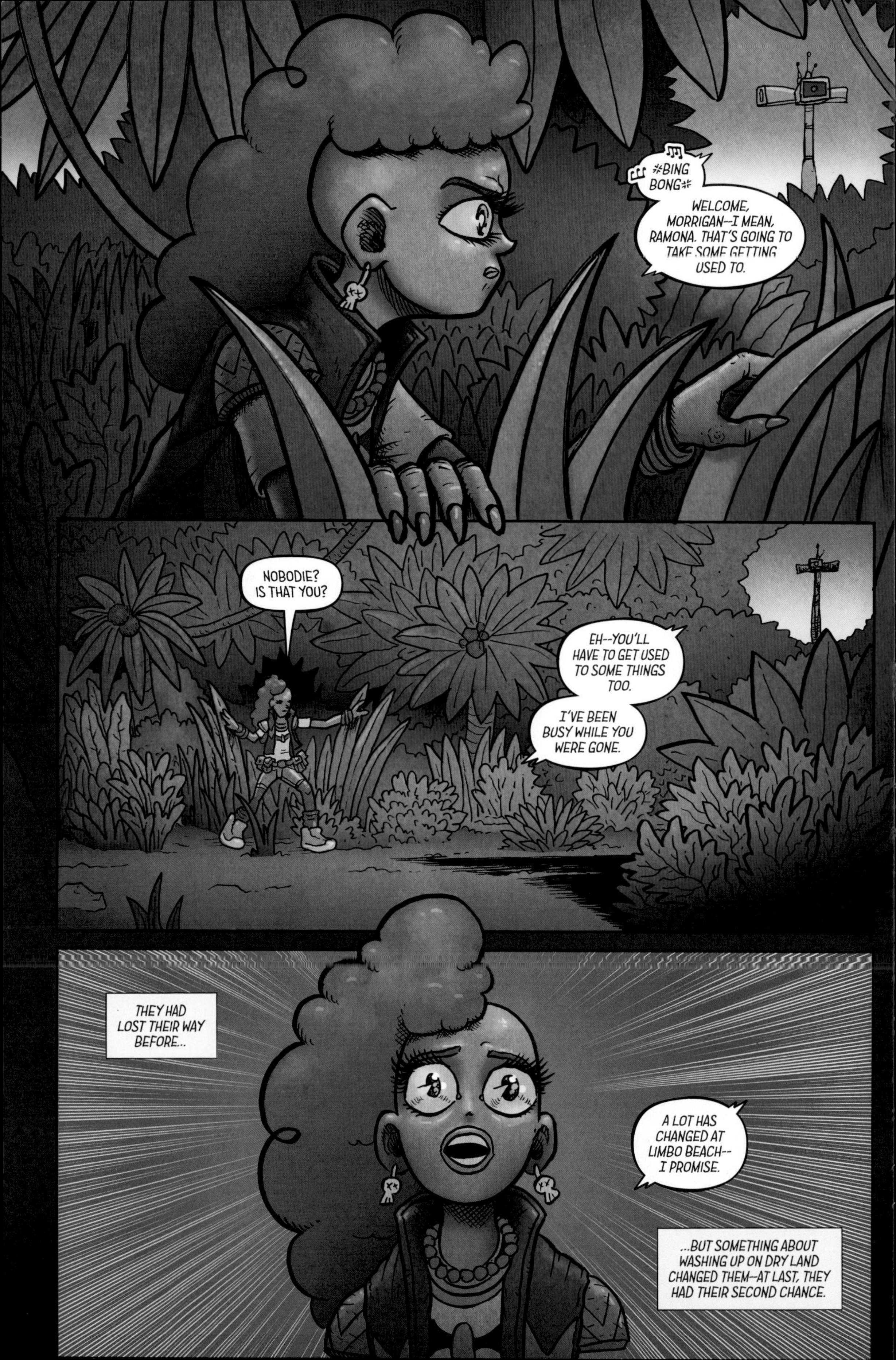

♯BING BONG♯
WELCOME, MORRIGAN--I MEAN, RAMONA. THAT'S GOING TO TAKE SOME GETTING USED TO.
NOBODIE? IS THAT YOU?
EH--YOU'LL HAVE TO GET USED TO SOME THINGS TOO.
I'VE BEEN BUSY WHILE YOU WERE GONE.
THEY HAD LOST THEIR WAY BEFORE...
A LOT HAS CHANGED AT LIMBO BEACH-- I PROMISE.
...BUT SOMETHING ABOUT WASHING UP ON DRY LAND CHANGED THEM--AT LAST, THEY HAD THEIR SECOND CHANCE.

THE END

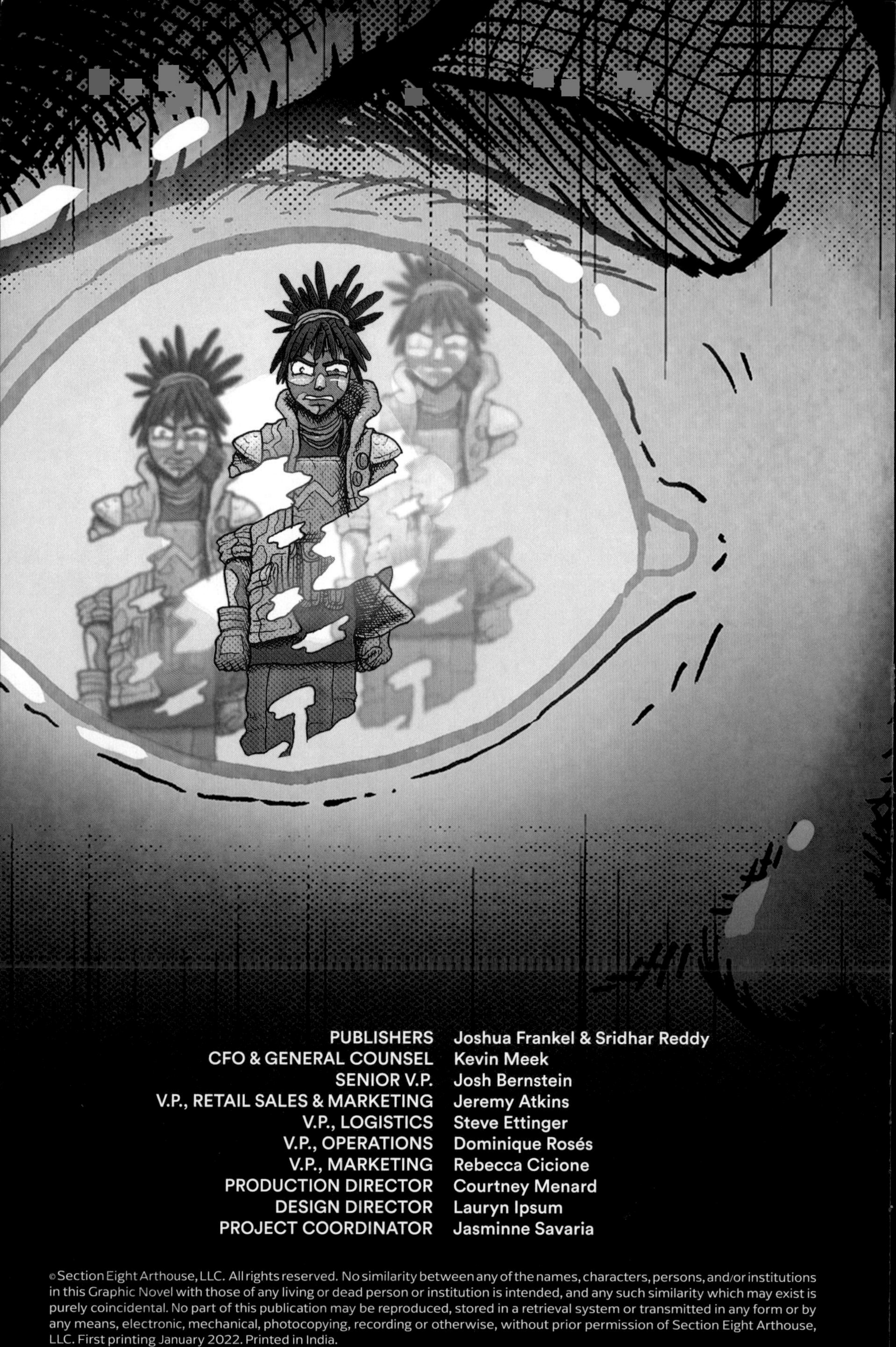

PUBLISHERS	Joshua Frankel & Sridhar Reddy
CFO & GENERAL COUNSEL	Kevin Meek
SENIOR V.P.	Josh Bernstein
V.P., RETAIL SALES & MARKETING	Jeremy Atkins
V.P., LOGISTICS	Steve Ettinger
V.P., OPERATIONS	Dominique Rosés
V.P., MARKETING	Rebecca Cicione
PRODUCTION DIRECTOR	Courtney Menard
DESIGN DIRECTOR	Lauryn Ipsum
PROJECT COORDINATOR	Jasminne Savaria

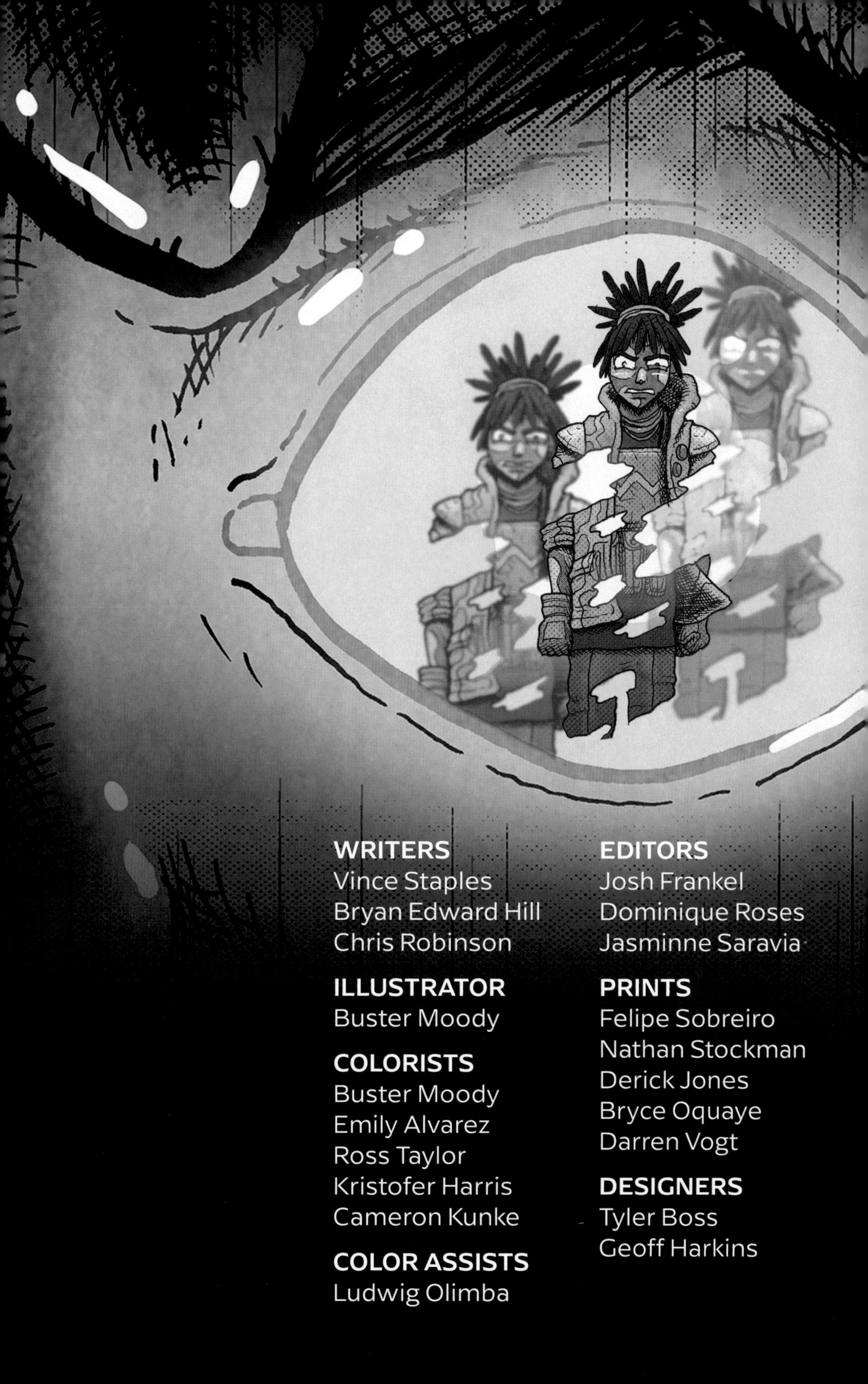

WRITERS
Vince Staples
Bryan Edward Hill
Chris Robinson

ILLUSTRATOR
Buster Moody

COLORISTS
Buster Moody
Emily Alvarez
Ross Taylor
Kristofer Harris
Cameron Kunke

COLOR ASSISTS
Ludwig Olimba

EDITORS
Josh Frankel
Dominique Roses
Jasminne Saravia

PRINTS
Felipe Sobreiro
Nathan Stockman
Derick Jones
Bryce Oquaye
Darren Vogt

DESIGNERS
Tyler Boss
Geoff Harkins

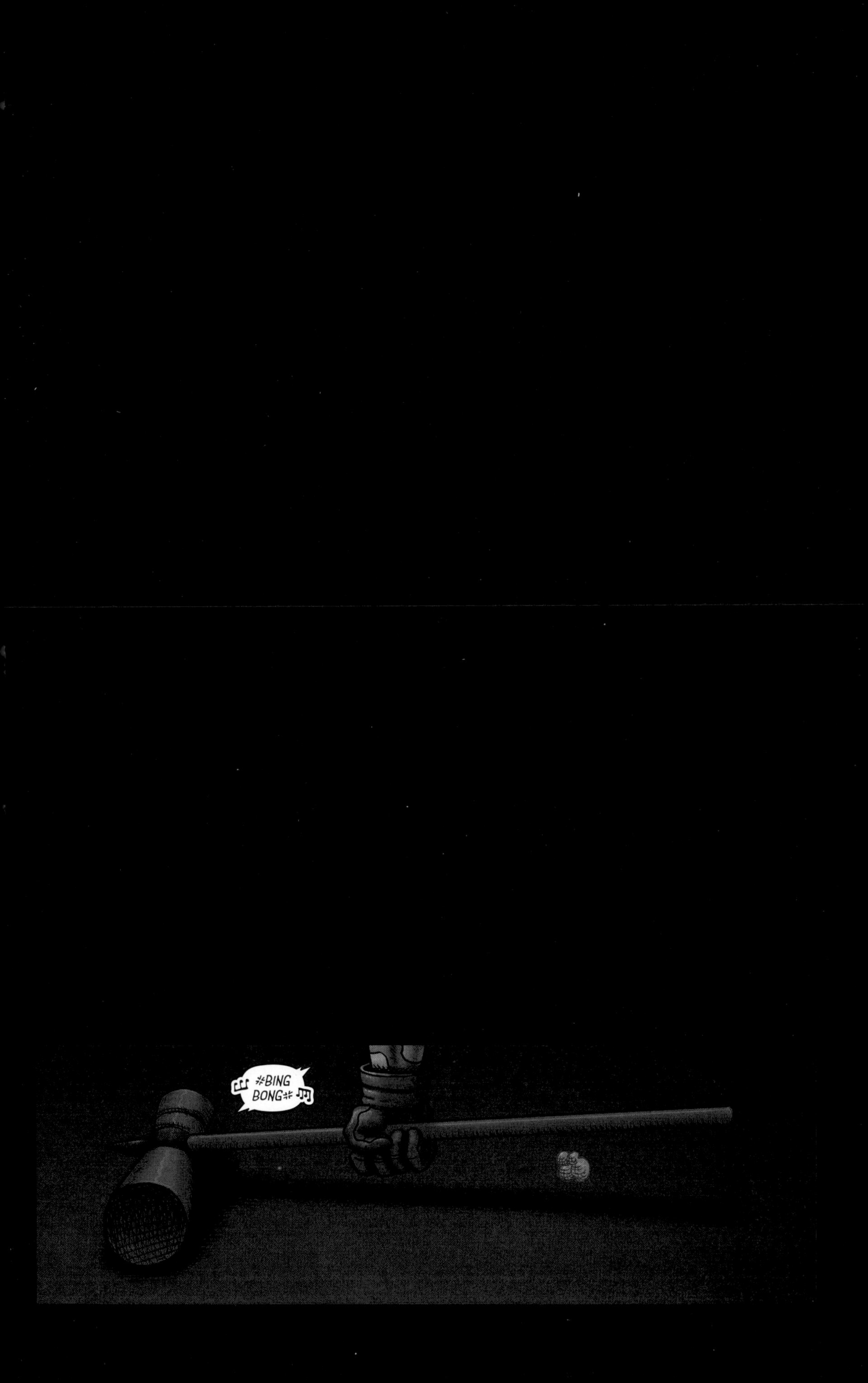
♯BING BONG♯

GALLERY

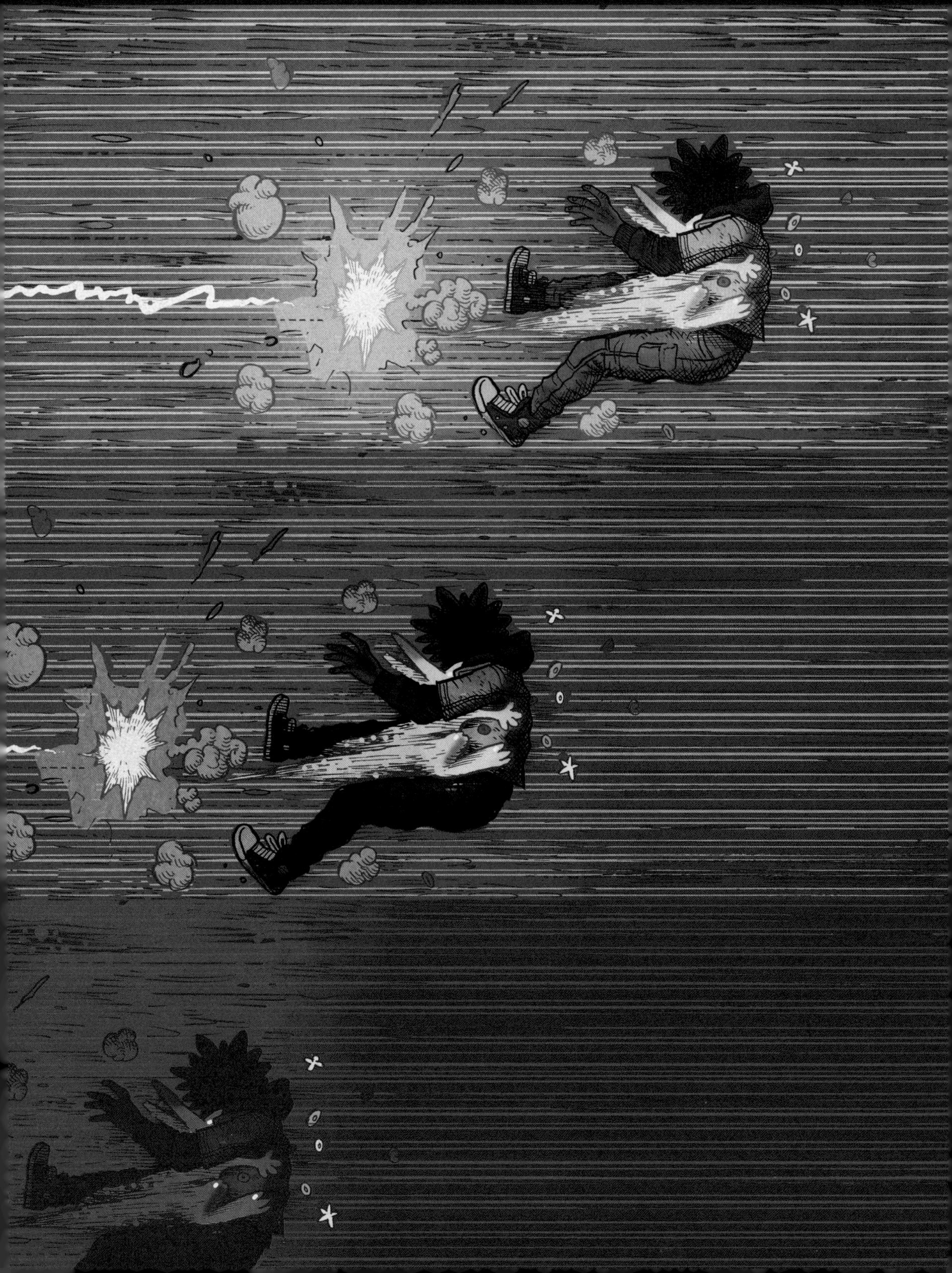

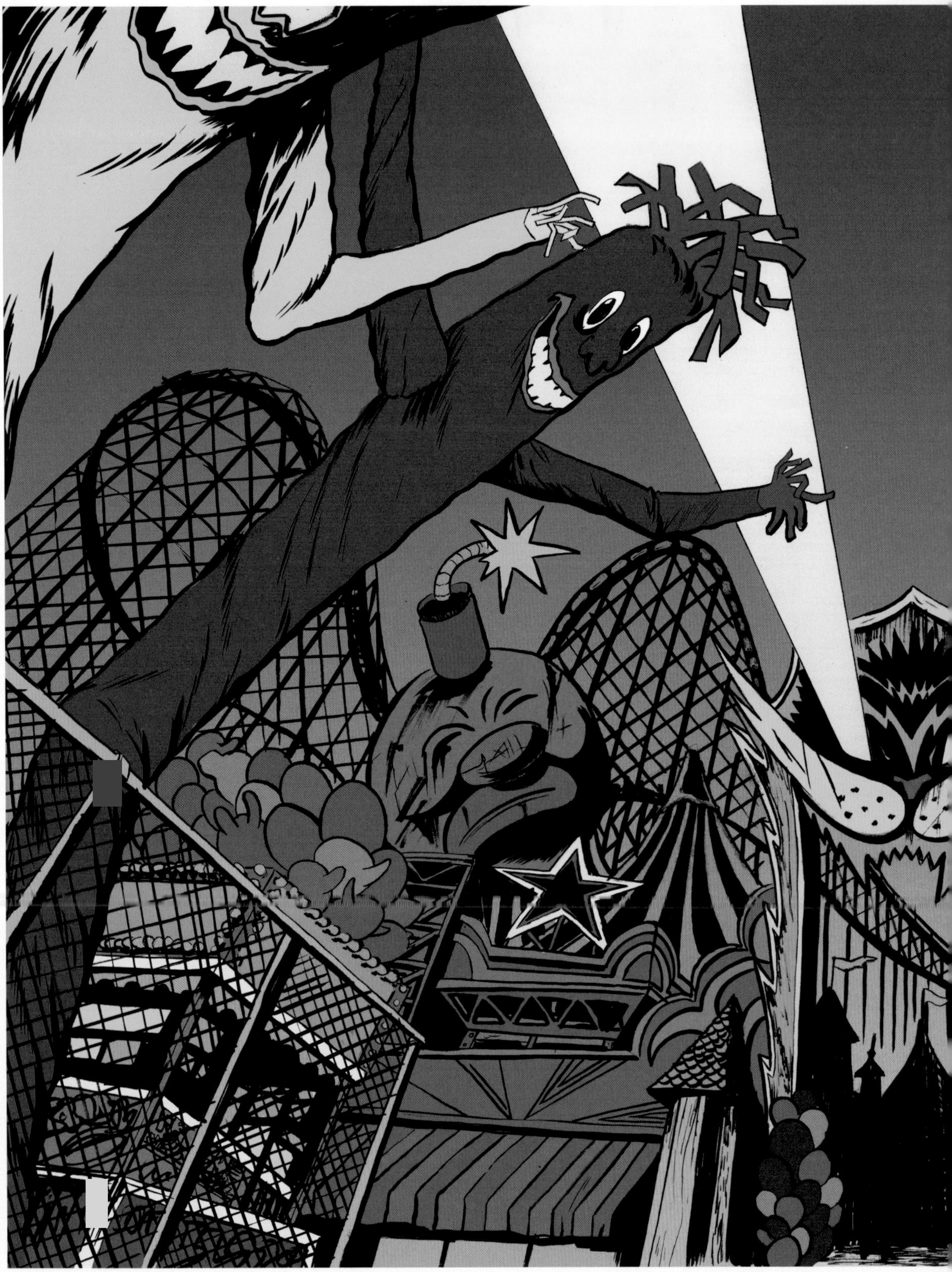

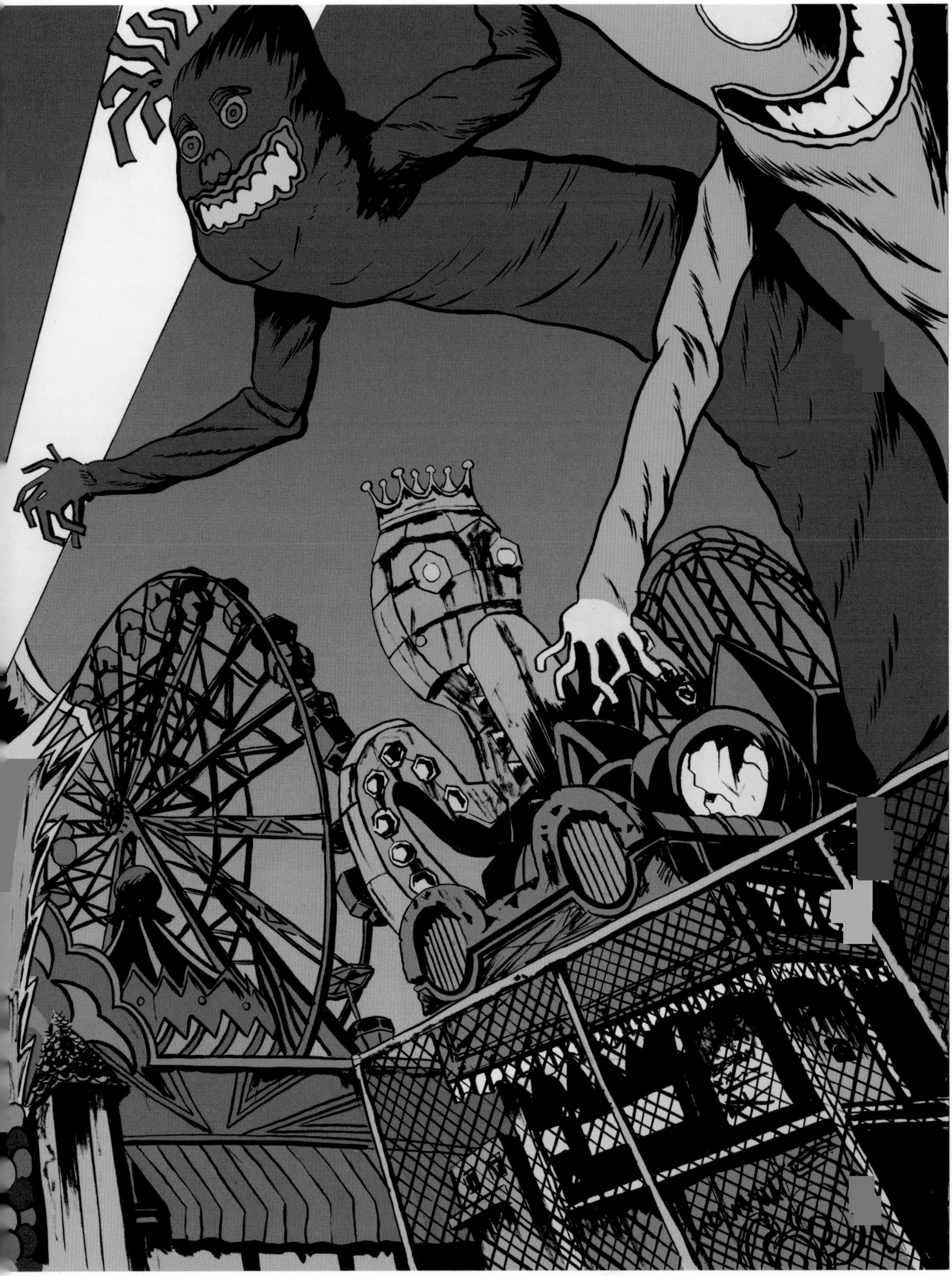

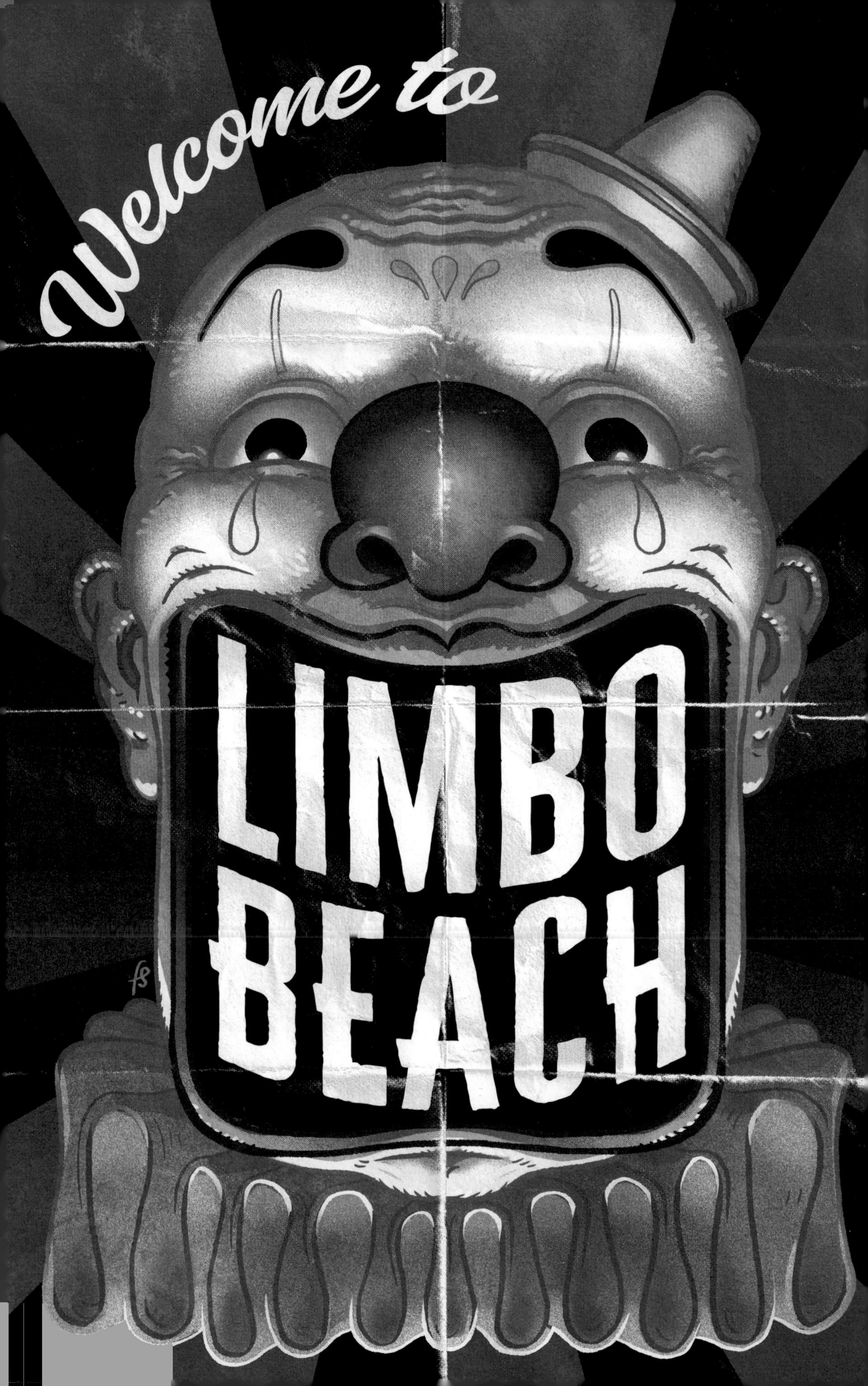
Welcome to
LIMBO
BEACH

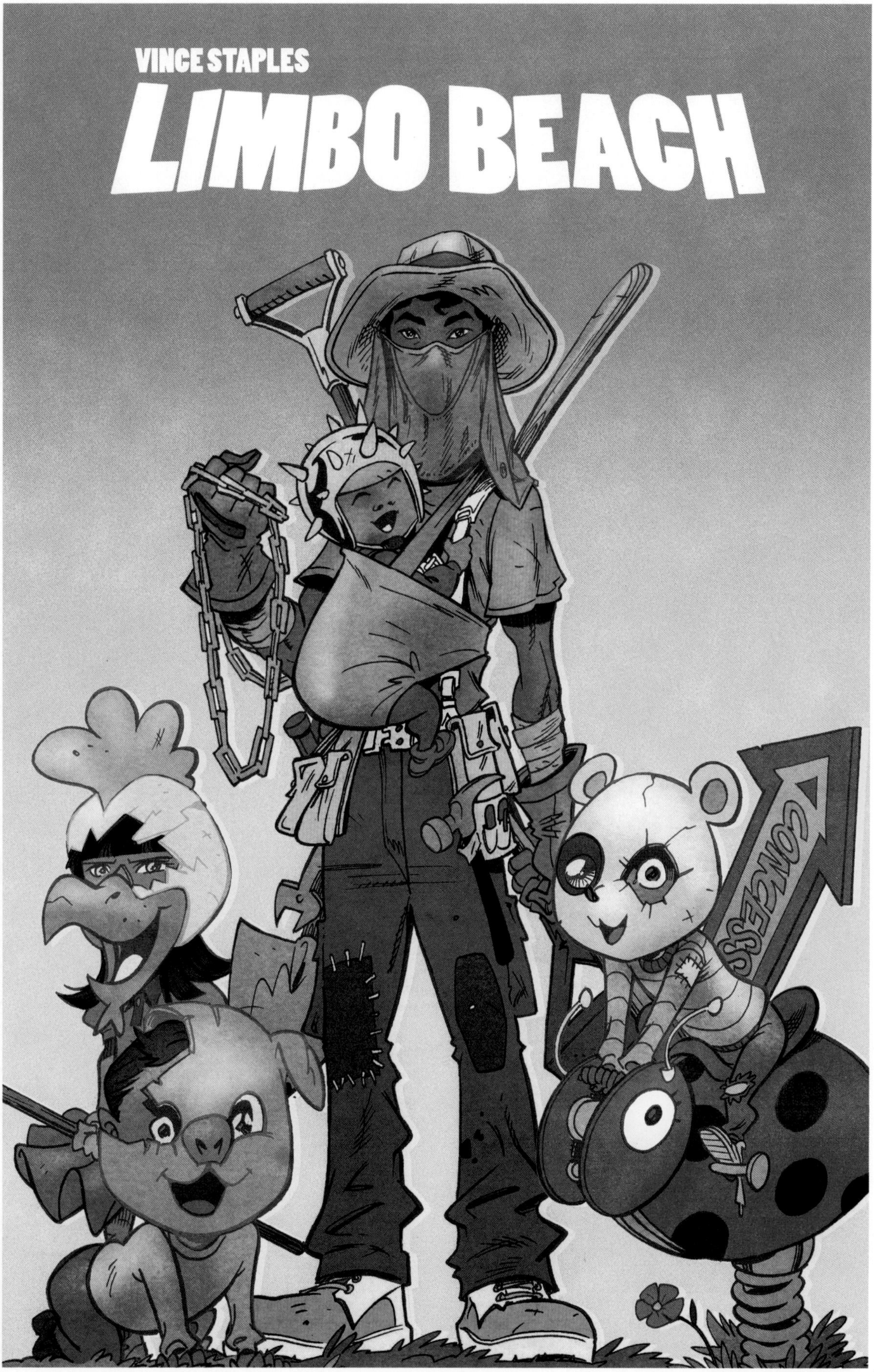
VINCE STAPLES
LIMBO BEACH

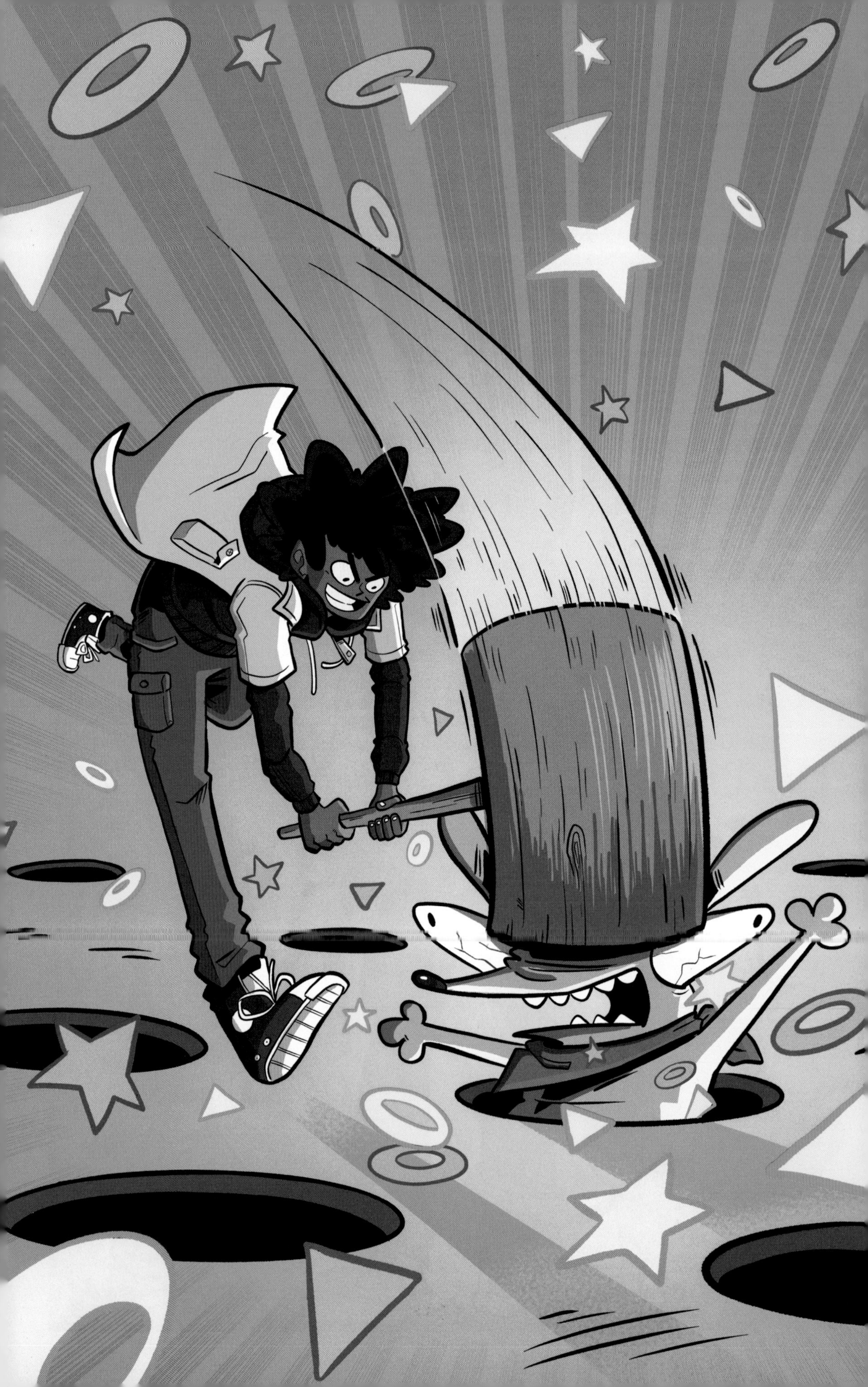